"THE CHILD WAS FOUND
THE NEXT DAY
IN THE BATHTUB. DEAD."

"Jesus," said Kevin.

"After you're with us for a while, Kevin, you'll stop saying that," Mr. Milton said. Kevin looked confused. "It shouldn't surprise you that the world is full of pain and suffering. And Jesus doesn't seem to be doing much about it," Mr. Milton explained.

"But I just don't see how you can get used to it."

"You do, or at least you get hard enough to do your job well," Mr. Milton said.

Mr. Milton slid a folder across the table to Dave who passed it on to Kevin. Despite his desire to get started on something exciting, Kevin felt icicles slide down his back. All eyes were on him now, so he smiled quickly.

"It's going to be an exciting case, Kevin; you will be baptized in fire," Mr. Milton said. "But there isn't a man here who hasn't been, and just look at them now."

Kevin looked around the room to see the other associates gazing at him. Each had a brilliant, eager intensity. He felt as if he were joining more than a law firm; he was joining some kind of brotherhood of blood . . .

Books by Andrew Neiderman

The Dark
The Devil's Advocate
Immortals
Imp
Night Owl
Tender Loving Care

Published by POCKET BOOKS

THE DEVIL'S ADVOCATE

ANDREW NEIDERMAN

POCKET BOOKS

New York   London   Toronto   Sydney   Tokyo   Singapore

This book is a work of fiction. Names, characters, places, and incidents are products of the author's imagination or are used fictitiously. Any resemblance to actual events or locales or persons living or dead is entirely coincidental.

An *Original* Publication of POCKET BOOKS

POCKET BOOKS, a division of Simon & Schuster Inc.
1230 Avenue of the Americas, New York, NY 10020

ISBN: 0-671-01410-2

First Pocket Books printing March 1990

10 9 8 7 6 5 4 3 2

POCKET and colophon are registered trademarks of Simon & Schuster Inc.

Printed in the U.S.A.

For Anita Diamant
One Classy Lady

Prologue

Richard Jaffee hurried down the steps of the court building in New York's Federal Plaza more like an attorney who had just lost a case than an attorney who had just won. Strands of his thin raven-black hair broke loose and danced about his head as he raced down the stone steps. Passersby took only casual notice of him. People in New York were always rushing to make a train, to make a cab, to beat out a changing light. Often they were just being carried along by the momentum moving through Manhattan's arteries, pumped by the invisible yet omnipresent giant heart that made the city pulsate like no other city in the world.

Jaffee's client, Robert Fundi, lingered behind to absorb the attention of reporters who clustered around him with the mindless energy of worker bees.

They were all shouting similar questions: What did the owner of a major private sanitation firm in the Lower East Side think of his being declared innocent of all charges of extortion? Was the trial just political because there had been talk of him running for borough president? Why didn't the prosecution's key witness tell all that he had allegedly told the prosecution?

"Ladies . . . gentlemen . . ." Fundi said, pulling a Cuban cigar from his top pocket. The reporters waited as he puffed life into it. He looked up and smiled. "You'll hafta direct all questions to my attorney. That's why I paid him all that money," Fundi said and laughed.

As if all their heads were tied together, the pack of reporters turned in Jaffee's direction just as Richard stepped into the back of the John Milton and Associates limousine. One of the younger and more determined interviewers rushed down the steps, shouting, "Mr. Jaffee! Just a moment, please. Mr. Jaffee!" The small crowd of attending reporters and friends all laughed as the limousine door was closed and the chauffeur went around the car to get behind the wheel. In moments the vehicle pulled away from the curb.

Richard Jaffee sat back and stared ahead.

"To the office, sir?" the chauffeur inquired.

"No, Charon. Take me home, please."

The tall, olive-skinned Egyptian with almond-shaped eyes peered into the rearview mirror as if he were looking into a crystal ball. His butter-smooth face wrinkled at the corners of his eyes. There was a nearly indistinguishable nod, confirming what he saw, what he knew.

"Very good, sir," Charon replied. He sat back and

drove on with the stoical presence of an undertaker's assistant driving a hearse.

Richard Jaffee didn't change position, didn't shift his posture, didn't turn to his right or left to look at anything on the streets. The thirty-three-year-old man seemed to be aging every passing minute. His complexion paled; his light blue eyes became dull gray, and the creases in his forehead deepened. He brought his hands to his cheeks and patted them gently as if to be sure he had not already decomposed.

And then he finally sat back and closed his eyes. Almost immediately, he pictured Gloria the way she had been before they had moved to Manhattan. He saw her as she was when they had first met—bright, innocent, bubbly but gentle, and very trusting. Her optimism and faith had been so refreshing and so stimulating. It filled him with a driving desire to give her everything, to work hard to make the world as soft and as happy as she saw it, to protect and to cherish her until death did them part.

Which it had, less than a month ago, in a delivery room of the Manhattan Memorial Hospital, even though she had had the best care and what had seemed like a perfectly healthy and normal pregnancy. She had given birth to a beautiful son, his features perfect, his health excellent, but the effort inexplicably took her life. The doctors couldn't explain it. Her heart simply gave out, they told him, as if her heart had grimaced, sighed, and lost its breath.

But he knew why she had died. He had confirmed his suspicions, and he had placed the blame solely on himself, for he had brought Gloria here. She had trusted him, and he had delivered her as though she were a sacrificial lamb.

Now, back in their apartment, his son slept peacefully, fed hungrily, and grew normally, unaware that he was entering the world without his mother, that his fee for life included her death. Richard knew that psychiatrists would tell him it was natural to resent the child, but psychiatrists didn't know. They just didn't know.

Of course, it was difficult, if not impossible, to really hate the infant. He looked so helpless and so innocent. Richard tried talking himself out of resenting him, first using logic and then using his memory of Gloria and her wonderfully effervescent approach to life to light his way back to sanity.

But none of it had worked. He had turned his child over to the live-in nurse, rarely asking after him and only occasionally looking in on him. Richard never questioned why his son cried or inquired about his health. He simply had gone on with his work, letting it consume him so he wouldn't think so much; he wouldn't remember; he wouldn't spend most of his time suffering the guilt.

The work had served as a dam holding back the reality of his personal tragedy. Now it came rushing in over him in the memory of Gloria's smiles, Gloria's kisses, Gloria's excitement when she had discovered she was pregnant. Behind his closed lids, he replayed dozens of moments, dozens of images. It was as though he were in his living room watching home movies.

"We're here, sir," Charon said.

They were here? Richard opened his eyes. Charon had opened the door and was standing on the sidewalk. Richard gripped his briefcase tightly and stepped out of the limousine. He looked at Charon. At six feet four, the chauffeur was a good five inches taller than Richard, but his broader shoulders and piercing eyes made him seem even taller, a veritable giant.

Richard stared at him a moment and saw knowledge in the chauffeur's eyes. He was a silent man, but he absorbed what went on around him and looked like he had lived for centuries.

Richard nodded slightly, and Charon closed the door and went back to the driver's seat. He watched the limousine go off, then turned and entered the apartment building. Philip, the retired New York City policeman who served as daytime security, peered over his newspaper and then snapped to attention, springing up from the stool behind the counter in the lobby.

"Congratulations, Mr. Jaffee. I heard the news bulletin. I'm sure it felt good to win another case."

Richard smiled. "Thank you, Philip. Everything all right?"

"Oh, just fine and dandy, Mr. Jaffee. Just like always," Philip said. "A man can grow old working here," he added, as he always did.

"Yes," Richard said. "Yes."

He went to the elevator and stood back stiffly as the doors closed. When he closed his eyes, he recalled the first time he and Gloria had driven up to the building, recalled her excitement, the way she squealed with delight when they looked at the apartment.

"What have I done?" he muttered.

His eyes snapped open as the elevator doors opened on his floor. Richard stood there for a moment and then walked out and to his apartment door. As soon as he entered, Mrs. Longchamp came out of the nursery to greet him.

"Oh, Mr. Jaffee." The nurse was only fifty, but she looked like everyone's grandmother—completely gray-haired, chunky, with soft brown eyes and a chubby face. "Congratulations. I just saw the news bulletin. They interrupted the soaps!"

"Thank you, Mrs. Longchamp."

"You haven't lost a case since you started with Mr. Milton's firm, have you?" she asked.

"No, Mrs. Longchamp. I haven't."

"You must be very proud of yourself."

"Yes," he said.

"Everything's all right with Brad," she offered, even though he hadn't asked. He nodded. "I was just getting ready to give him a bottle."

"Go on with it, by all means," Richard said.

She smiled again and returned to the nursery.

He put his briefcase down, looked around the apartment, and then strode slowly through the living room to the patio that afforded him one of the nicest views of the Hudson River. He didn't stop to admire it, however. He walked with the intent of someone who had always known exactly where he was going. He stepped onto the lounge chair so he could get his left foot securely on the wall, pulling himself up by grabbing hold of the cast-iron railings. Then, in one swift and graceful move, he reached down as if grabbing for the hand of someone to pull up and went head over heels fifteen flights to the pavement below.

1

Twenty-eight-year-old Kevin Taylor looked up from the papers spread out over the long chestnut-brown table before him and paused, pretending to think deeply about something before cross-examining the witness. These little dramatic gestures came naturally to him. It was a combination of his histrionics and his knowledge of psychology. The dramatic pause between asking questions and looking at documents usually unnerved a witness. In this case he was trying to intimidate the principal of an elementary school, Philip Cornbleau, a slim, dark-haired, pale-skinned, fifty-four-year-old, nearly bald man. He sat impatiently, his hands clasped over his chest, his long fingers jerking up and down against each other.

Kevin glanced quickly at the audience. The old expression, "You could cut the air with a knife," seemed appropriate. The anticipation was that thick.

It was as if everyone were holding his or her breath. The room suddenly brightened as sunshine poured through the large windows in Blithedale's courthouse. It was as if a lighting technician had thrown a switch. All that was left was for the director to shout, "Action!"

The courtroom was packed, but Kevin's gaze settled on a distinguished-looking, handsome man in the rear who was staring at him with the kind of loving, proud smile Kevin would have expected from his father, not that this man was old enough to be his father. He was probably in his early forties, Kevin thought, and he had a very successful air about him. Conscious of wealth and style, Kevin recognized the Giorgio Armani charcoal-gray pin-striped suit. He had looked at that suit covetously before buying the one he wore today, a double-breasted dark blue wool. He'd bought it at a discount store for half the price of the Armani.

The man acknowledged Kevin with a slight nod.

The silence in the courtroom was punctured by sharp coughs scattered here and there. Lois Wilson, a twenty-five-year-old fifth-grade teacher, was on trial for sexually abusing children in the small Nassau County community of Blithedale. It was a bedroom community; almost all the residents were New York City commuters. Quite rural in appearance, Blithedale was an oasis of sorts with upper-middle-class homes and landscaped grounds, clean, wide streets lined with red maples and oak, and a relatively quiet business area. There were no large malls, no overly developed strips of stores, gas stations, restaurants, and motels. Signs had to meet strict codes. Gaudiness, bright colors, obese posters were prohibited.

THE DEVIL'S ADVOCATE

The inhabitants liked the feeling of being in a cocoon. They could go into and out of New York as they wished, but when they returned, they returned to their well-guarded, "Alice in Wonderland" existence. Nothing overt happened. It was the way they wanted it.

Then, Lois Wilson, one of the new teachers in the elementary school, was accused of sexually abusing a ten-year-old girl. A school investigation uncovered three more similar occurrences. Background information and the local rumor mill established Lois Wilson as a confirmed lesbian. She was renting a house on the outskirts of Blithedale with her girlfriend, a foreign-language teacher in a nearby high school, and neither went out with men or had any male relationships.

No one in the firm of Boyle, Carlton, and Sessler was happy that Kevin had taken this case. He had actually sought it out, offering his services to Lois Wilson once he heard about her problem; and once he had the case, he had threatened to leave the firm if any of the senior partners actually forbid him from taking it. He had been growing more and more impatient with the firm, impatient with its conservative approach to law and with the direction he knew his life would take if he remained there much longer. This was the first dramatic case he had had, the first case with meat in it, the first case in which he could show his skill and acumen. He felt like an athlete who had finally entered a significant event. Maybe it wasn't the Olympics, but it was more than the local high school tournament. This case had already made the metropolitan newspapers.

The district attorney, Martin Balm, offered Kevin a

9

deal immediately, hoping to keep the story out of the media and avoid any sensationalism. The most important consideration of all, he stressed, expecting Kevin's sympathy, was keeping the children out of the courtroom and having them go through the horror once again. If Lois plead guilty, she would get five years probation and psychological counseling. Of course, her teaching career would be over.

But Kevin advised her not to take the deal and she agreed with him. Now she sat demurely, staring down at her hands in her lap. Kevin had told her not to look arrogant, but to appear wounded, suffering. From time to time, she took out her handkerchief and dabbed her eyes.

He had actually had her rehearse this posture in his office, showing her how to look intently at witnesses, how to look hopefully at the jury. He recorded her on video and played it back, giving her pointers about how to use her eyes, how to wear her hair, how to hold her shoulders and use her hands. It was the visual age, he told her. Icons, symbols, posturing were all important.

Kevin turned to look quickly at his wife Miriam four rows back. She looked nervous, tense, worried for him. Like Sanford Boyle, she had advised him not to take the case, but Kevin was committed to it more than he had been committed to anything else during his three years of practicing law. He wouldn't talk about anything else; he spent hours and hours doing research, investigating, working on weekends, doing far more than the retainer and fee justified.

He flashed Miriam a confident smile, and then he spun around abruptly, almost as if a spring had snapped.

"Mr. Cornbleau, you interviewed the three girls by yourself on Tuesday, November 3rd?"

"Yes."

"The alleged initial victim, Barbara Stanley, told you about them?" Kevin nodded to confirm the answer before he received it.

"That's correct. So I invited them into my office."

"Can you tell us how you began once they arrived?"

"Pardon?" Cornbleau frowned as if the question were ridiculous.

"What was the first question you asked the girls?" Kevin stepped toward the jury. "Did you ask if Miss Wilson had touched them on their buttocks? Did you ask if she had put her hands under their skirts?"

"Of course not."

"Well, what did you ask?"

"I asked them if it were true they were having the same sort of trouble Barbara Stanley had had with Miss Wilson."

"The same sort of trouble?" He grimaced at the word *trouble*.

"Yes."

"So Barbara Stanley told her girlfriends what allegedly happened to her and the three young girls related similar experiences to her, but none of the three had ever told anyone else before. Is that what you're saying?"

"Yes. That was my understanding."

"Quite a charismatic ten-year-old girl," Kevin quipped, acting as if he had merely spoken a private thought aloud. Some members of the jury raised their eyebrows. A bald-headed man in the front right corner tilted his head thoughtfully and stared intently at the principal.

When Kevin turned and looked at the audience, he saw that the dignified-looking man in the rear had widened his smile and was nodding encouragingly. Kevin half wondered if he might not be a relative of Lois Wilson, maybe an older brother.

"Now, Mr. Cornbleau, can you tell the court what kind of grades Barbara Stanley was getting in Lois Wilson's class."

"She was doing low C."

"Low C. And had she had any problems with Miss Wilson previously?"

"Yes," the principal muttered.

"Excuse me?"

"Yes. On two occasions, she had been sent to my office for refusing to do her work and using bad language in class, but . . ."

"So you can safely say Barbara was not fond of Miss Wilson?"

"Objection, your honor." The district attorney stood up. "Counsel is asking the witness to make a conclusion."

"Sustained."

"Sorry, your honor." Kevin turned back to Cornbleau. "Let's get back to the three girls, Mr. Cornbleau. Did you ask each of them to relate her experiences to you in your office that day?"

"I thought it was best to get right to it, yes."

"You're not telling us that while one told her story, the other two listened?" he asked, twisting his face to indicate his shock and incredulity.

"Yes."

"Wasn't that inappropriate? I mean, exposing the girls to these stories . . . alleged experiences . . ."

"Well, it was an investigation."

"Oh, I see. You've had experience with this sort of thing before?"

"No, never. That's why it was so shocking."

"Did you advise the girls that if they were making things up, they could be in serious trouble?"

"Of course."

"But you tended to believe them, correct?"

"Yes."

"Why?"

"Because they were all saying the same thing and describing it the same way." Cornbleau looked satisfied with himself and his answer, but Kevin stepped closer, his questions coming in a staccato manner.

"Then couldn't they have rehearsed it?"

"What?"

"Couldn't they have gotten together and memorized their stories?"

"I don't see . . ."

"Isn't it possible?"

"Well . . ."

"Haven't you ever experienced children this age lying?"

"Of course."

"And more than one lying at the same time?"

"Yes, but . . ."

"Then isn't it possible?"

"I suppose."

"You suppose?"

"Well . . ."

"Did you call Miss Wilson in and confront her with these stories immediately after speaking with the girls?"

"Yes, of course."

"And what was her reaction?"

"She wouldn't deny it."

"You mean she refused to be interrogated about such matters without benefit of counsel, don't you?" Cornbleau shifted his seat. "Isn't that so?" Kevin demanded.

"That's what she said."

"So you went ahead and informed the superintendent and then called the district attorney?"

"Yes. We followed school board policy for such matters."

"You didn't investigate further, call in other students?"

"Absolutely not."

"And before Miss Wilson was indicted on this matter, you and the superintendent suspended her, correct?"

"As I said . . ."

"Please, just answer the question."

"Yes."

"Yes," Kevin repeated, as if that were an admission of guilt. He paused, a slight smile on his face as he turned from Cornbleau to the jury and then back to Cornbleau.

"Mr. Cornbleau, did you on more than one previous occasion have words with Miss Wilson about her bulletin boards?"

"I did."

"Why?"

"They were too small and not up to standards."

"So you were critical of her as a teacher?"

"Room decor is an integral part of a teacher's effectiveness," Cornbleau said pedantically.

"Uh-huh, but Miss Wilson didn't have . . . let us

14

say . . . the same sense of high regard for bulletin boards."

"No."

"She was, in fact, according to what you wrote on her chart, 'disdainful.'"

"Unfortunately, most of the newer teachers are not given the same good background in college." Cornbleau smirked.

Kevin nodded. "Yes, why can't everyone be like us?" he asked rhetorically, and some people in the audience snickered. The judge rapped his gavel.

"You also have been critical of Miss Wilson's clothing, have you not?" Kevin continued more directly.

"I think she should dress more conservatively, yes."

"Yet Miss Wilson's department head has continually given her high marks for her teaching abilities," Kevin interrupted, raising his voice. "On her last report she said"—Kevin looked at his document— "'Lois Wilson has an intrinsic understanding of children. No matter what the obstacle, she seems to be able to reach them and get them stimulated.'" He put the document down. "That's quite a nice review, isn't it?"

"Yes, but as I said . . ."

"No further questions, your honor."

Kevin went back to his desk, his face red with fury, something he had the ability to do at a moment's notice. All eyes were on him. When he looked back at the elegant man in the audience, he saw that the smile had left his face, but it had been replaced with a genuine look of awe. Kevin felt buoyed.

Miriam, on the other hand, looked sad, sad enough to burst into tears. She looked down quickly when he gazed at her. *She's ashamed of me,* he thought. *My God, she's still ashamed of me. She won't be much longer,* he concluded confidently.

"Mr. Balm? Any further questions for Mr. Cornbleau?"

"No, your honor. We would like to call Barbara Stanley to the stand, your honor," the district attorney said, a tone of desperation in his voice.

Kevin patted Lois Wilson's hand reassuringly. He had driven the prosecution to the heart of their case.

A chubby girl with curly light brown hair trimmed just below her earlobes came down the aisle. The ten-year-old wore a light blue dress with a frilly white collar and frilly white sleeves. The baggy garment seemed to add to her girth.

She anxiously took her seat and raised her hand to be sworn in. Kevin nodded to himself and shot a knowing look at Martin Balm. She had been well schooled in what to expect. Balm had done his homework, too; but Kevin felt he had done more, and that would make all the difference.

"Barbara," Martin Balm began, approaching her.

"One moment, Mr. Balm," the judge said. He leaned toward Barbara Stanley. "Barbara, do you understand what you have just sworn to do . . . to tell the truth?" Barbara glanced quickly at the audience and then turned back to the judge and nodded. "And do you understand how important what you say here can be?" She nodded again, this time more softly. The judge leaned back. "Carry on, Mr. Balm."

"Thank you, your honor." Balm moved up to the witness chair. He was a tall, lean man, on his way to a promising political career. He was uncomfortable with this case and had hoped Kevin and Lois Wilson would take his offer, but they hadn't, and here he was, relying on the testimony of ten-year-old children. "I'd like you to tell the court just what you told Mr. Cornbleau that day in his office. Go slowly."

The chubby girl looked quickly at Lois. Kevin had told her to stare at all the children intently, especially the three who were confirming Barbara Stanley's accusations.

"Well . . . sometimes, when we had special arts . . ."

"Special arts. What's that, Barbara?"

"Special arts is art or reading or music. The class goes to the art teacher or the music teacher," the little girl recited, her eyes almost closed. Kevin could see she was trying hard to do it all correctly. When he looked around, he saw how members of the audience half smiled, silently rooting for the child. The gentleman in the back, however, looked intense, almost angry.

"I see," Balm said, nodding. "They go to another room, right?"

"Uh-huh."

"Please say yes or no, Barbara, okay?"

"Uh . . . I mean yes."

"Okay, sometimes when you had special arts . . ." Balm prompted.

"Miss Wilson would ask one of us to stay behind," Barbara replied on cue.

"Stay behind? Remain in class alone with her?"

"Uh . . . yes."

"And?"

"One time, she asked me to."

"And what did you tell Mr. Cornbleau about this time?"

Barbara turned herself a bit in the seat so she could avoid Lois's gaze. Then she took a deep breath and began.

"Miss Wilson asked me to sit by her, and she told me she thought I was growing into a pretty girl, but there were things I should know about my body, things adults don't like to talk about." She paused and looked down.

"Go on."

"She said there were places that were special."

"Special?"

"Uh . . . yes."

"And what did she want you to know about these places, Barbara?" Barbara shot a quick glance in Lois Wilson's direction and then turned back to Balm. "Barbara, what did she want you to know?" he repeated.

"That special things happen whenever . . . whenever anyone touches them."

"I see. And then what did she do?" He nodded to encourage her to continue.

"She showed me the places."

"Showed you? How?"

"She pointed to them, and then she asked me to let her touch them so I would understand."

"Did you let her, Barbara?"

Barbara pressed her lips together tightly and nodded.

"Yes?"

"Yes."

"Where exactly did she touch you, Barbara?"

"Here and there," Barbara said, pointing to her chest and between her legs.

"Did she just touch you there, or did she do something more?"

Barbara bit her lower lip.

"This is hard, Barbara, we know. But we've got to ask you so that the right things can be done. You understand, right?" She nodded. "Okay, tell the court. What else did Miss Wilson do?"

"She put her hand in here," she said, placing her own right hand between her legs, "and rubbed."

"Put her hand in there? You mean, in under your clothing?"

"Yes."

"Then what happened, Barbara?"

"She asked me if it felt special. I told her it just tickled, and she got annoyed and pulled her hand out. She said I wasn't ready to understand yet, but she would try again some other time."

"Did she?"

"Not with me," Barbara said quickly.

"With friends of yours, other girls in the class?"

"Uh-huh. Yes."

"And when you told them what Miss Wilson had done to you, they told you what she had done to them, correct?"

"Yes."

A low murmur trembled through the audience. The judge looked out with reproach, and everyone became quiet instantly.

"Then all of you told everything to Mr. Cornbleau?"

"Yes."

"Okay, Barbara. Mr. Taylor is going to ask you questions now, too. Just be as truthful with him as you have been with me," Martin Balm said and then turned toward Kevin and shook his head. He was capable of dramatics, too.

Pretty sharp, Kevin thought. *I've got to remember that one: just be as truthful with him as you have been with me.*

"Barbara," Kevin said before getting up. "Your full name is Barbara Elizabeth Stanley, right?" His tone of voice was light, friendly.

"Yes."

"There's another girl in your class named Barbara, too, isn't there, Barbara?"

She nodded, and Kevin stepped closer, still smiling.

"But her name is Barbara Louise Martin, and to differentiate, distinguish between the two of you, Miss Wilson called her Barbara Louise and you just Barbara, didn't she?"

"Yes."

"Do you like Barbara Louise?"

She shrugged.

"Do you think Miss Wilson likes Barbara Louise better than she likes you?"

Barbara Stanley looked at Lois, her eyes growing smaller.

"Yes," she said.

"Because Barbara Louise does better in class?"

"I don't know."

"And because Barbara Louise never got in trouble for using bad language in class like you did?"

"I don't know."

"Did you try to get the other girls to dislike Barbara Louise?"

"No."

"Now, Barbara, the judge told you, you have to tell

the truth when you testify in court. Are you telling the truth?"

"Yes."

"Did you pass notes to your friends making fun of Barbara Louise?

Barbara's lips trembled a bit.

"Didn't Miss Wilson catch you passing bad notes about her to other girls in class?" he asked, nodding. Barbara looked at Lois Wilson and then out in the audience toward her parents. "Miss Wilson keeps good records of whatever goes on in her classroom," Kevin said, turning toward Cornbleau. "She saved the notes." Kevin unwrapped a piece of paper. "'Let's call her Barbara Loser,' you wrote to somebody, and a number of other students started calling her that, right?" Barbara didn't reply. "In fact, the other girls who claim Miss Wilson did things to them joined you in calling Barbara Louise 'Barbara Loser,' right?"

"Yes." Barbara was close to tears.

"So you just lied when I asked you if you tried to get the other girls to dislike Barbara Louise, didn't you?" he asked with a sudden harshness. Barbara Stanley bit down on her lower lip. "Didn't you?" he demanded. She nodded. "And maybe you're lying again about the things you just told Mr. Balm, huh?" She shook her head quickly.

"No," the little girl said in a small voice. Kevin could feel the hateful glare of some members of the audience. A tear had broken free of Barbara's right eye and traveled unchecked down her cheek.

"You always wanted to be as popular with Miss Wilson as Barbara Louise is, didn't you, Barbara?"

She shrugged.

"In fact, you always wanted to be the most popular

girl in your class, popular with the boys as well as the girls, didn't you?"

"I don't know."

"You don't? Not lying again, are you?" He shot a glance at the jury. "You told Mary Lester that, right?" She started to shake her head. "I could ask Mary to come here, Barbara, so remember to tell the truth. Did you tell Mary you wished everyone hated Barbara Louise and everyone liked you more?" he asked, deepening his tone.

"Yes."

"So Barbara Louise is a popular girl, isn't she?"

"Uh-huh. Yes."

"You'd like to be popular, too, right? Who wouldn't?" he said, nearly laughing. Barbara didn't know whether she had to answer the question, but Kevin didn't need the answer. "Now, Barbara, you know that you and the other girls are accusing Miss Wilson of doing sexual things, bad sexual things to you. Right?"

Barbara nodded, her eyes a bit wider. Kevin held his gaze on her. "Yes," she finally said.

"Was this supposedly the first time sexual things were done to you or the first time you did something sexual, Barbara?" he asked quickly. There was an instant gasp from the audience and then an angry murmur. The judge rapped his gavel.

Barbara nodded slowly.

"Yes?"

"Yes," she said.

"But what about the time you and Paula and Sara and Mary invited Gerald and Tony to your house one afternoon after school when your parents weren't home, when no one in your family was home?" Kevin asked quietly. Barbara's face reddened. She looked about helplessly for a moment. Kevin moved closer and, almost in a whisper, asked, "Did you know that Mary told Miss Wilson about that afternoon, Barbara?"

Barbara looked terrified. She shook her head quickly.

Kevin smiled. When he glanced at Martin Balm, he saw the look of confusion on his face. Kevin nodded and smirked at the jury.

"You haven't been doing very well in Miss Wilson's class, have you, Barbara?" he asked, his tone becoming light and friendly once again.

"No." Barbara wiped away a tear. "But it's not my fault," she added quickly, happy the questioning had taken a different direction.

Kevin paused as if he were through, but then turned back to her.

"Do you think Miss Wilson doesn't like you and makes it tough for you?"

"Yes."

"So you wouldn't want her as your teacher anymore, would you?"

Barbara couldn't pull her eyes from Lois's intense gaze. She shrugged.

"No? Yes?" Kevin prompted.

"I just want her to stop picking on me."

"I see. All right, Barbara. When did the incident between you and Miss Wilson supposedly happen? What was the date?"

"Objection, your honor," Balm said, rising quickly. "I don't think this little girl can be expected to remember dates."

"Your honor, the prosecution is presenting this

little girl as one of its chief witnesses against my client. We can't pick and choose what she should and shouldn't remember about such an important allegation. If her testimony is inaccurate in any way . . ."

"All right, Mr. Taylor. You've made your point. Objection overruled. Ask your question, Mr. Taylor."

"Thank you, your honor. All right, Barbara, forget the date. Did it happen on a Monday, a Thursday?" Kevin asked quickly, practically leaping at the little girl.

"Um . . . a Tuesday."

"Tuesday?" He took another step toward her.

"Yes."

"But you don't have special arts on Tuesday, Barbara," he said quickly, seizing on an unexpected piece of good luck: the girl's confusion.

She looked about helplessly. "Um, I meant Thursday."

"You meant Thursday. You sure it wasn't a Monday?" She shook her head. "Because very often Miss Wilson goes to the faculty room when she has a break, and she wouldn't be in her room after the class left." Barbara just stared. "So it was a Thursday?"

"Yes," she said weakly.

"Didn't it supposedly happen to the other girls on a Thursday, too?" he asked, as if he were confused about the facts himself.

"Objection, your honor. She hasn't been schooled in everyone's testimony."

"On the contrary," Kevin said, "it's my contention that she has."

"By whom?" Balm demanded indignantly.

"Gentlemen." The judge rapped his gavel. "The

objection is sustained. Limit your questions to the testimony of this witness, Mr. Taylor."

"Fine, your honor. Barbara, when did you tell the other girls what had happened to you? Did you tell them right away?" Kevin asked before she could recover.

"No."

"Did you tell them at your house?"

"I . . ."

"Was it the day you had that party with Gerald and Tony?"

The little girl bit down softly on her lower lip.

"That's when you told them, right? Was there some reason why you picked that afternoon? Did something happen that gave you the idea to tell that story?"

Barbara's tears began to flow harder. She shook her head.

"If you want people to believe the story you are telling about Miss Wilson, you're going to have to tell everything, Barbara. All the girls are going to have to tell everything," he added. "Why you talked about Miss Wilson that afternoon, what you and the boys did, all of it." The look of terror on Barbara's face amplified.

"Unless, of course, you made it all up and then had the girls make it all up," he added, offering her a quick out. "Did you make it all up, Barbara?"

She sat like stone, her lips trembling slightly. Barbara didn't reply.

"If you tell the truth now, this is where it will end," he promised. "No one has to know anything else," he added, almost in a whisper. The little girl looked stunned. "Barbara?"

"Your honor," Balm said, "Mr. Taylor is badgering the witness."

"I don't think so, Mr. Balm," the judge said. He leaned toward Barbara. "Barbara, you have to answer the question."

"Did you lie to Mr. Cornbleau because you don't like Miss Wilson?" Kevin asked quickly. It was a great move; it assumed she had already answered in the positive. Out of the corner of his eye, Kevin saw eyebrows rise on members of the jury.

Barbara shook her head, but another tear escaped and then another as they started to trickle down her cheek.

"You know you could ruin Miss Wilson's career, Barbara?" Kevin said, stepping aside so that Lois Wilson could stare directly at the little girl. "This isn't a game, not like a game you play in your house, a game like 'Special Places,'" Kevin added in a loud whisper, and the little girl's face looked as if it had burst into flame. Her eyes widened. She looked frantically at the audience.

"If you didn't tell the whole truth before, it's better that you tell it now rather than keep telling the lies. Now, think and tell us the truth, Barbara," Kevin added, standing over her and glaring down with his eyes as wide as he could make them.

Kevin reached back like a prizefighter readying his knockout blow. "Miss Wilson never touched the other girls. They agreed to say it because of what they did at your house that afternoon, right? You said you would tell everyone if they didn't help."

Barbara's mouth opened wide. Her face was so flushed it looked as though all the blood in her body had been drawn into it. She looked widely at her parents. Kevin shifted his feet so he could block out the district attorney from her view.

"We don't have to talk about what happened at your house," he said mercifully, "but did you tell your friends what to say and how to say it? Barbara?" he pursued, hammering the answer he wanted into her. "When the other girls come up here, they will have to talk about the afternoon and the game, and they will have to tell the truth. But if you tell it now, we don't need to hear from them. Did you tell them what to say?"

"Yes," she muttered, grateful for the reprieve.

"What?"

"Yes." She started to cry.

"So they told Mr. Cornbleau what you told them to tell him," he concluded, driving the point home. Then he turned from her and looked at the jury, his face a wonderful combination of anger and sorrow. All of them looked at the little girl and then back at Kevin.

"But I didn't lie about what I told him. I didn't!" Barbara shouted through her tears.

"Seems to me, Barbara, you've been telling a number of lies while you sat here."

He turned and shook his head at the district attorney. Barbara was crying hard and had to be taken off the stand and led out a side door.

Kevin strutted back to his seat, gazing out at the audience as he did so. Most of them looked shocked, confused. Mr. Cornbleau looked enraged, as did a number of other indignant citizens. The gentleman in the rear was smiling at him, but Miriam shook her head and wiped a tear away from her own cheek.

Lois Wilson looked to him for some signal. He nodded, and then, just as he had instructed, when she looked at Barbara, she looked forgiving and wiped away her own well-timed and well-rehearsed tears.

The district attorney stood up. Facing the judge and audience with a vacant expression, he knew it was fruitless to go on.

2

The Bramble Inn was one of the better restaurants just outside of Blithedale. It was an English chophouse famous for its rack of lamb and homemade trifle. Kevin and Miriam Taylor loved the ambience, from the cobblestone walkway to the large foyer with hickory benches and brick fireplace. For the Taylors nothing seemed as romantic as going to the Bramble Inn on a snowy night to sit by the bar and drink cocktails while the fire crackled and snapped. As usual the inn was crowded with its upper-middle-class clientele, many of whom knew Kevin. Some stopped by to congratulate him. As soon as he and Miriam had a few quiet moments to themselves, he brushed his shoulder up against hers and kissed her cheek.

Almost a month ago, Miriam had bought the black leather skirt and jacket she wore tonight, but she had kept it hidden at the back of her closet, hoping she soon would have the occasion to bring it out and surprise Kevin. The snugly fitted skirt traced the soft, full curve of her hips and firm buttocks and revealed just enough of her slim, well-shaped legs to make her enticing but not obvious. Under the jacket she wore a white and green knit blouse that seemed to have been constructed directly over her perky breasts and petite shoulders.

At five feet nine, with rich, thick, wavy dark brown hair that curled up just above her shoulders, Miriam Taylor cut a place for herself in any crowd when she entered a room. She had taken a year's training at Marie Simon's Modeling School in Manhattan, and although she had never had any real modeling experience, she maintained a fashion model's posture and grace.

Kevin first had fallen in love with her voice—a deep, sexy, Lauren Bacall voice. He even had her recite one of his favorite movie lines: "You know how to whistle, don't you, Sam . . . you just put your lips together and blow."

When she looked at him with her bright hazel eyes and turned her shoulder, substituting "Kevin" for "Sam," it was as if a hand reached inside his stomach, grabbed his heart. He might as well wear a collar around his neck, he thought, and hand her the leash. There was nothing he wouldn't do for her.

"I'm guilty of uxoriousness," he told her. "The little-known sin of excessive love for one's spouse. From the moment I met you, I violated the First Commandment: Thou shalt have no other gods before me."

They had met at a cocktail party his firm—Boyle, Carlton, and Sessler—had thrown when they had opened their new offices in their recently constructed building in Blithedale. Miriam had come to the party with her parents. Her father, Arthur Morris, was the most prominent dentist in Blithedale. Sanford Boyle introduced Kevin to her and her parents, and from that moment on they orbited each other, pulling on each other with smiles and glances across the room until they came together and talked and talked up until the end of the party. She agreed to go to dinner with him that night, and from then on their romance was fast, hot, and heavy. He proposed in less than a month.

Now as they sat at the bar in the Bramble Inn toasting his success, Miriam considered the changes in him since they had first met.

How much he has grown, she thought. He looked years older than twenty-eight. There was a maturity, a control, a self-confidence in his jade-green eyes and his gestures that suggested a man of much greater experience and years. He wasn't a big man, but at six feet and one hundred seventy-five pounds, he was a trim, athletic-looking person with well-controlled energy. He had his bursts of exuberance when he needed them, but most of the time he paced himself well.

He was so organized, so healthy, so ambitious and determined that she used to kid him and sing those lines from an old pop song: "And he's oh so healthy in his body and his mind. He's the well-adjusted man about town . . ."

"So tell me what you really thought today while you sat there in court. Weren't you just a little proud of me?"

"Oh, Kevin, I'm not saying I wasn't proud of you. You were . . . masterful," she replied, but she couldn't expunge the terrified face of that little girl from her mind. She couldn't stop herself from reliving the moments of panic in the child's eyes when Kevin threatened to expose what she and her girlfriends had done at her house. "I just wish there had been another way for you to win the case than threaten that child with exposure, don't you?"

"Of course. But I had to do it," he said. "Besides, don't forget Barbara Stanley was using the threat of the same exposure to blackmail the others into testifying."

"She looked so pathetic when you tore into her," she said.

Kevin blanched. "I didn't bring the charges against Lois Wilson," he reminded her. "Marty Balm did. He was the one who brought Barbara Stanley into court and submitted her to the cross-examination, not me. I had a client to defend and her rights and future to think about first and foremost."

"But Kevin, what if she had talked the others into testifying with her because she was afraid to go it alone?"

"The prosecution should have developed its case another way then or objected, whatever. That's not my concern. I told you, Miriam, I was the defense attorney. I have to defend, use every available approach, otherwise I'm not doing my job. You understand that, don't you?"

She nodded. She had to agree, albeit reluctantly. What he said was true.

"Aren't you just a tiny bit proud of the way I handled myself in court?" he asked again, nudging his shoulder against hers.

She smiled. "You're a frustrated actor, Kevin Taylor. The way you moved about, directed yourself at the jury, timed your questions, and swung those eyes . . ." She laughed. "You could have been nominated for an Academy Award."

"It is like a performance, isn't it, Miriam? I can't explain what happens to me when I step into a courtroom. It's like the curtain goes up and everything's been written to follow. It's almost as if it doesn't matter who the client is or what the case is. I'm just there, destined to do what I do."

"What do you mean, it doesn't matter what the case is or who the client is? You wouldn't defend just anyone, would you?" He didn't reply. "Would you?"

He shrugged. "Depended on the money I was offered, I guess."

She studied him, her eyes narrowing. "Kevin, I want you to be honest with me."

He raised his right hand and turned to face her. "I swear to tell the truth, the whole truth . . ."

"I'm serious," she said, pulling down his hand.

"All right, what is it?" He turned around again and leaned over the bar to hug his drink.

"Put aside all the legal jargon, the role of the prosecution, the role of the defense attorney . . . all of it. You proved that the three girls lied, were forced to lie, or at least developed that impression, and I don't deny that Barbara Stanley looks like a manipulator, but did Lois Wilson abuse her? Take advantage of her? You questioned her, and you spent a lot of time with Lois Wilson."

"Maybe," he said. There was something in the way he moved his head that sent a chill through her.

"Maybe?"

He shrugged. "I defended her, as I explained to you,

found holes in the prosecution's case and attacked it where it was vulnerable."

"But if she was guilty . . ."

"Who knows who's guilty and who isn't? If we had to be absolutely positive of a client's innocence, beyond any possible doubt whatsoever, before taking a case, we'd all starve." He waved at someone and ordered another round of drinks.

For Miriam, it was as if a cloud had momentarily blocked the sun. She sat up and looked about the bar, her attention focusing on a handsome, distinguished-looking man with ebony hair and a dark complexion sitting alone at a corner table. Miriam was sure he was staring at them. Suddenly, he smiled. She smiled and quickly looked away. When she turned back, he was still staring at them.

"Kevin? Do you know that man in the corner who is looking so intently at us?"

"Man?" He turned. "Yes. I mean, no, but I saw him in court today."

The man smiled again and nodded. Kevin nodded back. The man, apparently taking that as a welcome, stood up and headed in their direction. He was a little over six feet tall with a trim build.

"Evening," he said. He extended his hand, a large palm with long fingers and manicured nails. On his pinky, he wore a flat gold ring with the initial "P" engraved in it. "Let me join in on the congratulations and add my name to the list of admirers. Paul Scholefield."

"Thank you, Paul. My wife, Miriam."

"Mrs. Taylor," he said, nodding. "You have good reason to look beautiful and proud tonight."

Miriam blushed. "Thank you," she said.

"I don't mean to intrude," Scholefield went on, "but I was in court today and saw you in action."

"Yes, I know. I remember seeing you." Kevin looked at him closely. "I don't think we've ever met."

"No. I don't live here. I'm an attorney with a firm in New York City. Would it be all right if I joined you for a moment?" he asked, indicating the seat beside Kevin.

"Sure."

"Thanks. I see you've just ordered a round of drinks; otherwise, I'd buy you both one." He signaled the waiter. "A champagne cocktail, please."

"What field of law are you in, Mr. Scholefield?" Kevin asked.

"Please, call me Paul. Our firm only handles criminal law, Kevin. Perhaps you've heard of it: John Milton and Associates."

Kevin thought a moment and then shook his head. "Sorry, no."

"It's all right." Scholefield smiled. "It's one of those firms you don't hear about unless you're in trouble. We've become specialists. Most of the cases we take on, other lawyers would avoid."

"Sounds . . . interesting," Kevin said cautiously. He was beginning to regret having him join them. He didn't want to talk shop. "I guess we'd better see about our table, huh, Miriam? Starting to get hungry."

"Yes," she said, picking up his hint. She signaled the maître d'.

"As I said," Scholefield continued, quickly understanding, "I don't mean to intrude." He took out a business card. "I didn't just drop in on your trial today. We've heard about you, Kevin."

"Really?" Kevin's eyes widened.

"Yes. We're always keeping an eye open for up-and-coming excellent attorneys who handle criminal cases, and it just so happens that we have an opening at our firm right now."

"Oh?"

"And after seeing you in action, I'd like to leave our card and ask you to consider it."

"Oh, well . . ."

"I know you'll probably be offered a partnership at the firm you're with, but at the risk of sounding a little snobby, let me suggest that working out here won't provide you with half the career satisfaction or half the income."

"Half the income?"

"Your table is ready, sir," the maître d' said.

"Thank you." Kevin turned back to Scholefield. "You said half the income?"

"Yes. I know what you'll make as a partner in your firm. Mr. Milton will double that immediately, and in a relatively short period you'll be earning a significant bonus as well. I'm sure." Scholefield stood up. "Please, don't let me take any more of your time. You two deserve a chance to be alone," he added, winking at Miriam.

Once again, she felt herself blush.

He pushed the card toward Kevin. "Just call us. You won't regret it. Once more," he added, lifting his glass, "congratulations on a splendid victory. Mrs. Taylor." He toasted again and left them.

For a moment Kevin didn't move. Then he looked down at the business card. The raised print seemed to lift off the card, magnifying itself. The soft dinner music, the low murmuring chatter around them, even Miriam's voice suddenly became distant. He sensed himself drifting.

"Kevin?"

"Huh?"

"What was that all about?"

"I don't know, but it sure sounds interesting, doesn't it?"

Scholefield returned to his table and smiled at her. Something cold tugged at her heart and made it flutter. "Kevin, our table's ready."

"Right," he said. He looked at the business card once more and then stuffed it quickly into his pocket and got up to join Miriam.

They took their seats at one of the intimate tables in a nook toward the rear of the restaurant. The small oil lamp on the table cast a soft, yellow, magical glow over both their faces. They ordered a white zinfandel and sipped it slowly while they talked softly, recalling other times, other romantic meals, other precious moments. The soft dinner music wove its way around and above them like background theme music in a film. He brought her hand to his lips and kissed her fingers. They gazed at each other so intently that the waitress felt guilty interrupting to ask them for their order.

It wasn't until after they had their food and had begun eating that Miriam brought up Paul Scholefield.

"You really never heard of his firm?"

"No." He thought about it and shook his head. Then he took out the card and stared at it. "Can't say I have, but that doesn't mean anything. Do you know how many firms there are in New York City alone? Nice location," he noted. "Madison and Forty-fourth."

"Isn't it a bit unusual for another lawyer to come watch you in action, Kevin?"

He shrugged. "I don't know. No, I guess not. What better way to judge someone than actually to see him on the job? And don't forget," he added with obvious pleasure, "this case has been in the New York City papers. There were two inches or so on it in the *Times* last Sunday."

Miriam nodded, but he could see she was bothered by something.

"Why do you ask?"

"I don't know. The way he said his piece and gave you his card . . . he was . . . so confident."

"Comes with success, I suppose. I wonder how serious that mention of money was . . . twice as much as I'd make as a partner at Boyle, Carlton, and Sessler?" He looked at the card again and shook his head.

"You'll make enough there, Kevin."

"You never make enough anymore, and there won't be many cases like this Wilson case. I'm only afraid I'll fall back into one of their areas, get inundated with corporate law or real estate, simply because there isn't going to be that much in the way of criminal law out here."

"It never bothered you before, Kevin."

"I know." He leaned forward, his eyes catching the heart of the small lamp's light as his face suddenly changed from soft and serene to hot and excited. "But there was something happening to me in that court-room this time, Miriam. I could feel it. I was . . .

glowing at times. It was like being on the edge continually, knowing that every word is critical, that there is more than just someone's land at stake. Someone's entire life is at stake. Lois Wilson's future was in my hands. I was like a heart or brain surgeon as compared to a GP setting a broken leg."

"It's not terrible to get some easy real estate work once in a while," she said in a low voice. His exuberance took her breath away.

"No, but the harder, the more critical the case, the sharper I can be. I know it. I mean, I'm not a pencil pusher, Miriam. I'm . . . I'm an advocate."

She nodded, her smile slowly wilting. There was something in his voice, something in his eyes that frightened her. She sensed that the life she had planned for them was not going to be enough for him.

"But Kevin," she said after a few moments, "you never brought this up before and probably wouldn't be bringing it up now if that man hadn't appeared tonight."

"Maybe not." He shrugged. "Maybe I don't know what I want." He looked at the card again and then put it in his pocket. "In any case, we'll have some time to think things out. I don't expect they'll offer me a partnership on Monday morning. Those three have to have a series of meetings. They believe things have to settle and harden." He laughed, but his laugh was different from his usual laugh. It was sharp, cold. "They probably never made love to their wives without first reviewing the pros and cons. Come to think of it, looking at their wives, I don't see how they could be impulsive about it anyway."

He laughed again, clearly disdainful this time, but Miriam didn't join him. Kevin had never been disdainful about the Boyles, Carltons, and Sesslers before. She had always assumed he wanted to be just like them.

"Isn't the lamb great tonight?" he asked, and she smiled and nodded, eager to put the discussion aside and slow down her heart beat so she could rid herself of the flickering butterfly wings just under her breast.

It worked. They didn't talk about law or the case. More content after their coffee and dessert, they went home to make love as passionately as she could ever remember.

But the following morning, she saw him go to the closet to find the pants he had worn to the Bramble Inn. He put his hand in the pocket and took out Paul Scholefield's business card, looked at it, and put it in the inside pocket of the jacket he would wear to work on Monday.

Throughout the weekend, Kevin had sensed a coolness in the community. The friends he had expected would call to congratulate him never called. Miriam had a conversation with her mother that he later found out was not pleasant. When he pressed for details, she finally told him that her mother had gotten into a fight with one of her so-called good friends defending him.

He almost got into a fight himself when he stopped at Bob's Service Station for gas Sunday morning and Bob Salter quipped that it was too bad the lesbians and gays were getting all the breaks in this country.

So he wasn't surprised at the cool reception he received at the office on Monday morning. Mary Echert, who served as his secretary and as the receptionist, barely said good morning, and Teresa London,

Garth Sessler's secretary, flashed a smile and looked away quickly as he made his way to his "hole in the wall."

Kevin wasn't in his office long before the intercom buzzed and Myra Brockport, Sanford Boyle's secretary, in a voice that made him think of a stern schoolteacher he had had in grade school, said, "Mr. Boyle would like to see you immediately, Mr. Taylor."

"Thank you," he replied and snapped off the intercom. He stood up and straightened his tie. He felt confident, elated. Why not? In three short years, he had made a nearly indelible mark on this well-established old firm. It had taken Brian Carlton and Garth Sessler a little over five years each to achieve a full partnership. In those days it was Boyle and Boyle, Sanford working with his father, Thomas, a man now in his mid-eighties, still sharp, still imposing opinions on his fifty-four-year-old son.

Kevin had feared Boyle, Carlton, and Sessler might resist offering him a partnership. There was a snobbery about them and about this firm. All three partners were sons of lawyers who were sons of lawyers. It was almost as if they considered themselves royalty, descendants of monarchs who inherited scepters and thrones, each with his own special kingdom, one with estate planning, another with real estate . . .

They had the biggest houses in Blithedale. Their children drove Mercedeses and BMWs and went to Ivy League schools, two already close to graduating law school. All the professional people in the community looked up to them, valued an invitation to their homes and their parties, and valued their attendance at their own parties. It was as if becoming their partner was becoming anointed.

Having been a member of the high society in this community all her life, Miriam was keenly aware of all this. They were at the point where they were going to build their dream house. Miriam talked about having children. Their upper-middle-class existence seemed guaranteed, and there was never any question about Kevin's desire to establish himself in the small Long Island community. He had been born and bred in Westbury, where both his parents still lived and ran his father's accounting firm. He had attended NYU Law and come back to the Island to find the girl of his dreams and work. This is where he belonged; this was his destiny.

Or was it?

He opened Sanford Boyle's office door and greeted the three senior partners, and then he took the seat in front of Sanford Boyle's desk, aware that it put him in the center, Brian Carlton seated on his left, Garth Sessler seated on his right. *It looks like they want me surrounded,* he thought, amused.

"Kevin," Sanford began. He was the oldest of the three, Brian Carlton being forty-eight and Garth Sessler being fifty, and he showed his age the most. He had the soft look of a man who had never had to do so much as mow his own lawn or take out his own garbage. He was nearly bald, his cheeks sagged, and his double chin trembled whenever he spoke. "You remember how we all felt about this case when you first announced you wanted to take it."

"Yes." He looked from one to the other. The three of them sat like austere judges in a Puritan court, all the lines and features of their faces sculptured deeply, each one looking more like a statue than the man himself.

"We all think you were absolutely masterful in that courtroom—precise and stinging. Perhaps too stinging."

"Excuse me?"

"You practically clubbed that little girl into submission."

"Had to do what I had to do," Kevin said, sitting back. He smiled at Brian Carlton. The tall thin man with a dark brown mustache leaned back, too, the tips of his long fingers pressed together as if he were there to oversee the discussion and not participate in it; while Garth Sessler, as impatient with small talk as usual, tapped his fingers on the side of his chair.

For some reason, Kevin never realized how much he disliked these three before. True, they were all bright, but they had as much personality as a data processing machine. Their reactions were as automatic and unemotional.

"I'm sure you know the whole community's buzzing. All of us have been on the phone most of the weekend with clients, friends . . ." He waved his hand in front of his face twice as if he were chasing away flies. "The fact is, the reactions are about as we expected. Our clients, on whom we are quite dependent for our living, are generally not happy with our position on this Lois Wilson thing."

"Our position? Haven't these people ever heard of innocent until proven guilty? I defended her and she was exonerated."

"She wasn't exonerated," Brian Carlton said, lifting the corner of his mouth sarcastically. "The prosecution just threw up its hands and backed out after you trapped a ten-year-old girl and made her admit she had been telling some lies."

"Same thing," Kevin replied.

"Hardly," Brian said. "But I'm not surprised you don't see the difference."

"What's that supposed to mean?"

"Let's get back to the point." Garth Sessler interrupted. "As we tried to explain to you before you became so heavily involved in the case, we have always steered away from these controversial cases. We're a conservative firm. We're not looking for notoriety or publicity. That sort of thing drives away the affluent clients in our community.

"Now then," he continued, taking the reins of the discussion firmly, "Sanford, Brian, and I have been looking over your history with our firm. We find you a dedicated, responsible person with a promising future."

"Promising?" Kevin turned instinctively toward Brian. He had entered this office believing his future had arrived. It was no longer just a promise.

"In criminal law," Brian said dryly.

"Which we are not interested in," Sanford concluded. For a moment Kevin thought they were the Three Stooges.

"I see. Then this is not a meeting to offer me a full partnership in Boyle, Carlton, and Sessler?"

"A full partnership is not the kind of thing we just hand out overnight, you know," Garth said. "Its value lies not only in the financial rewards but in what it means, and that meaning comes from the investment one makes in the community as well as in the firm. Why . . ."

"However, we see no reason why you won't become a full partner rather quickly in some firm that specializes in criminal law," Sanford Boyle said. He flashed a polished smile and sat forward, his hands folded on his desk. "Not that we aren't happy with everything you've done here. I want to repeat that."

"So you're not firing me so much as letting me know I'd be better off someplace else," Kevin said sharply. He nodded and relaxed in the chair. Then he shrugged and smiled. "Actually, I was considering tendering my resignation anyway."

"Pardon?" Brian said, leaning forward.

"I already have another offer, gentlemen."

"Oh?" Sanford Boyle looked quickly at his partners. Brian remained stone-faced. Garth raised his eyebrows. Kevin knew they didn't believe him, as if there was no possibility of his ever having thought of going to another firm. Their arrogance began to get under his skin. "With another firm in the area?"

"No. I'm . . . not at liberty to say any more just yet," he replied, the lie almost forming itself on his lips. "But I assure you, you will be the first to know the details. Excepting Miriam, of course."

"Of course," Sanford said, but Kevin knew these three often made personal decisions without consulting their wives. That was another thing he despised about them—their relationships with their wives and children were too impersonal. He shuddered to think that someday the four of them might have been sitting around this office offering a partnership to a bright young attorney like himself who could easily have a much more satisfying and exciting career someplace else but who might be easily tempted to accept the security and respectability of (suddenly he thought, God forbid) Boyle, Carlton, Sessler, and Taylor.

"Anyway, I'd better get back to my desk and finish up my paperwork on the Wilson case. Thank you for your half-assed expression of confidence in me," he added and left them staring at his wake.

When he closed the door behind him, he experienced a sense of delicious freedom as if he were free-falling from an airplane. In a matter of minutes, he had defied his so-called destiny and stood back like someone in firm control of his future.

Myra couldn't understand the wide smile on his face. "Are you all right, Mr. Taylor?"

"I'm fine, Myra. Feeling better than I have in . . . in three years, to be exact."

"Oh, I . . ."

"See you later," he said quickly and returned to his office.

For a long time, he sat behind his desk, thinking. Then he slowly reached into his pocket and took out the business card Paul Scholefield had given him. He laid it before him on the desk and stared down at it, but he was no longer looking at it; he was looking beyond it, into his own imagination, where he saw himself in a city court defending a man accused of murder. The prosecution had a strong, circumstantial case, but they were up against him, Kevin Taylor of John Milton and Associates. The jury hung on his every word. Reporters followed him through the courthouse corridors, pleading for information, predictions, statements.

Mary Echert tapped on his door and brought in his mail, interrupting his daydream. She smiled at him, but he could see from the expression around her eyes that the chatter had already begun.

"I don't have any appointments today that I might have forgotten, do I, Mary?"

"No. You are down to meet with Mr. Setton about

his son tomorrow morning and asked me to get you the police report."

"Oh. Yes. That's the sixteen-year-old kid who took a joy ride in his neighbor's car?"

"Uh-huh."

"Fascinating case."

She tilted her head, confused by his sarcasm. As soon as she left, he dialed John Milton and Associates and asked to speak to Paul Scholefield.

Fifteen minutes later, he was on his way to Manhattan, and he hadn't even called Miriam to tell her what had happened.

3

Boyle, Carlton, and Sessler had comfortable, tasteful offices back in Blithedale. Almost twenty years ago, Thomas Boyle had converted a small, two-story Cape Cod house into his and Sanford's offices. Part of the charm of the office was its homey atmosphere. One did feel relaxed there; perhaps too relaxed, Kevin thought. He had never had that reaction before. He had always appreciated the domestic touch in the curtains and drapes, the carpets and fixtures. He left one home every morning to go to another. That was his original way of thinking.

But the moment he entered John Milton and Associates, all that changed. He had gotten off the elevator on the twenty-eighth floor, which had a spectacular view of downtown Manhattan and the East River. At the end of the hall were the oak double doors with scripted writing that proclaimed "John Milton and Associates, Attorneys." He entered and found himself in a plush reception area.

The wide open space, the long tan leather couch, leather settee, and leather chairs announced success. Over the couch was an enormous brightly colored abstract painting that looked like an original Kandinsky. This was the way a successful law office should look, he thought.

He closed the door behind him and stepped over the lush, velvety tan carpet, feeling as though he were walking over a layer of marshmallow. The sensation brought a smile to his face as he approached the receptionist, who sat behind a half-moon teak desk. She turned from her word processor to greet him, and he widened his smile instantly. Instead of being greeted by the homey, plain-faced Myra Brockport or the gray-haired, pale-skinned, and dull-eyed Mary Echert, who greeted clients back at Boyle, Carlton, and Sessler, Kevin was greeted by a scintillating dark brunette who could easily have been a contestant in a Miss America pageant.

She had straight coal-black hair that lay softly over her shoulders, the ends nearly touching her shoulder blades. She looked Italian, like Sophia Loren with her straight Roman nose and high cheekbones. Her dark eyes were almost luminous.

"Good afternoon," she said. "Mr. Taylor?"

"Yes. Nice office."

"Thank you. Mr. Scholefield's anxious to see you. I'll take you to him directly," she said and stood up. "Would you like something to drink . . . tea, coffee, a Perrier?"

"Perrier would be fine. Thank you." He started to

follow her across the lobby toward the corridor at the rear.

"Twist of lime?" she asked, turning back to him.

"Yes, thank you."

He was mesmerized by the movement of her body as she led him down the corridor, stopping at a small kitchen area. She was at least five feet ten and wore a black knit skirt and white blouse with long sleeves. The skirt clung so tightly to her hips and buttocks, he could see the wrinkle as her muscles extended. It took his breath away. He laughed to himself, thinking how disapproving Boyle, Carlton, and Sessler would be.

She handed him a tumbler filled with the sparkling liquid on ice.

"Thank you."

The look in her eyes and the warmth in her smile sent a trickle of excitement down into his loins, making him blush.

"Right this way."

They passed one office, a conference room, and then another office before stopping at the door that had Paul Scholefield's nameplate. She knocked and opened it.

"Mr. Taylor, Mr. Scholefield."

"Thank you, Diane," Paul Scholefield said, coming around his desk to greet Kevin. She nodded and walked off, but Kevin was unable to pull his eyes from her for a moment. Scholefield waited with understanding. "Kevin, good to see you."

"Wonderful offices." Paul Scholefield's office was twice the size of Sanford Boyle's. It had a high-tech decor, the furniture glossy black leather, the bookshelves and desk glossy white. To the left of his desk were two large windows that looked out over the city to the East River. "What a view."

"Breathtaking, don't you think? All the offices have such views. Yours does, too."

"Oh?"

"Please, sit down. I've already told Mr. Milton you're here, and he wants to see you after we're through."

Kevin settled back in the black leather chair in front of Scholefield's desk.

"I'm glad you decided to give our offer serious consideration. We're literally inundated with new work," Paul Scholefield said, his eyes brightening. "So, did your present law firm offer you a partnership?"

"Not quite. They offered me an opportunity to find something else more suited to my nature," Kevin replied.

"What?" Paul held his smile.

"Apparently, the Lois Wilson case and the manner in which I conducted it has proven to be an embarrassment to them. Legal devices, technique, all of it is all right as long as it's done discreetly. You know, like manipulating some grandmother so they can get a piece of her estate or finding loopholes in the tax laws to fatten the pockets of their affluent clients," Kevin explained bitterly.

Paul shook his head and laughed. "Myopic. Quite provincial and narrow-minded. It's why you don't belong there, Kevin. Mr. Milton's right about you," he added, his expression becoming serious. "You belong here . . . with us."

"Mr. Milton said that?"

"Uh-huh. He was the one who spotted you first, and he's usually right when it comes to analyzing people. The man has remarkable insight."

"Have I met him?" Kevin asked, wondering how someone could be so sure of him without having met him.

"No, but he's always looking for bright, new prospects . . . likes to scout lawyers, go to hearings and trials like baseball scouts go to high school games. He saw you in action first and then he sent me. It's the way he went about hiring all of us. You'll meet everyone today—Dave Kotein, Ted McCarthy, and our secretaries. But let me show you your office first, and then we'll see Mr. Milton."

Kevin took a final sip of his Perrier and rose to follow him out the door and down the corridor. They stopped at an office door that had obviously just had its nameplate removed.

"Must have been something to tempt whoever it was away from this firm," Kevin commented.

Paul's eyes grew smaller as he nodded. "It was. A personal tragedy. He killed himself not long after his wife died in childbirth. His name was Richard Jaffee, and he was a brilliant attorney. Never lost a case while he was here."

"Oh, I didn't know."

"Mr. Milton is still quite upset about it, as you can imagine all of us are. But having you join us, Kevin," he added, putting his hand on Kevin's shoulder, "is going to cheer us up."

"Thank you," Kevin said. "But it sounds like I have big shoes to fill," he added.

"You can do it. If Mr. Milton thinks you can, you can," Paul said, nodding. Kevin almost laughed at the zealous expression of faith, but he could see **Paul Scholefield** was deadly serious.

Scholefield opened the door, and Kevin entered his prospective new office.

How many times during the past three years had he sat back in his closet of an office at Boyle, Carlton, and Sessler and dreamed of what it would be like to be a famous New York attorney with a plush office with a view.

Now before him was an L-shaped desk with a soft leather desk chair, a soft leather settee, and another leather chair at the front of the desk. The carpet was just as plush as the lobby's carpet, and the curtains were a bright beige. The walls were covered with light hickory paneling that gave the room a fresh, clean look.

"Everything looks brand new."

"Mr. Milton had the office redone. Hope you like it."

"Like it? I love it," Kevin said. Paul nodded. To Kevin the office was dazzling, from the sophisticated gold-plated phone system to the solid gold pen and pencil set. There were even silver picture frames waiting for his photos and frames on the walls awaiting Kevin's degrees and awards, the same number of frames he had hanging in his office back at Blithedale. What a coincidence, he thought. Good omen.

Kevin walked to the windows behind the desk. Just as Paul had said, there was the magnificent view of the city.

"Well?" Paul asked.

"Beautiful." He crossed to the bathroom and looked in on the shiny new fixtures and tiled floor and walls. There was even a shower stall. "I could move right in." Kevin inspected the books in the bookcase that took up most of the left wall. "I don't have to bring in a thing." Kevin laughed and looked around his office again. "This is . . . incredible."

"Mr. Milton will be glad to know you're happy with what he's done, Kevin." Paul looked at his watch. "It's time we met the man."

"Sure." He stopped to look back as they started out and shook his head. "It's exactly how I dreamed my office would be. It's as if . . ." He turned to the smiling Paul Scholefield. "As if he had gotten into my dreams."

After knocking, Paul opened the door and stepped back for him to enter first. Kevin had to admit he was nervous. Paul had built up John Milton so much in his mind, he had no idea what to expect.

The same carpet that covered the lobby area and flowed down the corridor spilled through the doorway of John Milton's office and covered his floor. At the center rear of the room was a dark mahogany desk and high-backed dark brown leather chair. There were two chairs set in front of the desk. Behind the desk were three large windows, nearly the height and width of the wall, providing an open, wide vista of the city and sky, an almost Godlike view.

At first Kevin was so taken with the radiance and brightness of the room that he did not see John Milton sitting in his chair. When Kevin stepped farther in and did see him, it was as if he had materialized out of the shadows.

"Welcome to John Milton and Associates, Kevin," he said. Kevin immediately heard a warmth in the man's mellow voice; it reminded him of the same open, friendly, and soothing tone Reverend Pendleton of the Blithedale Episcopalian Church had, a tone that put you quickly at ease. Kevin often tried to imitate it in court, secretly calling it his "Sunday voice."

John Milton looked like he was in his early sixties, with a curious combination of youthful and elderly traits. He had a full head of thick hair neatly trimmed and brushed, but it was all gray. As Paul closed the door behind them, Mr. Milton rose, his torso unfolding to a six-feet-two-inch frame and his smile bursting out of what at first looked to be a face locked in alabaster. He wore a dark gray silk suit with a ruby tie and ruby pocket handkerchief.

Kevin noted how his shoulders rose when he offered him his hand. He was in wonderful physical shape, which added to the strange but interesting mixture of youth and age. Moving closer, Kevin could see the crimson blush in his cheeks. He seized Kevin's hand firmly, as though he had waited ages to meet him.

"Pleased to meet you, Mr. Milton."

John Milton's eyes seemed to metamorphose while he and Kevin gazed at each other, changing from a dull, quiet brown to a shimmering rust. He had a straight, full nose with soft lines that at times made his face appear ageless. Even the lines around his eyes looked like someone had penciled them in only moments ago. His thin lips had an orange tone, and his jawbone was sharp, the skin tight, yet he had a fatherly look, a face full of wisdom.

"Paul has shown you what would be your office, I hope."

"Oh yes. It's fantastic. Love it."

"I'm glad, Kevin. Please, have a seat." He gestured toward the high-backed tan leather chair with smooth, dark mahogany arms. Hand-carved in them were figures from Greek mythology: satyrs, minotaurs. "Thank you, Paul," he added. Kevin looked back to see Paul Scholefield leaving.

John Milton returned to his own chair. Kevin noticed he had a firmness about him, something regal in the way he held his head and shoulders. He sat down like a monarch assuming his throne.

"As you know, we've been considering you for some time, Kevin. We would like you to start next week. Short notice, I know, but I already have a case earmarked for you," he added, tapping a thick folder to his right on the desk.

"Really?" He wanted to ask how he knew Kevin would accept a position here, but he thought that might seem impolite. "What's it about?"

"I'll give it to you in due time," John Milton said firmly. Kevin saw how easily Mr. Milton moved from warm and friendly tones to determined and resolute ones. "First, let me explain my philosophy when it comes to my associates, who, as you will learn, are more than mere associates. In most ways they are my partners, but even more than that, they are my family. We are a true team here, devoted to each other in many more ways than our mere professional relationships. We care for each other and each other's family. No one works in a vacuum; home, life, all problems have an effect on your work. Understand?"

"Yes, I do," Kevin said and couldn't help wondering about the man he was replacing. Was Mr. Milton leading up to that?

"I thought you would," John Milton said, sitting back until his face was covered by a shadow as a cloud slipped over the sun outside. "And for that reason, you wouldn't think it odd that I make suggestions, even try to help you in ways that are not, it would seem, directly related to your work here.

"For example," he continued, "it would surely help if you lived in the city. Now it just so happens I own a rather luxurious apartment complex in an ideal part of Manhattan, and I have an apartment available in it, one I would like you to take rent-free."

"Rent-free?"

"Exactly. That's how committed I am to my associates and their families. I have a way of writing it all off, too," he added. "Not that that's important. The important thing is to be sure you and your wife have a comfortable, enjoyable life while you're with us. I realize you and your wife have family ties to where you are presently located," he continued quickly, "but you won't be all that far away, and"—he leaned forward out of the shadow to smile—"you will have a new family here."

Kevin nodded. "It sounds . . . wonderful. Of course, I'll have to discuss it with my wife," he added quickly.

"Of course. Now," John Milton said, rising, "let's just talk about the law for a moment and let me give you my philosophy.

"Law should be strictly interpreted and strictly enforced. Justice is a resulting benefit, but it is not the reason for the legal system. The legal system is designed to maintain order, keep all men in check." He turned at the corner of his desk to look down at Kevin and smile again. "All men, the so-called agents of good as well as the criminal element.

"Compassion," John Milton continued, like a lecturing college professor, "is admirable in its place but has no place in the system because it's subjective and imperfect and subject to change, whereas law can be perfected and remain timeless and universal."

He paused and looked at Kevin, who nodded quickly.

"I think you understand everything I am saying and agree with it."

"Yes," Kevin said. "Maybe I haven't put it exactly in those terms, but I do."

"We are advocates, first and foremost, and as long as we remember that, we will succeed," John Milton said, his eyes blazing with determination. Kevin was mesmerized. When John Milton spoke, he spoke in undulating rhythms, so soft at times that he felt as if he was reading the man's lips and repeating phrases in his own voice. And then, suddenly he would be dynamic, his voice forceful and vibrant.

Kevin's heart beat quickly, a flush coming into his face. The last time he remembered feeling this excited was when he was on the high school basketball team and they were playing the game that would determine their league championship. Their coach, Marty McDermott, had made a locker-room speech that sent them sailing out on the court with enough fire in their hearts to burn away the whole league. He couldn't wait to get his hands on the ball. Now, he couldn't wait to get back into court.

John Milton nodded slowly. "We understand each other more than you imagine, Kevin; and as soon as I realized that, I instructed Paul to make overtures." He stared at Kevin for a moment and then smiled. It was almost an impish smile. "Take this last case you tried . . ." John Milton settled back in his seat, a more relaxed posture this time.

"Lois Wilson, the schoolteacher accused of abusing children?"

"Yes. Your defense was brilliant. You saw the weak spots in the prosecution's case and you surged forward, concentrating on them."

"I knew the principal had it in for her and I knew the other little girls were lying . . ."

"Yes," John Milton said, leaning forward, his arms extended over the desk as if he wanted to embrace Kevin. "But you also knew Barbara Stanley was not lying and that Lois Wilson was guilty."

Kevin just stared.

"Oh, you weren't completely sure, but in your heart you thought she had abused Barbara Stanley and that Barbara Stanley, afraid to come forward by herself, worked her friends into a frenzy and got them to join her. That idiot principal was anxious to get the teacher . . ."

"I don't know all that for sure," Kevin said slowly.

"It's all right," John Milton said, smiling again. "You did what you had to do as her advocate." John Milton stopped smiling. In fact, he looked angry. "The prosecution should have done the kind of homework you did. You were the only *real* attorney in that courtroom," he added. "I admire you for it and want you here working with me. You're the kind of attorney who belongs here, Kevin."

Kevin wondered how John Milton knew so much about the Lois Wilson case, but that curiosity didn't linger. There were too many distractions, too many wonderful things to think about now. They went on to talk about salary, and he discovered Paul Scholefield had not exaggerated. It was twice what he was making at his present firm. Mr. Milton said he would make arrangements for Kevin and Miriam to move into their apartment immediately if Miriam approved. As soon as he finished, Mr. Milton buzzed his secretary and asked her to fetch Paul Scholefield. Paul arrived instantly, as if he were just standing outside the door, waiting.

"He's back in your hands, Paul. Kevin, welcome to our family," John Milton said, extending his hand. Kevin took it and they shook firmly.

"Thank you."

"And as I told you, all the arrangements for your moving into the apartment will be taken care of before the weekend. You can bring your wife in any time to look at it."

"Thanks again. I can't wait."

John Milton nodded with understanding.

"Quite a man, isn't he?" Paul said softly as they left the office.

"Extraordinary how he gets right to the heart of things. There's a no-nonsense air about him, yet I didn't feel he was all business. He was very warm, too."

"Oh yes. To be honest," Paul said, pausing in the corridor, "all of us love the guy. He's like . . . a father."

Kevin nodded. "Yes, that's the way I felt." He looked back. "As if I was sitting and talking with my father."

Paul laughed and put his arm around Kevin, and they continued down the corridor, stopping at Dave Kotein's office. Dave was closer to Kevin's age, being only thirty-one. He, too, was a graduate of NYU Law, and they immediately reminisced about the professors they had in common. Dave was a slim, five-feet-ten-inch-tall man with light brown hair cut short, almost as close as a military cut. Kevin thought Miriam would find him cute because he had baby blue eyes and a soft, pleasing smile and in some ways reminded him of her younger brother, Seth.

Despite his slender frame, Dave had a deep, resonant voice, the kind of voice chorus directors sell their souls to get into their ensembles. Kevin imagined him in court, cross-examining a witness, his voice reverberating over the heads of an attentive audience. From their introduction, Kevin sensed that Dave Kotein was a sharp, highly intelligent man. Later Paul would tell him Dave Kotein had graduated in the top five of his class at NYU and could have worked at a number of prestigious New York or Washington firms.

"Let me continue the tour," Paul said. "You and Dave will have many opportunities to get to know each other, as will your wives."

"Great. Any children?" Kevin asked.

"Not yet, but soon," Dave replied. "Norma and I are at about the same point you and Miriam are," he added. Kevin started to smile but then thought how odd it was they knew about his personal life, too.

Paul anticipated the thought. "We make a complete study of a prospective associate," he said, "so don't be surprised at just how much we already know about you."

"Sure this isn't a branch of the CIA?"

Dave and Paul looked at each other and laughed.

"I felt the same way when Paul and Mr. Milton were considering me."

"We'll talk to you later," Paul said, and he and Kevin left to go to the law library.

The law library was twice the size of Boyle, Carlton,

and Sessler's and fully updated. There was a computer which Paul Scholefield explained was tied into police records, even federal records, as well as a mainframe that would feed them precedent cases and investigative information so they could understand and examine police reports and forensic evidence. One of the secretaries was at the keyboard entering in new information provided by one of their private investigators.

"Wendy, this is Kevin Taylor, our new associate. Kevin, Wendy Allan."

The secretary turned around, and once again Kevin found himself taken aback by a beautiful face and figure. Wendy Allan looked to be twenty-two or twenty-three years old. She had peach-colored hair layered softly with sweeping bangs that were feathered over her forehead. Her chestnut brown eyes brightened as she smiled.

"Hi."

"Hello."

"Wendy will double as your secretary and Dave's until we hire a new one," Scholefield explained. Kevin smiled to himself with the thought that soon he would have his own secretary.

"Look forward to working with you, Mr. Taylor."

"Likewise."

"We'd better catch Ted," Paul whispered. "I just remembered he's got to take a deposition this afternoon."

"Oh, sure."

He followed Paul out, looking back once to ingest the smile Wendy Allan still offered.

"How do you keep your mind on your work with such beautiful women around?" Kevin asked, half kidding. Paul stopped and turned to him.

"Wendy and Diane are beautiful, and as you will see, so are Elaine and Carla, but each is a top-notch secretary, too." Paul smiled and looked back at the library. "Mr. Milton says most men have a tendency to think beautiful women are not intelligent. He once won a case because a prosecutor thought just that. Remind me to ask him to tell you about it one day. By the way," he added, lowering his voice, "Mr. Milton hired all the secretaries personally."

Kevin nodded, and they continued on to Ted McCarthy's office.

In many ways McCarthy reminded Kevin of himself. He was two years older and about Kevin's height and of similar build, only he had black hair, a much darker complexion, and dark brown eyes. But both had been born and bred on Long Island. McCarthy had lived in Northport and attended Syracuse University Law School.

Like Miriam, Ted McCarthy's wife had also been brought up on the Island. She had been a physician's receptionist in Commack. They, too, had no children yet but were planning to have some soon.

Kevin sensed that Ted McCarthy was a precise man. He sat behind a large black oak desk, his papers neatly organized beside a large silver-framed photograph of his wife and another silver-framed photograph of him and his wife on their wedding day. His office was rather spartan compared to Dave Kotein's and Paul Scholefield's, but there was more of a sense of order and tidiness.

"Pleased to meet you, Kevin," McCarthy said, rising from his seat when Paul introduced them. Just like Dave and Paul, Ted had an impressive speaking voice with sharp, clear diction. "From the way Mr.

Milton and Paul described you, I knew you'd be with us soon."

"Seems everyone knew before I did," Kevin quipped.

"It was the same way for me," Ted said. "I had been working in my father's firm and had absolutely no intention of leaving, when Paul approached me. By the time I came up here to meet Mr. Milton, I was already working out how I would break the news to my father."

"Extraordinary."

"There's hardly a day that passes without something exciting happening. And now with you joining us . . ."

"I'm really looking forward to it," Kevin said.

"Good luck and welcome aboard," Ted said. "I have to run off to take a deposition involving a client accused of raping his next-door neighbor's teenage daughter."

"Really?"

"Tell you about it at our staff meeting," Ted said.

Kevin nodded and started to follow Paul out. He paused at the doorway. "One thing I'd like to know, Ted," Kevin said, wondering how Miriam, her parents, and his would react to his decision.

"Sure."

"How did you break the news to your father?"

"I told him how much I wanted to specialize in criminal law and how impressed I was with Mr. Milton."

"But you had a family firm to inherit, didn't you?"

"Oh . . ." Ted smiled and shook his head. "After a short while you'll see that this is a family firm, too."

Kevin nodded, impressed with Ted's sincerity.

Kevin returned to what would be his office and sat behind the big desk. He leaned back in the chair, his hands behind his head, and then spun around to look out over the city. It made him feel like a million dollars. He couldn't believe his luck—a rich firm, a rent-free luxury apartment in Manhattan . . .

He turned back and looked into the drawers of the desk. Clean pads, new pens, a fresh diary book—everything was there. He was about to close the lower side drawer when something caught his eye. It was a small jewelry case.

He took it out and opened it and looked down at a gold pinky ring with the initial "K" carved into it.

"Trying the chair out for size?" Paul said, stepping in.

"What? Oh. Yeah. What is this?" He held out the ring.

"Found that already, huh? Just something from Mr. Milton, a welcoming gift. He did it for all of us."

Kevin took the ring out of the case gingerly and tried it on. It was a perfect fit. He looked up with surprise, but Paul didn't seem at all amazed.

"It's those little things, the way he takes the time to show us how committed he is to us as people, that makes the difference here, Kevin."

"I can see that." Kevin thought for a moment and then looked up from his ring. "But how did he know I would take the job?"

Paul shrugged.

"Like I said, he's a great judge of character."

"Amazing." He looked around the office. "This man . . . Jaffee?"

"What about him?"

"No one could see it coming?"

"We knew he was depressed. Everyone pitched in. Mr. Milton hired a nurse for the infant. We did all that we could, called him, visited with him. We all feel guilty; we all felt responsible."

"I wasn't implying . . ."

"Oh no," Paul said. "We all live in the same apartment building. We should have been able to help him."

"All of you live in the same apartment building?"

"And you will, too. In fact, you'll be taking over Jaffee's apartment."

Kevin just stared. He wasn't sure how Miriam would take to that.

"How did he . . . did he do it?"

"He jumped from his patio. But don't worry," Paul said, smiling quickly, "I don't think the apartment is cursed."

"Just the same, it might be wise for me to hold back that information from my wife."

"Oh, by all means. At least until you're settled in and she can see for herself how safe and comfortable you are. In time a herd of wild elephants won't be able to drag her away!"

4

It wasn't until Kevin was about to turn off the expressway that he realized just how much of his and Miriam's life he would be changing. Not that he regretted any of it—quite the contrary, he couldn't remember ever being as excited about his life and his career. It was just that as he drew closer to the idyllic little community in which he and Miriam had planned to spend their lives, he realized he was going to take them far away from the life they had pictured.

But the changes were all good changes, ones Miriam should want, too, he thought. How could she not? More money meant an even bigger dream house than they'd envisioned. Their lives would become more cosmopolitan, and they would get away from what he now saw as a stifling provincialism.

Perhaps most importantly, they would expand their circle of friends and meet far more interesting people, heads and shoulders above the so-called sophisticated upper class of Blithedale. He had taken an immediate liking to the two other attorneys working in John Milton's firm and felt confident that Miriam would as well.

He returned to his law office, checked on his messages. Miriam had called, but he decided he would speak to her when he got home.

He and Miriam lived in Blithedale Gardens, a complex of cedar wood town houses just outside the village proper in a wooded, rustic setting. The townhouses were comfortable and spacious two-floor apartments with wood-burning brick fireplaces. The complex had a community pool and two clay tennis courts. In no sense of the word had Miriam and he been roughing it during these early years, but when he looked at the town on the quick ride home, he found himself suddenly critical. There was something here he had not seen before—the area had a way of lulling its residents, making them complacent. Now he saw greater things and how unattainable those things would be if they stayed here.

He pulled into his garage, but before he had a chance to open the front door, Miriam had it opened for him. She stepped back into the foyer, a look of worry on her face. "Where have you been? I thought you would call me before lunch and we might get together, and you know I was waiting to hear what Sanford Boyle had to say."

He stepped in, closing the door softly behind him. "Forget Boyle; forget Carlton; forget Sessler."

"What?" She brought her right hand to the base of her throat. "Why? They didn't offer you the partnership?"

"Partnership? Hardly. Just the opposite."

"What do you mean, Kevin?"

He shook his head. "They didn't fire me so much as they suggested I find something more suitable to my . . . my nature," he said. He walked past her to the living room and flopped on the couch.

She remained behind, looking stunned. "It was this last case, wasn't it?"

"The straw that broke the camel's back, I suppose. Look, Miriam, I wasn't meant for them and they weren't meant for me."

"But Kev . . . after three years with only good things happening." She grimaced. "I knew you shouldn't have taken this case. I knew it. Now look what's happened," she cried. She couldn't keep her heart from pounding. How would it look? Kevin defends a known lesbian and then loses his position at one of the most prestigious firms in the community? She could hear her mother saying "I told you so."

"Relax." He smiled up at her.

"Relax?" She tilted her head. Why wasn't he more upset? "Where have you been, Kevin?" She looked at the clock on the fireplace mantel. "And aren't you home early?"

"Uh-huh. Come on in. Sit down." He patted the cushion beside him. "I have a lot to tell you."

"Your mother called," she said, almost as if she foresaw his words and wanted to start reminding him of his ties to the area.

"I'll call her in a while. Everything all right?"

"Oh yes. She wanted to congratulate you on the court victory," she added dryly.

"Good. She's going to be even happier now."

"Why, Kevin?" Miriam decided to sit across from him, folding her hands in her lap.

"Don't look so nervous, honey. All we're going to do from now on is improve our lives."

"How?"

"Well, obviously I'm going to leave Boyle, Carlton, and Sessler. Thank God for that."

"You used to be very proud of working there," she said sadly.

"Used to be. What did I know? I was a kid, just out of law school, happy to get anything like that, but now . . ."

"What? Tell me," she asked more forcefully.

"Well," he said, leaning forward, "remember that man who came up to us at the bar in the Bramble Inn Friday night and gave me his card?"

"Yes."

"Well, after I had my cheerful discussion with the Three Stooges, I looked into it."

"What did you do?"

"I called him and drove into Manhattan. It was like . . . like entering one of my daydreams. Talk about your rich New York firms. Wait until you see this. They're on the twenty-eighth floor. The view is magnificent. Anyway, they're literally inundated with work; that's how fast their reputation has grown in New York. They desperately need another attorney."

"What did you do, Kevin?"

"First let me tell you that Paul wasn't kidding. They will be paying me twice as much as I would have earned at Boyle, Carlton, and Sessler this year even if they had done the right thing and made me a full partner. And that's a lot of money, Miriam. Second,

I'd only be doing what I want to do, trying criminal cases."

"But what if it doesn't work out? You're secure here; you're building something here."

"What do you mean, doesn't work out? That's some vote of confidence from my wife." He worked up a look of disappointment instantly, as if he were in court.

"I'm just trying to . . ."

"I know. Any big move like this is scary, but once you meet everyone . . . and this is the best part as far as we're concerned, Miriam: the other associates, Ted and Dave and Paul, are all married, and none of them have children yet. Dave and Ted and their wives are about our age. We'll be able to socialize with people with whom we have something in common. I mean, what do you really have in common with Ethel Boyle or Barbara Carlton or Rita Sessler? You know they still think themselves a step better than us because I'm not a partner, and don't tell me you haven't complained that they treat you like a child."

"But we have other friends, Kevin."

"I know. But it's time we expanded our horizons, honey. These people live and work in New York. They go to shows, concerts, art galleries, take great vacations. You're going to finally do the things you've always wanted to do."

She sat back, thinking. Maybe he was right; maybe she had been too cloistered all her life. Maybe it was time to break out of the cocoon. "You really think this is going to be a good move, Kev?"

"Oh, honey," he said, getting up and going to her. "It's not just a good move; it's a great move." He kissed her and sat beside her, taking her hands in his. "I wouldn't do anything that would make you unhappy, no matter how happy I think it would make me. It just couldn't work. We're too . . . too much a part of each other."

"Yes." She closed her eyes and bit down softly on her lower lip. He touched her cheek, and she opened her eyes.

"I love you, Miriam. I don't see how any man could love a woman more."

"Oh, Kev . . ." They kissed again, and then she saw his new pinky ring.

"Where did you get that, Kevin?" She took hold of his hand to bring the ring closer. "Your initial?"

"You won't believe this. It's a gift from Mr. Milton, sort of a welcome gift."

"Really? But how could he know you would accept his offer?"

"When you meet Mr. Milton, you'll understand. The man radiates confidence, authority, success."

She shook her head and looked at the ring again.

"Twenty-four-karat gold, solid," he said, waving his hand.

"You're really taken with them."

"I know," he confessed.

"But Kevin, what about the commuting? You never wanted to get into that."

He smiled. "Mr. Milton has a wonderful solution." He shook his head. "It all seems too perfect to be true, but it is."

"What? Tell me," she said, bouncing on the settee. He laughed at her impatience.

"Well, it seems that as a result of a case he had years ago, Milton took over a Riverside Drive apartment building and there is an apartment available in it right now."

"Riverside Drive? You mean we would move into New York?" She checked her budding excitement. He knew she wasn't keen on living in the city.

"Guess what the apartment sells for."

"I have no idea."

"Six hundred thousand dollars!"

"But Kevin, how can we afford that?"

"We don't have to afford it."

"I don't understand."

"It's ours until we're ready to build our dream house. No rent, nothing. Not even an electric bill."

Miriam's mouth dropped open so dramatically, he had to laugh again.

"And get this . . . Ted McCarthy and his wife, Jean; Dave Kotein and his wife, Norma; Paul Scholefield and his wife, Helen, live in the same building, too."

"Where does Mr. Milton live?"

"In a penthouse apartment in the same building. It's just as Ted McCarthy told me today . . . John Milton and Associates is one big family."

Her resistance began to falter. She couldn't help but be more interested. "What about Mr. Milton? Doesn't he have a wife and family of his own?"

"No. Perhaps that's why he treats his associates like his family."

"What is he like?"

Kevin sat back. "Miriam," he began, "John Milton is the most charismatic, charming man I have ever met." As Kevin was describing the meeting to her, he had the uncanny feeling that he was actually reliving it. Every detail had remained vivid in his mind.

Later, after a quiet dinner, they went to sleep

mentally exhausted. In the morning, Kevin would blame that mental exhaustion on his vivid nightmare. He was in court, arguing the Lois Wilson case again, only this time, when he looked up at the judge, the judge was Mr. Milton, who smiled down at him approvingly. Kevin turned toward Barbara Stanley, who sat naked on the witness stand. Lois Wilson stood right behind her and leaned over to run the tips of her fingers over the little girl's nipples. Then she looked up at him and smiled lasciviously before leaning over again to reach down between the little girl's thighs.

"No!" he cried.

"Kevin?"

"No!" He opened his eyes.

"What is it?"

"Huh?"

"You were shouting."

"What? Oh." He rubbed his face vigorously to wash away the vivid images that lingered in his eyes. "Just a nightmare."

"Wanna talk about it?" Miriam asked in a very groggy voice.

"No. I'll go back to sleep. I'm all right. It's nothing," he said. She moaned gratefully and fell asleep quickly. Moments later, he permitted his eyes to close.

When he awoke, Kevin called the office to say he wasn't coming in and asked Mary to reschedule his appointment with the Settons. The secretary was surprised and wanted to know more, but Kevin ended the call abruptly. Then they dressed, ate breakfast, and left for the city. It had snowed nearly two inches, the second significant snowfall of the year, and it wasn't even December. There was a soft carpet of milky white fresh flakes that crunched underfoot and put Miriam in the mood for Christmas. Sleigh bells tinkled in her memory, and when she had looked up on the way to the car, she saw a patch of blue sky through an opening in the clouds. The sun's rays came pouring through and turned the snowy branches into glistening sticks of cotton candy.

The heavy commuter traffic over the Grand Central Parkway, however, quickly changed the same clean white flakes into greasy-looking black and brown slush. Automobiles ahead of them slung the icy muck into their windshield. The wipers cleared it away with a monotonous regularity. Directly ahead of them, low gray clouds lingered threateningly on the skyline.

"Commuting is not for me," Kevin muttered as they approached the toll booth. "I couldn't deal with the tension and the wasted time."

"On the other hand, living in the city isn't all peaches and cream, Kevin. Parking problems, traffic . . ."

"Oh, no parking problems, honey. There's a secure private parking garage in the basement of our building."

"Really?"

"I won't need to drive to work, either. Mr. Milton has a limo for us that takes us to work and back every day. He told me it would become a sort of second office . . . Paul, Ted, Dave, and I discussing cases, et cetera."

"What about Mr. Milton?"

"Keeps different hours, I guess." She stared at him. "I don't know it all yet, honey. But I will. I will," he chanted.

She sat back as they entered the city. As soon as

Kevin turned down Blazer Avenue and approached Riverside Drive, Paul Scholefield stepped out of the John Milton and Associates limo that was parked in front of the apartment building and signaled for him to turn into the parking garage under the building.

The gate opened and he drove in.

"You guys have 15D," Paul said, pointing to their spaces. "Might as well get into the right one."

Kevin backed up and parked. Paul opened Miriam's door and helped her out of the car as Kevin came around to greet him.

"Great to see you again, Mrs. Taylor."

"Oh, please call me Miriam."

"Miriam. Please call me Paul," he countered with a smile. "There's an elevator right down here," he said, pointing to the right. "The parking lot gate opens with a clicker." He took one out of his jacket pocket and handed it to Kevin. "You have another one in your apartment on the kitchen counter." He turned back to Miriam. "I'm sure you've noticed that this garage is heated," he said proudly and pushed the button to request the elevator. The door opened instantly, and he gestured for them to step in first.

"How long have you and Helen been living here, Paul?" Kevin asked.

"We moved in soon after Mr. Milton acquired it. It's been . . . six years."

"This is a very nice area in the city, isn't it?" Miriam asked.

Paul smiled and nodded. "We're close to Lincoln Center, galleries, not far from the theater district. New York will be at your fingertips, Miriam," he said, and the elevator door opened. He held it open for them and indicated that they should go out and to their right.

Paul stopped before 15D, which, like the other apartments, had a wide, dark oak door with a small metal mallet for a knocker.

"How quaint," Miriam said, looking at the knocker. "I just love antiques."

Paul took out the door keys, unlocked the door, and stepped back after swinging it open. At the opposite end of the wide foyer and visible on entering was the dining room, the gold-trimmed deep blue velvet curtains pulled back so that the row of windows was uncovered. Even on so gray a day as this, the light poured in.

"Bright . . . airy," Miriam said as soon as they entered.

They stepped into the foyer which had hardwood floors. To the right about eight feet in was the entrance to the stepdown living room which had a white marble fireplace. The carpet, which looked brand new, was a light blue, not quite as bright as the carpet they had back in Blithedale. The room was not empty, however. In the right corner was a spinet.

"Oh, Kev!" Miriam exclaimed. She brought her hand to the base of her throat. "What I've always wanted!" She stepped down the two steps into the living room and tapped the keys. "It's in tune!" She played the first few bars of "Memory."

"Miriam can play well," Kevin explained. "We were talking about buying a piano, but we figured we'd wait until we had our house."

"How come it's here?" Miriam inquired.

"Belongs to Mr. Milton," Paul stated simply. He shrugged. "He always had it here."

She ran her hand over the top of the piano lovingly and smiled. "What a wonderful surprise," she muttered.

"Glad you'll make use of it," Paul said.

Miriam shook her head in astonishment and continued on to the dining room. "I was going to put up paper something like this in our own dining room. In fact, I went to a store nearby and picked it out."

Miriam glanced up at the sparkling chandelier and continued on to the long, lemon-yellow kitchen, shaking her head at the brand-new appliances, the long counter and work space. There was a large window in the breakfast nook with the same view of the Hudson River the dining room had.

But it was the master bedroom that took her breath away. Even Kevin was speechless. It was nearly twice the size of their master bedroom in Blithedale, and there was a long marble vanity table built on a landing to the right of the bathroom. The mirrors extended the width of the wall.

"Our bedroom set is going to look tiny in here, Kev. We'll need some more furniture."

"Uh-huh!" He shifted his eyes toward Paul. "It starts already. We need this, we need that."

"Well, we will, Kev."

"All right, all right."

"Don't worry about it, Miriam. Kevin can afford it now," Paul said.

"Thanks a lot for your support, buddy."

Paul laughed. "The same thing happened to me, my friend. My wife's still out there on a shopping safari."

Miriam oohed and ahhed over the master bathroom with its whirlpool tub and brass fixtures and then went on to inspect the second bedroom.

78

She returned declaring that whoever had lived here before had obviously made it into a nursery. "There's wallpaper with cartoon characters on the walls," she said.

"Well, you can change anything you want to change," Paul remarked.

"Oh no. A nursery is just fine. We were planning on starting our family soon anyway," she replied, looking to Kevin for confirmation. He nodded, smiling.

"I suppose this means you could be happy here?" Paul Scholefield teased.

"Happy? How fast can we move in?" she said, and even Kevin had to laugh at her unexpected enthusiasm. He had been anticipating all sorts of resistance, no matter how nice the apartment was. Even though Blithedale and the surrounding communities had grown considerably more urban during the last decade, she liked to think of herself as a country girl. There was always the question of safety and having to deal with congestion and pollution. Both her parents and his reinforced these negatives, not only because they believed they were true but because they wanted Kevin and Miriam to remain where they were. But Miriam seemed to have forgotten all that. At least for the moment.

"Oh Kev, I didn't even notice the patio," she said, moving across the living room to the glass doors. Kevin looked at Paul, but Paul didn't show any emotion, even though from that patio a highly successful attorney and good friend had tossed away his life. Miriam opened the doors and stepped out. "Kevin, come here."

He joined her, and they both stood there taking in the magnificent view.

"It takes my breath away," Miriam said. "Just imagine sitting out here on warm nights, sipping wine, looking up at the stars."

He nodded, but he couldn't help wondering about Richard Jaffee. What went through a man's mind to make him do such a thing? Because of the way the railing was shaped, he must have climbed up and swung himself over. It wasn't something that could be done easily, impulsively. He had to have thought it through, felt there was no other course of action. How depressing.

"Kevin, don't you think so?"

"Huh? Oh, yeah, yeah. It's . . beyond words," he said. He was grateful for the sound of the doorbell.

"Guests already?" Paul mused.

The three of them went to the foyer and opened the door. Norma Kotein and Jean McCarthy came rushing in like a fresh breeze of spring air, both women laughing and talking at once.

"I'm Norma Kotein."

"And I'm Jean McCarthy."

"Obviously you must be Miriam," Norma said. "We couldn't wait. Dave said to give you two a chance to settle in, but Jean said . . ."

"Whatever for? That's our job anyway: helping you settle in."

"Hi," Norma said, taking Miriam's hand in hers. Miriam just stood there smiling. "I'm in 15B."

"I'm in 15C," Jean said. She took Miriam's hand the moment Norma released it.

Then they paused to catch their breath.

"Paul?" Norma demanded.

"Oh. This is Kevin and Miriam Taylor. You know who they are already."

"Just like an attorney," Jean said. "Won't waste a word unless he's being paid for it."

They both laughed, almost in unison. In some ways they did look like sisters. Although Norma's hair was trimmed into a neat pageboy and Jean's was long and scooped up at the ends which lay softly over her collarbone, both had light brown hair, Norma's barely a shade darker. They were both about five feet six inches tall, with firm, petite figures, Norma a little more buxom.

Kevin thought they were the two most bubbly women he had ever met. Norma's light blue eyes sparkled like jewels under ice, and Jean's green eyes twinkled with a similar glitter. Both had soft, smooth complexions with bright, healthy cheeks and rich red lips. Dressed in jeans and similar dark blue sweatshirts with pink LA Gear sneakers, it was as if they were wearing some sort of uniform.

"You'll come to my apartment for coffee. I've got these great sugarless muffins," Jean said, scooping her arm under Miriam's. "There's this bakery just over on Broadway and Sixty-third . . ."

"She acts like she discovered it. I found it first," Norma whined playfully.

Miriam had to laugh as they practically turned her toward the door. She glanced helplessly at Kevin.

"It's all right," he said. "Paul and I are going to the office. I'll be back in a couple of hours . . . to rescue you," he added and laughed.

"Rescue her?" Norma straightened up. "That's what we're doing. Why would she want to have anything to do with all that boring legal gibberish when we have loads of shopping information to pour into her?"

"At least she won't be bored while I'm away," Kevin muttered.

"There'll never be a boring day in her life again," Paul said, but he said it with such arrogance and determination, Kevin had to look at him to be sure he wasn't deliberately exaggerating to be humorous.

He wasn't.

"Where's your wife, Paul?"

"Helen's a little more laid back than those two, but she's just as friendly once you get to know her," he said. "Anyway, let's be on our way. The limo's out front."

Kevin nodded. He looked back before they closed the door behind them and heard Norma and Jean's peal of laughter, followed by Miriam's.

Wasn't this all wonderful? Wasn't this all good?

He wondered why he even had to ask himself the questions.

"Coffee?" Paul asked. He leaned over to pour them both a cup from the pot the chauffeur had prepared and left on the warmer built into the cabinet.

"Sure." Kevin sat back in the smooth, black leather seats and ran his hands appreciatively over the cushions as the limo pulled away from the curb. It was a Mercedes limousine with some interior customizing. "This is really the way to travel through New York."

"I'll say." Paul handed him his cup. "You don't even notice the city from in here." He sat back in the seat across from Kevin and crossed his legs. "Every morning we have our coffee. There's always a copy of the *Wall Street Journal* on the seat so we can relax before getting into the war. I've been doing it so long, I just take it for granted now."

"You've been with Mr. Milton for six years?"

"Yes. I was working upstate, a little village called Monticello, mostly handling real estate work with an occasional traffic accident. Mr. Milton spotted me when I defended a local doctor against a malpractice suit."

"Really? **How** did you do?"

"Complete victory." He leaned toward Kevin. "Even though the bastard was guilty of the most arrogant, insensitive, irresponsible behavior."

"How did you manage to win under those circumstances?"

"Confused the defendant badly on the stand for one thing. He had been treated for an eye injury and this doctor failed to examine him for days. He went off on a golfing holiday and forgot to tell his partner to look in on the poor slob. In the interim, his eye drained and he lost it."

"Oh Christ."

"He was a poor schnook, a highway department laborer. His sister was the one who pushed him into the lawsuit, but he couldn't remember when the doctor looked at him, what the doctor really did, and, fortunately for us, the hospital kept poor records. Of course, I had a specialist from New York testify for the doctor that his cohort had done all the right things. Paid the bastard five thousand dollars for an hour's work, but saved the physician quite a bundle."

"What about the poor schnook?" Kevin asked before he had a chance to check his own thoughts.

Paul shrugged. "We had made his lawyer an offer, but the greedy bastard thought he was going to win a bundle." He smiled. "We do what we have to do, buddy. You know that now.

"Anyway," he continued, "shortly after that, Mr. Milton stopped by to see me. We went to lunch together and talked, and the next day I came into the city to visit him. Been here ever since."

"Never regretted it, I imagine."

"Not for a moment."

"Well, I am impressed with everything and especially with Mr. Milton." Kevin thought for a moment. "In all the excitement yesterday, I never got to ask him about himself. Where is he from?"

"Boston. Yale Law School."

"One of those wealthy families? Father a lawyer, too?"

"Wealthy, but he wasn't a lawyer. He doesn't like to talk about his past that much. His mother died giving birth to him, and he didn't get along with his father, who eventually threw him out."

"Oh."

"Apparently that was the best thing that could have happened. Forced to be on his own, he worked hard and built himself a reputation quickly. He's a self-made man in every sense of the word."

"How come he's not married? He's not . . ."

"Hardly. He has his women; he's just wary of commitments. A confirmed bachelor, but happy. Hugh Hefner should have it so good," Paul quipped. Kevin laughed and gazed out the window at the crowds of people crossing the street. It was exciting to be here, to be working in New York, to be surrounded with success, and to be offered so much.

What had he done to deserve it? he wondered, but picking up on his grandfather's favorite warning not to look a gift horse in the mouth, he didn't question it anymore. He was just eager to get started.

As soon as they entered the office, Diane informed them that Mr. Milton, Dave, and Ted were waiting for them in the conference room.

"Oh, I almost forgot, we have a staff meeting. Actually, that's very fortunate," Paul added, patting Kevin on the shoulder. "You'll get baptized immediately."

5

The conference room was a brightly lit, dark gray rectangular room with no windows. Except for a large IBM clock high on the rear wall, there were none of the elaborate paintings that hung in the lobby and corridor. The bland walls and immaculate gray floor tile gave Kevin the feeling he was in a hospital examination room. The room had no smell, pleasant or otherwise. A very low-sounding air-conditioning system forced sterile, cool air into the room.

Mr. Milton was at the head of the long black table which, along with the chairs, was the only furniture. Dave and Ted sat across from each other at the center with folders and papers neatly placed before them. There was an empty seat between them and Mr. Milton on both sides. Carla was serving coffee.

"Morning," Mr. Milton said. "How does your wife like the apartment?"

"It's fantastic. I don't think I'll get her out of it today."

Dave and Ted nodded knowingly at each other. They had obviously been through a similar experience with their own wives. Kevin saw that John Milton had a way of holding his smile tightly around his eyes almost as if every part of his face had an independent reaction to things. His mouth remained firm, his cheeks taut.

"Oh, and before I forget, thank you very much for the ring."

"Been into your desk drawers already, huh?" John Milton turned to Dave and Ted, who smiled widely. "Told you this was an enthusiastic young attorney." Everyone looked at Kevin approvingly. "Kevin, why don't you sit to the right of Dave."

"Fine," Kevin said, looking down at Dave. "Morning." Both Ted and he responded. Paul took the seat to the right of Mr. Milton and put on his reading glasses as he opened the folder.

"We're just about to begin," John Milton explained. "I'm glad you could make this. Nothing formal, but we do have these meetings periodically so we can all be aware of what everyone's doing."

"Coffee?" Carla asked softly.

"No thank you. I've already had too many cups this morning."

She retreated quickly to the chair behind Mr. Milton, where she had a pad and pen. Then she looked up, poised.

"Ted, why don't you begin?" Mr. Milton said. Ted McCarthy gazed down at his folder.

"All right. Martin Crowley lives on the second floor of an apartment house on Eighty-third and York. He's a short-order cook at Ginger's Pub on Fifty-seventh and Sixth. He's had this job for nearly four years. The owners and the manager have only good things to say about him: hard worker, responsible. He's been a bachelor all his life, no family in New York. He's stout but keeps his hair short, about as short as Dave's," he added, looking up at Dave and smiling. Dave did not smile.

"Go on," Mr. Milton said softly, his eyelids closing as though Ted's words gave him a sensual pleasure.

"Anyway, his neighbors, other than the Blatts, of course, don't have much to say about him. He's a loner, friendly, but keeps to himself. Has a hobby . . . model airplane construction. His place is literally inundated with them."

"How old is he?" Dave asked.

"Oh. He's forty-one."

"Get to the girl," Mr. Milton commanded.

"His next-door neighbors, the Blatts, have two children, a boy ten and a daughter fifteen. The daughter, Tina, came home one night hysterical, claiming Martin had invited her into his apartment to show her his model planes and while she was there, subdued her and raped her. They called the police."

"Was she taken to a doctor?"

"She was. When no semen was found, she claimed Martin wore a condom." Ted looked up. "She said that even though he was raping her, he told her he was concerned about AIDS."

"Getting it or giving it?" Dave quipped.

"She didn't say."

"What do they have, then, besides the girl's testimony?" Mr. Milton demanded, his tone of voice pulling everyone back on track.

"Well, there were some abrasions on her shoulders and arms. Her panties had been ripped. A subsequent search of Martin's apartment produced a pearl hair comb Tina's mother claimed was Tina's."

"Even if it were hers, that only proves she was in the apartment, not that she was raped," Paul commented.

"Martin said nothing incriminating?" John Milton asked.

"He was smart enough to refuse to answer any questions until he had an attorney."

"Was he home at the time she alleged she was attacked?"

"Yes. And alone, claiming to be working on a new model plane."

"What else?"

"Well . . ." Ted looked at his notes. "About six years ago, he was accused of raping a twelve-year-old in Tulsa, Oklahoma. It never went to trial."

"No problem. Even if you put him on the stand, they can't ask about prior accusations, only prior convictions."

"I don't think we have to put him on the stand. I did some digging around at the girl's school today. She has a reputation for being sexually promiscuous. I found two high school boys who would be willing to testify. I can discredit her quickly. In fact, I'm leaking that to the family now. Maybe we won't even go to trial."

"Very good, Ted." Mr. Milton's smile trickled down from his eyes, trembled through his cheeks, and reached the corners of his mouth. "Very good," he repeated softly. "I'd like to read the details of the Tulsa incident, though," he added and made a small gesture with his right hand that started Carla scribbling on her pad. "Dave?"

Dave Kotein nodded and opened his folder. Then he looked up to preface his remarks. "Looks like I'll have the headlines this week."

"Good, we could use the publicity," Paul said. Mr. Milton turned to him and they exchanged a look of satisfaction.

"Dave has a rather highly publicized case, Kevin," Mr. Milton said. "Perhaps you've read about it: a number of coeds have been raped and viciously murdered, their bodies mutilated, the murders covering an area from the upper Bronx, through Yonkers and into Westchester. A man has been arrested and charged."

"Yes. Wasn't a victim found just last week?"

"Tuesday," Dave said. "At a corner of the parking lot at the Yonkers race track. Wrapped in a plastic garbage bag."

"I remember. It was particularly gruesome."

"You only read half of it." He pulled out a sheaf of papers and held them toward him. "Here's the rest. The coroner's report reads like a detailed description of a Nazi torture chamber, which, by the way," he said, turning to Mr. Milton, "the prosecution intends to point out."

"Why's that?" Kevin asked. He couldn't help his spontaneous interest.

"My client, Karl Obermeister, was in Hitler's Youth Corps. Claims he was just a child, of course, and did what he was told, but his father distinguished himself by being a guard at Auschwitz."

"Doesn't matter. His family's not on trial here," Mr. Milton commented, waving off the references.

"Right," Dave said and turned to his documents again.

"What else was in that coroner's report, though?" Mr. Milton inquired. "Perhaps Kevin should hear it."

Kevin turned, surprised. "Well, that's okay, I . . ."

"Besides being sliced across the breasts, a heated rod was inserted in the woman's vagina," Dave began quickly.

"So much for semen as evidence," Ted said.

"Christ," Kevin said.

"We've all got to have strong stomachs, Kevin. We'll be dealing with gruesome crimes as well as white-collar crimes in this firm," Mr. Milton said. His voice was tight, hard. It was as close to a reprimand as Kevin imagined it could be.

"Of course," he said softly. "Sorry."

"Go on," Mr. Milton commanded.

"Obermeister was stopped in the general vicinity. A patrolman became suspicious. He seemed too anxious to accept a speeding ticket. In the morning after the body had been discovered, this patrolman remembered Karl Obermeister. They went to his apartment to question him, only an overly ambitious young detective went a lot further. He searched his place without a warrant and found wire fasteners similar to the ones used to bind the victims. They took Karl in and kept him in a holding tank for five hours, questioning him until he confessed."

"So he confessed," Kevin muttered.

"Yes," Dave said and smiled, "but I scrutinized everything the police had done. We're going to get it thrown out of court for sure. All that time they held him at the station, they never gave him an opportunity to phone an attorney. He wasn't properly Mirandized, and the alleged evidence the detective found is all inadmissible. They don't have anything,

91

really. Karl will soon be walking," he added and turned to Mr. Milton, who smiled at him. Dave closed and opened his eyes as though he were receiving a benediction.

"Very, very good, Dave. That's good work; that's really good work."

"Congratulations, Dave," Paul said.

"Beautiful," Ted added. "Absolutely."

Kevin stared at the associates, all of whom looked so content. It flashed through his mind that Dave Kotein was Jewish and that successfully defending someone with a Nazi background should have bothered him. But there was no sign of it. If anything, his eyes radiated pride.

"Even so," Mr. Milton said, "I'd like to go over that coroner's report. Have a copy made for me, Carla," he said without turning to her. She made a note on her pad. He looked at Paul and then at the rest of them. "And now Paul has a biblical case for us to consider."

Ted and Dave smiled.

"Biblical?" Kevin queried.

"Cain and Abel," Paul said. He looked at John Milton.

"Precisely. Describe it, please, Paul."

Scholefield opened his folder. "Pat and Morris Galan are both in their late forties. Pat's an interior decorator. Morris owns and operates a small bottling works. They have an eighteen-year-old son, Philip, but when Pat was forty-one, they had a second son, Arnold. It was one of those should we, shouldn't we decisions. From what they say, they couldn't make up their minds and time ran out. They had the child, but a baby at their ages seemed burdensome. Pat wanted to keep working and eventually resented the new child."

"She admitted to this?" Mr. Milton asked.

"She was seeing a psychologist and is open about her feelings concerning the baby because she feels that contributed to it all. The Galans had marital problems, too," he continued. "Each didn't think the other was doing enough when it came to caring for the new baby. Pat accused Morris of resenting her work. Eventually they both went into counseling.

"In the meantime much of the responsibility for Arnold fell to Philip, who, being an active teenager with a life of his own, resented the burden, too. At least this is the picture I see."

"Describe the crime," Mr. Milton directed.

"One night while bathing his younger brother, Philip lost control and drowned him."

"Drowned him?" Kevin asked. Paul had said it so nonchalantly.

"He was washing his hair; Arnold is . . ." He looked at his papers. ". . . five years old at the time. He puts up resistance, complains . . . Philip loses his temper and holds the boy's head under water too long."

"My God. Where were their parents?"

"That's just it, Kevin. They were out on the town, as usual, pursuing their own lives. Anyway, Mrs. Galan has asked us to defend her son Philip. Her husband doesn't want anything to do with him."

"Does Philip have history of violence?" Dave asked.

"Nothing out of the ordinary. Some fighting in school but no previous police involvements. Good student, too. Generally well liked. The thing is, he's not very remorseful."

"What do you mean?" Kevin asked. "Doesn't he realize what he has done?"

"Yes, but . . ." Paul turned to John Milton. "He's not sorry. It's so clear that he has no regrets that the prosecution is going for premeditated murder. They're trying to create the scenario that he wasn't told to give his brother a bath. He did it just to kill him. Under questioning, the mother admitted she didn't tell him he had to bathe Arnold.

"I don't want to put him on the stand. The way he talks about his dead brother . . . if I were on the jury, I'd convict him, too."

"Could he have planned it?" Kevin asked.

"Our job is to show that he didn't," John Milton said quickly. "We're defending him, not working for the prosecution. How are you going to handle it, Paul?"

"I think you were right about the parents. I'll work them over, show them for what they are, and illustrate that the boy was put under enormous pressure. Then I'll bring in Dr. Marvin to confirm his unstable mental state . . . confused roles, all this at a time when he's undergoing other adolescent pressures, the kind of pressures that have turned teenage suicide into an epidemic."

He turned to Kevin.

"I don't know if he could have planned it, Kevin. As Mr. Milton says, Mrs. Galan hired me to defend him, not prosecute him. Besides, even though he's still hard-nosed about what he has done, I really think he has been twisted and victimized by his parents and their attitudes.

"When they returned that night, he was asleep in

his bed. They didn't even look in on Arnold. It wasn't until the next morning that Mr. Galan found his five-year-old son in the tub."

"Jesus."

"After you're with us a while, Kevin," Mr. Milton said, "you'll stop saying that." Kevin looked confused. "It shouldn't surprise you that the world is full of pain and suffering. And Jesus doesn't seem to be doing much about it these days."

"I know. But I just don't see how you can get used to it."

"You do, or at least you grow tough enough to do your job well. You know a little about that already," John Milton said, smiling. His insinuation was a clear reference to Kevin's defense of Lois Wilson. Kevin felt himself blush. He looked around to see how the others were gazing at him.

Paul looked as serious as Mr. Milton. Dave wore a look of concern. Ted was smiling.

"I guess it just takes time," Kevin said, "and more experience."

"That's so true," John Milton replied. "Time and experience. And now that you've heard about the firm's present workload, you can begin to think about your own case."

John Milton slid a folder to Dave, who passed it on to Kevin. Despite his desire to get started on something exciting, he felt icicles slide down his back. All eyes were on him now, so he smiled quickly.

"It's going to be an exciting case, Kevin; you will be baptized by fire," John Milton said. "But there isn't a man here who hasn't, and just look at them now."

Kevin turned from one to the other. Each had the

intensity of an Ahab searching for his Moby Dick. He felt as if he were joining more than a law firm; he was joining some kind of fraternity, brotherhood of blood, advocates of the damned. They made fortresses out of the law and procedure; they made weapons out of it. Whatever they chose to do, they were victorious, successful.

Most importantly, they were eager to please John Milton, who now sat back, contented, satiated by their stories and plans for court battle.

"Next time we meet, Kevin, we'll be listening to you," John Milton said and stood up. They all stood up and watched him leave, Carla right behind him. As soon as they were gone, Dave, Ted, and Paul turned to Kevin.

"I thought he was going to get angry there for a moment," Dave said. "When you said 'Jesus . . .'"

"Why would that anger him?"

"If there's one thing Mr. Milton can't tolerate, it's an attorney feeling sorry for a victim when he has a client to defend. That has to be first and foremost," Paul explained.

"It's especially true for Dave's case," Ted said.

"Why is that?"

"Because Dave's client, unlike our two, hasn't got a pot to piss in. Mr. Milton is bankrolling his client all the way."

"You're kidding?"

"We kid you not," Dave said. "He saw a breakdown in the system and he went after it. That's his style."

"And that's why we're so successful," Ted said proudly, even arrogantly.

Kevin nodded and looked at his new associates

again. They weren't knights and this wasn't the Round Table in Camelot, but they would become just as legendary, Kevin thought. He felt sure of that.

Miriam feared her face would remain permanently creased in a smile. She had been smiling and laughing since Kevin left. Norma and Jean were unendingly entertaining. When one slowed down, the other picked up. At first Miriam thought those two had to be on something, uppers. How could two women be so energetic, so talkative, so ecstatic for so long a period without being juiced?

But their philosophies about life seemed to suggest otherwise. Both were health fanatics, which explained the sugarless muffins; and Miriam had to admit they looked like prime examples of the good life: trim figures, clear, creamy complexions, beautiful white teeth, bright eyes, positive self-images.

Although neither worked or pursued a career, both appeared to have full lives. They went so far as to schedule and organize their days in order to be able to do all that they wanted. Cleaning and cooking took place in the morning, followed by their aerobics classes Monday, Wednesday, and Friday. Tuesday was set aside for grocery shopping. Thursdays they went to the museums and galleries; and of course, Saturdays and Sundays they went to the theater and movies. Most of their evenings were plotted out with dinners, shows, regular get-togethers.

Furthermore, it was immediately obvious to Miriam that Norma and Jean, along with the yet unmet Helen Scholefield, formed a close-knit, self-sufficient group. They didn't talk about any other people.

Apparently, the three couples went everywhere together, even taking vacations together whenever court schedules permitted it.

As Kevin had suggested, these urban women were continually on the go, their lives comfortable, interesting. She couldn't imagine them spending an afternoon leafing through magazines, watching soap operas, just waiting for their husbands to return from work, as she had been doing lately. It had become increasingly more difficult to get any of her Blithedale friends to come into the city for a show or shopping or anything. It was always "such an effort to buck the traffic and crowds."

But these two were absolutely impervious, oblivious to any difficulties the city might present, and they lived just as well, if not better, here—no sense of insecurity or fear for their safety, no inconvenience, and, most importantly, perhaps for someone like Miriam who had been brought up on the Island, no feeling of being closed in. Their homes were just as spacious and bright as hers.

Norma's apartment was done in a traditional decor, much like hers and Kevin's back in Blithedale, only Norma and Dave's colors were more conservative. Jean's apartment was brighter, with light colors and wider spaces, her furniture ultramodern, lots of squares and cubes, plastic and glass. Although Miriam wasn't fond of it, it was interesting. Both apartments had the same beautiful views as hers and Kevin's.

"We've been talking and talking," Norma finally realized. They were sitting in her living room sipping white wine from large goblets. "And not giving you a chance."

"That's all right."

"No, it's impolite," Jean said, sitting back and crossing her legs. They were long and slim, and she had a gold ankle chain spotted with small diamonds on her left ankle. Miriam hadn't missed much about their affluence. Both apartments contained expensive things, from their oversized television sets and state-of-the-art stereos to their furnishings, decorations, and ornaments.

"To tell you the truth, I've just been sitting back and admiring your apartments. Both of you have such beautiful things."

"And so will you," Norma said.

She started to shake her head, her eyes tearing.

"What's wrong, Miriam?" Jean asked quickly.

"Nothing's wrong. I just can't believe how fast all this is happening. I feel as if I'm being ripped out of one world and placed into a completely different one overnight, not that it's not all wonderful . . . it's just . . . just . . ."

"Overwhelming," Norma said, nodding, her face serious. "It was the same for me."

"And me," Jean chimed in.

"But don't fret about it," Norma said, leaning over to pat Miriam on the knee. "You won't believe how quickly you'll adjust and enjoy. Right, Jean?"

"She speaks truth," Jean said, and the two of them laughed. Miriam had to smile, her anxiety slipping back again.

"Anyway, getting back to you. What have you been doing with yourself while your handsome young husband has been burning up the legal turf in—what did you call it—Blithedale?" Norma asked.

"Yes, Blithedale. Small community, but we love it. Loved it, I should say." She paused. "Funny, it's almost as if I've left it and been here for months," Miriam said softly. The feeling made her bring her fingers to the base of her throat. Both women stared, similar smiles of amusement on their lips. "Anyway," Miriam continued, "for a while, I tried to do some fashion modeling, but all I did was a department store show here and there. I quickly realized it wasn't the career I really wanted for myself. I helped my father . . ."

"Who is a dentist?"

"Yes. I worked as a receptionist for nearly six months and then I decided to concentrate on Kevin and our home life. We intend to have children this year."

"So do we," Norma said.

"Pardon?"

"Intend to have children this year," she said, looking at Jean. "In fact . . ."

"We've been conspiring to have them about the same time, although the boys don't know it." They laughed. "Maybe you'll join us now."

"Join you?" Miriam's smile widened in puzzlement.

"Actually, Mr. Milton suggested it to Jean at one of his parties. Wait until you see the penthouse. He's bound to have a party any day now, since there's a new associate in the firm."

"Oh, he gives wonderful parties, gourmet catering, music, interesting guests . . ."

"What do you mean, Mr. Milton suggested it?" She turned to Jean.

"He has a wry sense of humor sometimes. He knew we were planning on starting our families this year and he pulled me aside and said wouldn't it be something if Norma and I had our children about the same time, maybe even the same week. I told Norma, and she thought it was a great idea."

"We've been planning it like a campaign, marking days on our calendars when the forays will begin," Norma said, and they both laughed again. Then Jean stopped abruptly.

"We'll show you our plans and maybe you'll join us, unless you and Kevin have already . . ."

"No, we haven't."

"Good," she said, sitting back.

Miriam saw they weren't kidding. "You say your husbands don't know?"

"Not all of it," Norma said.

"You don't tell your husband everything you do, do you?" Jean asked.

"We're very close, and something as important as this . . ."

"So are we, close," Norma said, "but Jean's right. You've got to have some personal, woman secrets."

"We three have got to stick together," Norma said. "Men are wonderful, especially our men, but they are, after all, men!" She widened her eyes.

"You should say four," Jean corrected. Norma looked puzzled. "We *four* have got to stick together. You're forgetting Helen."

"Oh yes, Helen. It's just that we see so little of her these days. She's become . . . very introspective," she said, throwing her hand up dramatically. Both she and Jean laughed.

"What do you mean?"

"Actually, we're being unfair. Helen had something of a nervous breakdown after Gloria Jaffee's death and went on medication. She's into therapy, but she's a wonderful, kind person, and very attractive," Norma said.

"Gloria Jaffee?"

Norma and Jean looked at each other quickly.

"Oh, I'm sorry," Jean said. "I just assumed you knew about the Jaffees." She turned to Norma. "Put my foot in my mouth again, huh?"

"Seems you did, partner."

"Who are the Jaffees?" Miriam asked.

"I don't see how you wouldn't find it all out very soon anyway. It's just that I didn't want to be the one who threw some cold water on the fires of excitement and happiness here," Jean said.

"That's all right. I need something to bring me down. It's naive to think everything will always be peaches and cream," Miriam replied.

"Very good attitude," Norma said. "I like that. It's about time we had someone in our group who had some perspective. Jean and I get carried away sometimes, and with Helen so depressing these days, we just tend to avoid anything unpleasant."

"Tell me about the Jaffees," Miriam insisted.

"Richard Jaffee is the attorney your husband is replacing. He killed himself after his wife died in childbirth," Jean said quickly.

"My God!"

"Yes. They had . . . everything to live for. The baby was born healthy, a son," Norma said, "and Richard was brilliant. Dave says Richard was the sharpest attorney he'd ever met, including Mr. Milton."

"How tragic." Miriam thought for a moment and then looked up quickly. "They lived in our apartment, didn't they?" The girls nodded. "I thought so . . . the nursery . . ."

"Oh, I feel so bad about depressing you," Jean moaned.

"No, it's all right. How did Mr. Jaffee die?"

Norma smirked and shook her head.

"He jumped off the patio," Jean said quickly. "There, now I've told you all the horrible details, and if you're unhappy, Ted's going to blame me."

"Oh no, I'm sure . . ."

"Dave's not going to be ecstatic about my part in this, either," Norma said.

"No, really, it's all right. I'll deal with it. Kevin should have told me right away, that's all."

"He's just trying to protect you," Norma said. "Like a good husband. Dave and Ted are the same way, right, Jean?"

"Right. Can't fault them for that, Miriam."

"But we're not children!" Miriam exclaimed. Instead of being upset with her response, the two laughed.

"No, we're not," Norma said. "But we're loved, cherished, protected. You might not realize how important that is just yet, Miriam, but believe me . . . believe us, after a while, you'll see how wonderful it is. Why, Jean and I don't even ask about the grisly details of our husbands' cases anymore, and the boys don't talk about them around us."

"Isn't that thoughtful?" Jean added.

Miriam looked from one to the other. Then she sat back. Maybe it was thoughtful; maybe if she hadn't been so involved in the details of the Lois Wilson case, she wouldn't have been so upset about the way Kevin had handled it, and she could have taken more pleasure in his success, a success that had contributed to all this.

"After all"—Norma continued to pound home the point—"they're working hard to make things wonderful for us."

"The least we can do," Jean concluded, "is make it easier for them to do so." They laughed in unison and sipped some wine.

Miriam said nothing for a moment. "Tell me about Helen Scholefield," she said. "How is she?"

"Oh, she's improving. Therapy has helped a great deal. Mr. Milton recommended someone as soon as he heard she was having problems," Norma said.

"She's been painting again, too, and that's helped as well," Jean added.

"Oh yes. And she's good. I'm sure she will be happy to show you her work."

"Actually, it's very good. Reminds me of Chagall, but with a touch of Goodfellow. You remember that abstract artist we saw over at the Simmons Gallery in SoHo last month," Jean said. Norma nodded.

Miriam shook her head and smiled at them.

"What's wrong?" Jean asked.

"You two seem . . . so cosmopolitan," she said, thinking of Kevin's words. "You take everything so calmly and you're not afraid of doing things. It's wonderful. I admire you both."

"You know, I think you've actually been the one kind of cloistered out there in your Long Island world," Jean said, her face growing calmer and more serious-looking. "Am I right?"

Miriam thought for a moment. Sometimes she felt that way. Her parents had sent her to a private school when she was twelve and from there she went on to an exclusive junior college and then to college and modeling school, always pampered, always protected.

Kevin had certainly treated her that way since they were married. Now she even believed he had joined Boyle, Carlton, and Sessler and designed a life for them in Blithedale only because she had wanted it. Had she been holding him back? Could he have gotten them into this world even sooner? She hated to think that she had been selfish, and yet . . .

"I suppose that's true."

"Not that either Norma or I have had a rough time. Norma's father is a plastic surgeon on Park Avenue. She's lived on the exclusive East Side all her life, and I come from affluent parents in Suffolk County." She sat back. "My father's a broker and my mother's a real estate agent who probably could sell the Brooklyn Bridge," she added.

"She could. I met her," Norma said.

"But don't you worry," Jean said. "In a matter of days, you'll be just like us, doing many of the same, crazy things. Whether you want to be or not," she added prophetically. There was a moment of silence and then Norma laughed. Jean joined her, and just as Jean predicted, Miriam started laughing too.

6

Outside the conference room, the associates parted, each off to work on his own case. Kevin said his goodbyes and walked to his office while he looked over the case file Milton had given him. He sat down in the comfortable leather desk chair and continued reading through the folder, formulating tactics and making notes as he went along. Close to an hour later, he sat back, shook his head, and smiled. If the others had known what Mr. Milton had handed him, they hadn't shown it. It was the kind of case that could make a young attorney's reputation overnight because it would draw a great deal of media attention. And John Milton had decided to give it to him.

To him! Even his swollen ego and continually thirsty ambition didn't prepare him for such an opportunity, especially with three other attorneys in the firm, each much more experienced in criminal law than he was.

No wonder John Milton wanted him to begin work immediately. This case was just beginning to make the headlines. In fact, what John Milton was doing in the preface of this file was anticipating who his client would be, expecting him to be charged with the murder of his wife.

A little over twenty years ago, forty-one-year-old Stanley Rothberg had married Maxine Shapiro, the only child of Abe and Pearl Shapiro, owners of one of the biggest and most famous Catskill Mountain resort hotels, Shapiro's Lake House, located in Sandburg, a small upstate New York community not far from where Paul Scholefield first had practiced law. In fact, it occurred to Kevin that Paul would have been a more logical choice to take this case, since he was familiar with the area. However, Shapiro's Lake House had developed a national reputation because of the celebrities who performed there, the hotel's longevity, and the introduction about ten years ago of the Shapiro's Lake House Raisin Loaf, the recipe supposedly Pearl Shapiro's. It was a popular item in supermarkets and well advertised on television.

Both Abe and Pearl Shapiro were now dead. Stanley Rothberg had started as a busboy and then become a waiter in the Lake House dining room. He had met and romanced Maxine and (no secret from anyone), without Abe and Pearl's initial blessing, married Maxine and eventually became general manager of one of the biggest hotels in the resort area.

Maxine turned out to be a sickly woman, eventually developing brittle diabetes. She lost a leg and was confined to a wheelchair during the last few years. She had a full-time nurse. Last weekend she was found dead, as the result of an insulin overdose. Mr. Milton was positive Stanley Rothberg would be charged with first-degree murder. Everyone seemed to know that he had a girlfriend on the side. The Rothbergs had no children, so he was the sole heir to the multimillion-dollar tourist facility and bakery enterprise. There was clear motive and clear opportunity.

Kevin sensed John Milton's presence in his doorway and looked up quickly from the folder. One of the things that was beginning to amaze him about the man was how he seemed to change appearance every time Kevin saw him. Right now he looked wider, taller, and even a bit older. He saw lines in his face that he hadn't seen before, or was that just the trick of lighting?

"Got right into it, eh? That's good, Kevin. I like it when one of my associates grabs on tenaciously," he said, making a fist. "Keep that edge, keep that hunger, and you'll always be formidable in court."

"Well, I saw this story in Sunday's paper. As far as I know, no one's been charged yet; but I gather from this you expect Stanley Rothberg will be."

"No question about it," John Milton replied, stepping farther in. The lines lifted from his face. "My sources tell me an arrest is only days away."

"And obviously Mr. Rothberg is anticipating it, too. When did you meet with him?"

"Oh, I haven't seen him yet, Kevin."

"Pardon?"

"I wanted you to be familiar with the case when he arrived. He'll be a little nervous about someone as young as you taking his defense, of course; but once he sees how competent you are . . ."

"I don't understand." Kevin closed the folder and sat forward. "You're saying we don't actually have this case yet?"

"Not formally, but we will. Why don't I go ahead and plan a meeting between us and Stanley Rothberg early next week. It's my understanding that he won't be arrested until then anyway. I'll handle the arraignment and bail."

"But how do we know he'll come to us? Did he phone?"

John Milton smiled confidently, his eyes changing again to that shimmering rust, only a little brighter this time.

"Don't worry about where he will go when he finds himself in trouble. He'll know. We have mutual acquaintances who have already spoken to him. Trust me. Anyway, you should go through the medical data concerning his wife."

"Yes," Kevin said, staring, his thoughts complicated by a static of confusing impulses. Kevin was excited by the prospect of such a case, but he was also uneasy about it. Why had Mr. Milton given him, a new associate, an important case so quickly? Shouldn't he take something simpler, build up to a case like this?

"I bet you already have an idea for his defense. Something popped into your head?"

"Well, I was thinking . . . after reading how Maxine Rothberg suffered. She and Abe had no children; she was confined to a wheelchair and a restricted life in the midst of a glamorous and exciting world. She must have been terribly frustrated and unhappy."

"Precisely my theory . . . suicide."

"According to what we have here, she did inject

herself occasionally, even though she had a full-time nurse."

John Milton smiled again and shook his head.

"You're a very sharp young man, Kevin. I know I'm going to be more than satisfied with your work. Look into the nurse, too. There's a lot we can use, you'll see."

He started to turn away.

"Mr. Milton."

"Yes?"

"How did you get all this . . ." He ran his palm over the closed folder. ". . . this detailed information already?"

"I have private investigators on full-time duty, Kevin. I'll be introducing them to you from time to time so they can make direct reports, and I keep some things on my computer files." He laughed, a short, quiet laugh. "You've heard of ambulance chasers; well, we're crime chasers. It's important to be aggressive out there, Kevin. It pays, in more ways than you can ever imagine."

Kevin nodded and watched Mr. Milton leave. Then he sat back.

He had been right. The urban world was different and far more exciting. This was New York, where the best competed with each other, and only the best could compete. Boyle, Carlton, and Sessler paled before such a firm as John Milton and Associates, and to think, at one time during his neophyte legal existence, he had thought they were something special, they and their mesmerizing upper-middle-class existence. They were soft; they were actually dying, wallowing in comfort. Where was the challenge? When were they really on the edge, taking risks? Why, Kevin was already heads and shoulders above them. None of them had the guts to represent Lois Wilson, and now they were upset because their lily-white reputations might have gotten stained. The biggest adventure of their lives was going to a new gourmet restaurant. And he had almost become one of them!

John Milton had saved him; that's what he had done: saved him.

Kevin got up quickly, squeezing the folder securely under his arm, and started out.

"Oh, Mr. Taylor," Wendy called, ascending from behind her desk like some mermaid rising out of the water as soon as Kevin emerged from his office. "I'm sorry. I didn't see you go in."

"That's all right. I had just intended to stay for a few moments but got lost in some reading."

She nodded, her chestnut-brown eyes darkening as if she had an instant understanding of what would seize his attention so firmly. She brushed back her hair and looked at the folder under his arm.

"Oh, wait." She turned and hurried back to a cabinet behind her desk and took out a ruby leather attaché case. "I was going to give you this when you officially started, but since you've already begun . . ." She handed it to him. One side was engraved in dark brown script, the color of dried blood. It read, "John Milton and Associates." In the lower right-hand corner was printed, "Kevin Wingate Taylor."

"This is beautiful." He ran his fingers over the raised lettering.

Wendy smiled. "All the associates have the same one. Present from Mr. Milton."

"I've got to remember to thank him. And thank you, Wendy."

"Yes, sir. Is there anything I can do for you?"

He thought for a moment. "Yes. Work up all you can on diabetes and find out whatever you can about the history of Shapiro's Lake House, the Catskill resort."

Wendy's smile widened. "That's all been done, Mr. Taylor."

"Oh?"

"Mr. Milton asked for that last Wednesday."

"Oh. Great. Well, I'll drop by and start reading it. Thank you."

"Have a good day, Mr. Taylor."

He started down the corridor, looking in on Ted McCarthy, who was on the phone. Ted waved, and Kevin continued on. Dave Kotein's office door was closed, so he went on to the reception desk and asked Diane to call for the limo.

"It will be waiting for you right outside the front door, Mr. Taylor. Use it as you wish. Charon is not due back here until the end of the day."

"Thank you, Diane."

"Have a nice day, Mr. Taylor."

"You too."

He was practically bouncing over the thick carpet. The secretaries weren't just beautiful and pleasant, they were warm, sincere . . . titillating. Everything about this place was pleasing: the colors, the lushness, the newness. He hated to leave.

Kevin hummed in the elevator and waved to the security guard in the lobby, who waved back as if they were already old friends. As soon as he came through the revolving doors, he paused and squinted. The heavy cloud cover had thinned considerably, and rays of the noonday sun reflected off the glass, the sidewalk, and the shiny surface of the limo. Charon opened the limo door and stepped back.

"Thank you, Charon. I'll be heading back to the apartment first and then we'll be going to the Russian Tea Room for lunch."

"Very good, Mr. Taylor." He closed the door softly, and moments later they were on their way. Kevin sat back and closed his eyes. He had so much to tell Miriam that he was sure they would both be talking a blue streak at lunch and all the way back to Blithedale. And when he described his first assignment as a John Milton associate . . .

He opened his eyes and ran his hand over the attaché case, snapping it open and gazing in at the folder. It would soon grow in size. That was for sure. Kevin laughed to himself. Talk about well-prepared attorneys. All that material already worked up and waiting for him. What an office—private investigators, a computerized library, efficient secretaries . . . Kevin sat back, his self-confidence growing. With such a support network behind him, he had to do well.

Then something Wendy had said triggered a curious thought. He must have heard it wrong, he thought, but he opened the file and looked at the dates associated with some facts to be sure.

Had she said Mr. Milton had asked for the information on diabetes and Shapiro's Lake House last Wednesday?

Maxine Rothberg had been found dead in her bed just this past weekend. Why would Mr. Milton be interested as far back as last Wednesday?

Wendy must have been mistaken, or maybe he hadn't heard right, he thought, and closed the briefcase.

After all, what else could it be?

"More wine?" Norma offered. She tilted the bottle toward Miriam's glass.

"No, I think I'd better get back to my apartment. Kevin will be looking for me."

"So?"

"Let him find you," Jean said. She looked at Miriam and shook her head. "I can see we have some work to do here, Norma."

"Men have a tendency to take their women for granted sometimes," Norma advised. "We've got to keep them on their toes, keep the mystery alive, keep them thinking. Otherwise, you'll become just another one of their possessions."

"Kevin's not like that," Miriam said.

"Nonsense," Jean said. "He's a man. He can't help it."

Norma and Jean laughed again. For a moment the two of them appeared childlike to Miriam, their eyes brightening mischievously.

Before anyone could say anything else, they heard the doorbell. "That must be Kevin," Miriam said. They all got up. As they started for the front door, Norma put her arms around Miriam.

"Can't wait for you to move in," she said. "Catching you up will give us a chance to relive all our own wonderful discoveries." Jean opened the door to greet Kevin.

"Hi. So you found us out." She turned to Miriam and winked. "We thought you would eventually."

"Just simple deduction," he said and looked at Miriam. "Have a good time?"

"Yes, yes I did."

"You don't have to worry," Jean said, smiling and then winking again at Miriam. "She's already one of us."

"I hope that's good," Kevin kidded. He flirted with his eyes, and the two of them giggled. Norma hugged and kissed Miriam, and then Jean did the same.

"See you soon," Miriam said. They stood side by side in the doorway, smiling as she and Kevin retreated to the elevator.

"Looks like you three got off to a good start, huh?" Kevin asked.

"Yes."

"You don't sound enthusiastic," Kevin said cautiously.

Miriam was silent as they got into the elevator, but just before it opened on the lobby floor, she turned to him. "What didn't you tell me about the Jaffees?"

"Oh." He nodded. "I should have figured they would. Well," he said, taking a deep breath as they stepped into the lobby, "it's a depressing story and I didn't want to put an onus on the apartment." He turned to her. "Eventually, I would have told you. I'm sorry. It wasn't right to keep it from you. It's just that I want to surround you with pretty things, happy things. I want this to be the best time of our lives, Miriam."

She nodded. It was just as Norma and Jean had said—Kevin wanted to protect her from sadness and depression. She decided she shouldn't fault him for it.

"It is a tragic story, but I don't see why it should affect us," she concluded.

He beamed. "That's how I feel." He hugged her.

"Why are we getting out here?" she asked, realizing they had stepped into the lobby. "Shouldn't we have gone down to the parking garage?"

"I have a surprise." He nodded toward the front entrance. As they approached, Philip came out from behind his desk to greet them. "Oh. This is Philip, Miriam. He works day security."

"Pleased to meet you, Mrs. Taylor. You have any problems at all or you need anything, don't hesitate to call on me."

"Thank you very much."

Philip opened the door for them, and when they stepped out, Charon opened the limo door for them.

"What's this?" Miriam asked, looking from the limousine to Charon.

"It's the office limo, always at the disposal of the associates. Charon, this is my wife, Miriam."

Charon nodded, his almond eyes scrutinizing her so intently, she felt self-conscious and instinctively crossed her arms over her breasts.

"Hello," she said and got in quickly. She looked back as Kevin joined her.

"Where are we going?"

"Russian Tea Room," he said. "I made the reservation on the limo phone right after I left the offices. Cocktail, Madam?" he asked, opening the liquor cabinet. "I can make you your favorite, a Bloody Mary."

Cocktails in this plush Mercedes limo, lunch at the Russian Tea Room, a wonderful apartment on Riverside Drive, vibrant young new girlfriends—she shook her head. Kevin laughed at the look on her face.

"I think I'll make two and join you," he said. The drink only added to the high Miriam was experiencing. "So," he said, sitting back after he had made the drinks, "tell me more about your visit. What are they like?"

"They're a little overwhelming at first, especially when I think of the women I know in Blithedale. Sometimes they're so cosmopolitan and deep, and then sometimes they talk and act like teenage girls. But they're a lot of fun, Kev."

"I'm sorry I was gone so long, but . . ."

"Oh, I didn't even notice the time. They kept me pretty busy."

She began by describing Jean and Ted's apartment, and then going into Norma's. She rattled on, telling him every detail about her new girlfriends, except, of course, their plans for simultaneous births and how happy they were to discover that she wasn't pregnant yet.

She wanted to tell Kevin about that; she almost did once or twice at lunch, but every time she started to, she pictured Norma and Jean and how they would feel if they found out she had betrayed their first secret. It might ruin the friendship before it had even begun, and what was the difference anyway, she thought? It was a harmless, really humorous idea with, most likely, very little chance of turning out as they planned.

After lunch, they returned to their apartment for one more look before heading back to Blithedale. Miriam had to confirm the reality. Kevin waited by the front door as she walked through it again.

"It is a beautiful apartment, isn't it, Kev?" she

asked, as if she had to have her feelings reinforced. "How can he afford to give it to us rent-free? He could make a fortune renting it out, couldn't he?"

"He's writing this off as some kind of a tax deduction. Like my grandfather said, don't look a gift horse . . ."

"I know, but still . . ." A ripple of apprehension passed through her. Kevin's wonderful new job, this beautiful new home, great new friends . . . Did wonderful things really just happen like this?

"Why fight good luck?" he asked.

She turned to him, and he shrugged. She smiled. Kevin was right. Why not relax and enjoy it? she told herself. Kevin embraced her.

"I love you, Miriam. I want to do the best I can and give you as much as I can."

"I wasn't complaining before, Kev."

"I know, but why shouldn't we have these things if we can?"

They kissed, looked back at the apartment once more, and then left.

How different the ride back to Blithedale was in contrast to the ride into the city that morning, Kevin thought. On the way in, he could count Miriam's words on his fingertips. But from the moment they had gone to lunch at the Russian Tea Room to the moment they had pulled into their driveway in Blithedale Gardens, Miriam barely let up. Whatever fears he'd had about Miriam being unhappy with the changes in their lives he was proposing were totally obliterated by her streak of unchecked enthusiasm.

A few times on the way home, he tried to tell her

about the cases discussed at the staff meeting and his own case, but each time he began, she interrupted with another suggestion about their new apartment. It was as if she didn't want to hear anything about the work. Usually she wanted to know all the details about a case, even those boring real estate negotiations. Finally, he shook his head, sat back, and drove.

It wasn't until Blithedale itself came into view that Miriam slowed down her monologue. It was almost as if they had crossed back over some invisible boundary and returned from their dream world into reality. The morning clouds were completely gone, and the late November afternoon sky was a clear, crystal blue. Children were just getting off the school bus, their exhilarated voices preceding their bodies down the steps and out the door.

Solar heat had already softened and melted much of last night's snow, so that it lingered in patches only on lawns and here and there along the sidewalks. Almost as soon as they stepped off the bus, the young boys, and even some girls, began throwing snowballs at each other. Kevin smiled at their innocent play. A line of slow traffic followed the unloading bus through the tree-lined wide street. The relative rustic splendor and peace was in sharp contrast to the hustling, bustling, energized city world they had just left. It had a calming effect. Miriam sat back, a soft angelic smile on her face.

"I wish we could have both, Kev," she said, turning to him slowly. "The excitement of New York and the easy pace of Blithedale."

"We will. We can!" he realized, turning back to her, his eyes wide with excitement. "If we don't have to pay for an apartment in the city, we can think seriously about a weekend and summer house on the Island."

"That's right. Oh, Kevin, we're going to do it, aren't we? We're going to have it all!"

"Why not?" He laughed. "Why not?"

Kevin decided he wouldn't tell her about his first case at John Milton and Associates until he had returned from Boyle, Carlton, and Sessler, even though he was bursting with excitement about it. She was going to be just as excited and proud when she heard, he thought.

As soon as they had pulled into their driveway at Blithedale Gardens, he told her he had better go see Sanford Boyle and tell him what he had decided.

"I can't wait to rub it in—twice the salary! And they were so smug."

"Don't be arrogant, Kev," she warned. "You're bigger than they are, and anyway, arrogant people always get theirs in the long run."

"You're right. I'll contain myself just like . . . just like Mr. Milton would," he said. "The man's got class."

"I can't wait to meet him. From the way Norma and Jean talked about him and the way you talk about him, he sounds like Ronald Reagan, Paul Newman, and Lee Iacocca all wrapped up in one."

Kevin laughed. "All right, all right, I may be over-doing it a bit, I admit. I'm just excited, I guess, and you've always had your feet planted a little more firmly than I have. Anyway, I'm glad you're around to help me keep my perspective, Miriam."

"I must give that impression," she said. "Norma and Jean said something similar to me."

"Did they? Why not? They recognize a perceptive and intelligent person when they see one."

"Oh, Kev."

He kissed her on the cheek.

"I'd better call my parents," she said, getting out of the car. "What about yours?"

"I'll call them tonight."

She watched him drive off, the excitement building to a crescendo in her, too. She took a deep breath and looked around. She couldn't help liking it here. The serenity, the quaintness of the village, and the simplicity of this life gave her a sense of balance and left her at peace with herself. They had had a great deal going for them, already more than most people their age. Were they being greedy, or was Kevin right when he wondered aloud why other people, people who weren't any smarter or more clever than he was, were enjoying more?

It was wrong to hold him back, Miriam thought, and yet she couldn't keep those tiny butterfly wings from fluttering just below her breast. But there was nothing to worry about. It had to be a natural reaction, she concluded. Who wouldn't feel this way after so much had happened?

Miriam hurried on, filling her mind with thoughts and plans for the packing and moving that was soon to come.

The secretaries at Boyle, Carlton, and Sessler sensed something was happening with Kevin. Kevin could see it in Myra's face when he entered the offices.

"Is Mr. Boyle in, Myra?"

Her big brown eyes scrutinized him, but he wore his tight smile like a mask. "Yes."

"See if I can see him in ten minutes, will you, please? I'll be in my office."

How small, insignificant, even stifling his office appeared to him now. Kevin nearly laughed aloud when he walked into it. The desk looked half the size of his desk at John Milton's. He felt like a man going from a small Chevy or Ford to a Mercedes overnight.

And what did he have waiting for him here since his successful completion of the Lois Wilson case? He looked at the folders on his desk—that teenager who went joy riding, a will he had to draw up for the Benjamins, and a speeding ticket he had to handle for Bob Patterson. Whoopie-do.

He sat back in his chair and put his feet up on the desk. Goodbye to this closet, he thought. Goodbye to frustrations, to daydreaming and envy, goodbye to small-town minds with small-town futures.

Hello, New York!

Myra buzzed him. "Mr. Boyle will see you now, Mr. Taylor."

"Why, that's fine, Myra," he sang back. "Thank you."

He stood up quickly, sucked in his stomach, looked around his office one more time, and went into Sanford Boyle's office to tell him he was resigning.

"Oh, I see. So this other offer's panned out for you, has it?" Boyle's eyebrows turned in toward each other like caterpillars in pain.

"At twice the money I would make here, even with a full partnership, Sanford." Boyle's eyebrows nearly lifted off his head. "I'll be at John Milton and Associates."

"I can't say I ever heard of them, Kevin," Sanford Boyle said.

Kevin shrugged. It didn't surprise him. It was on the tip of his tongue to say, "You and your 'full' partners don't know much about the world outside of your precious little Blithedale, but believe me, Sanford, there's a bigger, wider, far more interesting world out there."

He didn't say it; Miriam's warnings about arrogance kept him in check. Instead, he returned to his office and packed up most of his personal belongings. Myra, Mary, and Teresa did not come by to wish him good luck. When he carried his things out to his car, they looked up with disappointed and disapproving eyes. He wrote off their censure. They were bucolic, intolerant of ambition, narrow-minded and insular. *Typical small-town minds,* he thought, *condemning me for wanting to improve my lot in life quickly, dramatically.* He was positive they thought he was ungrateful. *And they expect me to fall on my face,* he thought. *Won't they be surprised when they read about me in* The New York Times *as soon as the Rothberg case begins.*

Kevin felt a sense of relief and elation when he finally got into his car. But Mary Echert couldn't keep her indignation up as well as the other two. She had to follow him out to say goodbye.

"Everyone's very upset and sorry to see things turn out this way, Mr. Taylor," she offered.

"I was hoping some would be happy for me, Mary. I'm not going off to hell, you know." He got into his car and slammed the door. She stood there, her arms folded, looking down at him. He rolled down his window. "Anyway, thanks for all you've done. You were always an efficient, competent secretary, Mary, and I did appreciate you." He couldn't help the condescending tone; it just came naturally. She nodded, not smiling. He started his car, and she turned away. Suddenly she turned back, remembering something.

"I wasn't going to tell you," she said. "He was so nasty on the phone."

"Who?"

"Gordon Stanley, Barbara Stanley's father."

"Oh. What did he say? Not that it matters now."

"He said someday you'll realize what you've done and you'll hate yourself," she replied. He could see that for her it fit the occasion, like an all-occasion greeting card or something. He just shook his head and drove off, leaving her looking after him in the driveway.

It did add a note of depression and bring down his mood. But, thankfully, John Milton came to the rescue, almost as if he knew what Kevin would be going through. At home, Miriam greeted him at the door. Her face was as bright and as ecstatic as it had been when she had first set eyes on the New York apartment.

"Oh, Kevin. You can't imagine! What thoughtfulness!"

"What?"

"Just look," she said, leading him into the living room. "It came minutes after you left."

There on the living-room table was a large bouquet of two dozen blood-red roses.

"And he sent it to me!" Miriam exclaimed.

"Who?"

"Mr. Milton, silly." She picked up the card and read it. "'To Miriam, on the beginning of a wonderful new life. Welcome to our family. John Milton.'"

"Wow."

"Oh, Kevin, I never thought I would be so happy."

"Neither did I," he said. "Neither did I."

And like a torch burning away the darkness, John Milton's timely and thoughtful gift burned away any hesitation they had felt about leaving Blithedale.

7

Norma and Jean were waiting outside Kevin and Miriam's apartment when they arrived with the moving men. The girls were dressed in jeans and sweatshirts, their sleeves pulled up, ready for work.

"This is so nice of you!" Miriam exclaimed.

"Nonsense," Norma said. "We're like the Three Musketeers." They hooked her arms and sang, "One for all and all for one." Miriam laughed, and they began to unpack the cartons while Kevin directed the moving men until all the furniture had been brought up. As soon as Kevin had their stereo placed in the living room, Norma tuned it to an oldies station, and she and Jean began singing along, pulling Miriam into their festive mood, laughing and dancing to the beat of the music as they moved things from one place to another. Kevin shook his head and smiled. The three were already acting as if they had known each other forever.

He was so happy for Miriam. Her girlfriends back at Blithedale were staid, very conservative. She rarely had a chance to let go and be silly if she wanted.

They took a break for lunch, sending out for pizza. Afterward, Kevin showered and changed so he could go to the office for a little while. The women debated the placement of paintings, pictures, and knickknacks and then started to rearrange the furniture, again. When Kevin was ready to leave, he stood in the living-room doorway and announced his departure.

"I get the feeling this would all go smoother if I weren't in the way anyhow," he declared. No one disagreed. "Isn't anyone going to insist I stay?" The three women, all of one face, stopped and looked at him as if he were some stranger who had stepped in from the hallway. "All right, all right, don't beg. I can't stand that. See you later, honey," he said, kissing Miriam on the cheek.

He heard the girls' laughter as he closed the apartment door and headed for the elevator. Buoyed by how well it was all going, he felt a new energy and looked forward to getting to the office.

Just as he pushed the call button for the elevator, he heard a door open and close down the hallway. He turned to see a woman come out of the Scholefields' apartment. He figured it was Helen Scholefield. She was carrying a painting wrapped in brown paper. Like someone in a trance, she moved slowly, with deliberate steps. As she emerged from the shadows and into the light, Kevin made out her physical characteristics.

She was a tall woman, nearly Paul's height, with straw-blond hair and a light complexion. She had her hair pinned on the sides and brushed down just to the center of her shoulder blades. Although she looked a little stiff, her posture was stately. She wore a thin white cotton blouse with a frilly collar and frilly sleeves. The blouse was so thin, he could easily make out the fullness of her bosom. Her breasts were high and firm, and even though she was wearing a long, flower-patterned peasant skirt, he could see she had long legs and slim hips. Her brown leather sandals were fastened with straps that snaked around her ankles.

The elevator door opened, but Kevin was mesmerized by her approach and didn't even notice the doors close again. Helen turned to him, her smile beginning around her soft aqua eyes and then moving quickly down to her light orange lips. There were tiny apricot freckles over the bridge of her nose and the tops of her cheeks. Her skin was so thin at her temples that he could make out the webbing of tiny veins.

Kevin nodded. "Hi. Are you Mrs. Scholefield?"

"Yes, and you're the new lawyer," she replied, stating it so firmly it was as if she were labeling him for life.

"Kevin, Kevin Taylor." He extended his hand, and she took it in her free one. Her fingers were long but graceful-looking. Her palm felt warm, even a bit hot, the palm of someone running a fever. There was a slight flush in her cheeks.

"I was just on my way to your apartment with a welcoming gift." She lifted the painting to indicate that it was the gift. Because it was wrapped, he couldn't see what sort of painting it was. "I did it especially for you."

"Thank you. That's very kind of you. Miriam told

me you were an artist. Miriam's my wife," he said. "When we came to see the apartment, she visited with Norma and Jean, and I guess they gossiped about everything and everyone. Not that men don't do that. It's just . . ." He stopped, feeling as though he were babbling. She held her smile, but her eyes grew smaller and moved from side to side as she scanned his face. "They're all in there," he added, pointing toward his doorway, "in the apartment . . . spinning the furniture round and round." He laughed.

"I bet." She looked into his eyes so intently, he felt self-conscious and nodded nervously.

"I got to . . . got to go over to the office for a little while."

"Of course."

He pressed the call button again. "I'm sure we'll see a lot of each other," he said when the doors opened again.

She didn't reply. She just shifted her feet so she could turn and look into the elevator at him as the doors closed. He thought she wore an expression of pity. He felt like a coal miner going down into the bowels of the earth to contract black lung.

What a contrast she was to the other two, he thought. So subdued. It was probably as Paul had suggested—she was shy, withdrawn. And yet he couldn't remember anyone looking at him so closely. Maybe it was part of being an artist. Sure, artists are always studying people's faces, searching for new ideas, new subjects, he concluded. So what? He actually thought she was rather attractive. There was a softness in her face, a peaceful quality that made her seem angelic. And even though he had seen her for only a short time, he was intrigued by the mystery of her long legs and firm bosom. He liked women who were subtly sexy. Women like the ones who worked at John Milton's offices were alluring, but they were so obvious, there wasn't anything special about them. They were erotic but not deep, he thought. Yeah, that's it. Helen Scholefield was deep.

He shook her out of his thoughts and hurried on through the lobby to the waiting limo.

Everyone, from the doorman to the secretaries, greeted him so warmly and looked at him with such admiration in their eyes, he couldn't help feeling very important. He wasn't in his office five minutes before John Milton buzzed him and asked him to come to his office.

"Kevin, everything going all right?"

"Perfect. And Miriam wanted me to be sure to thank you for those lovely roses. Very thoughtful."

"Oh, I'm glad she liked them. You have to remember to do things like that, Kevin," he advised in a fatherly tone. "Women like to be pampered. You've got to remember to tell her how important she is to you. Adam neglected Eve in Paradise and paid dearly for it later."

Kevin didn't know whether to laugh or nod. John Milton wasn't smiling. "I'll remember."

"I'm sure you treat your wife well anyway, Kevin. Have a seat. Well," John Milton said, sitting back, "it happened just as I told you it would. This morning Stanley Rothberg was arrested and booked, charged with the murder of his wife. It will be in the papers and on the news all day and night."

Kevin nodded, holding his breath. It was all going to happen. Just like that, he was going to be launched into what most lawyers would consider the most exciting case of their careers. Many worked years to get something like this, and most never did, he thought.

"I know things are kind of hectic for you right now, with the moving and all, but do you think you could be ready by tomorrow morning for our meeting with Rothberg?"

"Sure," Kevin said. He'd work all day and all night if he had to.

"As I told you, you'll have to study up on all the aspects of the case, show him you're knowledgeable and show him you're going to be aggressive on his behalf."

"I'll get right on it."

"Good." John Milton smiled, his eyes brightening. "That's the attitude I expected you'd have. Well, don't let me keep you. And don't hesitate to call me at any time if you have any questions. By the way," he added, reaching into his top drawer and taking out a business card, "this is my home phone number. It's unlisted, of course."

"Oh, thank you." Kevin took it and stood up. "What time will Rothberg be here?"

"Our meeting will be at ten A.M. in the conference room."

"Okay." Kevin swallowed. His heart was pounding with excitement. "I better get busy. Thank you for your confidence in me," he added and left the office.

Wendy had the files he had asked for on his desk. First, he read up on diabetes, familiarizing himself with the symptoms and the treatments.

A second file was devoted to Maxine's nurse, a fifty-two-year-old black woman named Beverly Morgan. Beverly had served as Maxine's mother's nurse during her final years after she had suffered a stroke. Her nursing experience was impeccable, but her personal life was filled with tragedy. She had two sons, but her husband had deserted her when the boys were young. One of them had a considerable criminal record by the time he was in his early twenties and had served time twice. He eventually died from a heroin overdose when he was twenty-four. The other had married and had two children and, like his father, had deserted his family and was now working on the West Coast.

Apparently, Beverly Morgan's hard life had caught up with her, and although she wasn't a confirmed alcoholic, she was heavily enough into drinking to attract attention. How else had Mr. Milton's investigators discovered the incidents in the hotel bar and the fact that she kept a bottle in her room? Kevin reasoned. No wonder Mr. Milton had told him to look over this information. She could have easily made a mistake with Maxine Rothberg's insulin. In any case it provided a good red herring, something to confuse the jury and twist up the prosecution's case. If the prosecution intended to use Beverly Morgan as a witness against Stanley Rothberg, he knew how to discredit her testimony now.

The most damaging thing was Stanley Rothberg's affair. Apparently, from what Kevin read, it had begun just about the time Maxine became ill. He would have to decide on a strategy for that. His initial feeling was to have Stanley own up to it quickly and develop the argument that he couldn't bring himself to leave his wife, especially after she had become so ill;

and yet, he was a man, with a man's needs. Kevin would generate an argument somewhere along those lines, he thought. Juries appreciate honesty, even when someone's confessing to an immoral act. He envisioned Rothberg breaking up on the stand, regretting the tragedy of his life. Stanley Rothberg loved, he enjoyed, but oh how he suffered through it all.

The violins were playing. Kevin shook his head. Look, he told his conscience, it could be true; it could very well be the way it was. He had yet to meet Rothberg and decide about the man, but thinking it through from his own point of view, as a man, he could see it as a feasible argument.

He opened the third file to read about Maxine Rothberg's personal medical history and quickly saw how her physician, Dr. Cutler, could be an effective witness for the defense. He would have to testify that he had instructed Maxine Rothberg in how to give herself the insulin shot and how much to give. And apparently he also had some negative things to say about Beverly Morgan, strongly suggesting that she should be replaced. Of course, Kevin had yet to see what sort of case the prosecution had, but all this preliminary information buoyed his confidence.

He looked up when he heard a knock on his door. Paul Scholefield poked his head in. "How's it going?"

"Oh, great, great. Come on in."

"Don't want to interrupt. I know you've had a big case thrown into your lap."

"Big isn't the word for it. The Rothberg case!"

Paul smiled and sat down, but Kevin thought he didn't seem all that surprised.

"You know, the case that's been in the papers

almost every day for the past week or so," he emphasized.

Paul nodded. "That's Mr. Milton's way. When he has confidence in someone . . ."

Kevin looked at the open doorway and then leaned across his desk to speak softly to Paul. "At the risk of sounding ungrateful or falsely modest, Paul, I don't understand why he has such confidence in me. He barely knows me and the kind of work I've done up to this point . . ."

"All I can tell you is he hasn't been wrong about a person yet, whether it was one of us, a client, or a witness. Anyway, I stopped by to tell you if there's anything I can do to help . . ."

"Oh, but you have your own cases . . ."

"That's all right. We all make time for each other. Each of us might be out on a separate assignment, but we all pull together. Mr. Milton compares each of us to the tentacles of an octopus. In a way he's right—by feeding the firm, we feed ourselves. So . . . everything all right back at the apartment?"

"Great. Oh, I met your wife on the way out."

"Oh?"

"Very attractive woman."

"Yes, she is. We met in Washington Square. I think I fell in love with her before I turned my head to look her way."

"She has such a peaceful aura about her."

"Yes, she does," Paul said, smiling. "I remember how hyper I used to be when we first got married. Everything was a tragedy, you know. You're carrying the world on your shoulders, but the moment I got home, it was as if I left the world outside my door."

Kevin stared at him a moment. It was good to see that another man loved a woman as completely as he loved Miriam.

"She was bringing us a painting, something she had done especially for us."

"Really? I wonder what it could be. I didn't see anything new." He looked troubled by the information. He hesitated a moment and then looked down.

"Something wrong?"

"I'm afraid so. We got some bad news yesterday."

"Oh. I'm sorry. Anything we can help with?"

"No, nobody can help. We've tried to have children and failed. Helen's doctor has now confirmed that she's . . . incapable of becoming pregnant."

"Oh, I am sorry."

"Just one of those things. As Mr. Milton said this morning when I told him, you just have to go on from there. Play whatever hand you're dealt."

"I guess that's good advice." Kevin wondered for a moment how he would react to discovering either he or Miriam was sterile. Having his own child had always been so important to him. Like any prospective young parent, he often daydreamed about taking his son to baseball games or buying his daughter dolls. He would start their college funds the day they were born. They had already decided they wanted a boy and a girl and would go as far as trying four times to have them. With the money he was going to make, he could afford four children if he had to.

"Yes, well, we've discussed adopting."

Kevin nodded. "Whatever happened to the Jaffees' child?"

"Richard's brother took him, and guess what—his

brother is an attorney, too. He told Mr. Milton he would do everything he could to make it possible for Richard's son to follow in his father's footsteps."

"Mr. Milton knew him?"

"He took charge after Richard's . . . Richard's suicide. That's the kind of guy he is. Well," he said, rising, "I'll let you get back to work. Good luck. Oh"—he turned from the doorway—"scuttlebutt around here is Mr. Milton will be having a party in honor of you in his penthouse very soon. And believe me, when Mr. Milton throws a party, it's a party."

Miriam sat back on the couch, exhausted. Excluding lunch, she hadn't stopped from the moment they got up this morning. Norma and Jean were a wonderful help, but she thought they got a little silly at the end, arguing over who would invite her and Kevin over for dinner first. Finally, she told them to toss a coin, and Norma won. Kevin and she would go there tomorrow night and then to Jean's the night after.

But the most trying moments of the afternoon came when Helen Scholefield stopped by. It was weird the way she suddenly materialized like a ghost. No one heard the doorbell or heard her come in. Norma, Jean, and she had just stopped for a moment after pushing the couch from one side of the living room to the other and then back again, laughing at their indecisiveness. Miriam sensed someone else was in the room and turned toward the doorway. She thought Kevin might have come back because he had forgotten something.

But there she was, clutching the wrapped painting against her body and staring at them with a soft smile on her face. She made Miriam think of an older woman caught smiling enviously at young children at play.

"Oh," Miriam exclaimed. She looked quickly to the other girls.

"Helen," Norma said. "We didn't hear you come in."

"How are you?" Jean asked quickly.

"I'm all right," she replied and turned her attention to Miriam. "Hello."

"Hi."

"Helen, this is Miriam Taylor," Norma said quickly. "Miriam, Helen Scholefield."

Miriam nodded again.

"I brought you something, a welcoming gift," Helen said, stepping forward and handing her the wrapped painting. "I hope you like it."

"Thank you."

"I'm sure Helen painted it herself," Jean said.

Miriam looked up quickly from the package.

"Yes, yes I did, but don't be afraid to say you don't care for it. My work is . . . special, different. Not everyone appreciates it, I know," she said, looking pointedly at Norma and Jean.

If that were the case, Miriam wondered, staring at Helen, why bring someone one of your paintings as a welcoming gift? Why not find out first if they appreciate the kind of art you do?

"Kevin and I have absolutely no artwork to hang. I'm afraid we're both a little ignorant when it comes to that sort of thing."

"You won't be for long," Norma warned.

"Maybe Helen will come with us to the Museum of Modern Art this week," Jean said.

All eyes were on Helen. She widened her smile. "Maybe," she said with a tentative tone.

"Can I get you a cup of coffee?" Miriam asked, not yet having unwrapped the painting.

"Oh no, please. You're very busy."

"We should take a break," Jean said. "We're getting a little stupid, moving pieces of furniture one way and then another."

"I can't stay anyway," Helen said. "I have a doctor's appointment."

"Oh, I'm sorry," Miriam replied.

"I just wanted to stop by and say hello."

"Perhaps you'll stop by later, when you return," Miriam suggested.

"Yes," Helen said, but there was no promise or hope in it. She looked around. "Your apartment is going to be lovely, as lovely as . . ." She looked from Norma to Jean. "As ours are."

"I'm excited about living here—the views, the proximity to so many museums and good restaurants . . ."

"Yes. We're close to everything, good things as well as bad."

"We don't want to think about anything bad," Jean said quickly, in a reproachful voice.

"No . . . no, I don't suppose you do. Why should you? Why should anyone?" she asked rhetorically. She suddenly looked as if she were all alone, thinking aloud. Miriam turned to Norma, who shook her head. Jean raised her eyes toward the ceiling and then looked away.

"Is Charon going to take you to your appointment?" Norma asked her, obviously anxious to see her move along.

"Charon takes us everywhere," Helen replied. "That's his purpose."

Miriam's eyes widened. What a strange way to put it, she thought.

"Well, maybe he's waiting for you downstairs," Jean suggested.

Miriam noticed Helen's expression change from a soft, esoteric look to a sharply knowing one as she focused on the two women. Then she smiled warmly again and turned to Miriam. "I'm sorry my first visit is so short, but I wanted to be sure to stop by to say hello and welcome you before going to my appointment."

"Thank you. And thanks a lot for the painting. Oh, I didn't even unwrap it. How rude. I was just . . ."

"That's all right," Helen said quickly. She touched Miriam's hand, and Miriam looked into her eyes to see what she thought was excruciating mental anguish. "It's different," she admitted, "but it makes a statement."

"Really? That sounds interesting." She started to unwrap it. Helen stepped back and looked at Norma and Jean, both fixed on the painting being unwrapped. Miriam pulled all the paper off before holding it up.

For a long moment, no one said anything. The colors were vibrant, so bright it seemed as if there was a bulb behind the canvas. At first, Miriam wasn't sure which side was up. Since Helen didn't say otherwise, she assumed she was holding it correctly.

The top of the painting was done in long, soft strokes of sapphire emerging from a wafer at the center which was the color and texture of a Communion wafer. Directly below the blue was a dark green area shaped like palisades, the edges sharp, the incline very steep. Pouring over the palisades was a female figure stretched and twisted into a liquid form, but there was a distinct face caught up in an expression of agony and dread as her body spilled over the brink and down into what looked to be a sea of boiling blood. There were tiny, bone-white bubbles popping up out of the sea.

"Well," Norma said, "that certainly makes a statement."

"What colors!" Jean remarked.

"I've never seen anything like it," Miriam said and then wondered if she had sounded negative. "But I . . ."

"If you don't want it, I'll understand," Helen said. "As I said, my work is special."

"No, no, I want it. I want it very much. I can't wait to see Kevin's reaction . . . anyone's reaction, for that matter." She turned to Helen. "It's definitely the kind of thing that draws attention and sets everyone talking. Thank you." She stared at Helen for a moment. "It was very special to you, wasn't it?"

"Yes."

"Then that makes it even more valuable to me," Miriam said, trying to sound sincere but realizing she sounded too patronizing. "Really," she added.

"If it isn't now, it will be," Helen said prophetically. Miriam looked to Norma and Jean. Both pressed their lips together as if to contain their laughter. "Well, I'm sorry I have to go so quickly, but . . ."

"Oh, no . . . no. I understand." More than you think, Miriam thought. "You go on. We'll catch up later. Once I get settled here, I want you and Paul to come over for dinner."

Helen smiled as if Miriam had made the most

ridiculous suggestion. "Thank you," she said and started away.

"And thank you," Miriam called after her. No one said anything until Helen left.

Then Norma and Jean looked at each other and burst into laughter. Miriam shook her head, smiling.

"What am I supposed to do with this?"

"Hang it in the hallway closet."

"Or on the outside of your front door," Jean suggested. "It'll serve as a deterrent, keeping burglars and salesmen away."

"I just felt so sorry for her. She is disturbed. This painting." She held it up again. "It's like a nightmare!"

"It makes a statement," Norma quipped, and Jean and she laughed again.

"Yes, it says 'aarrgh'!" Jean exclaimed, seizing her own throat and falling to her knees. Norma and Miriam laughed.

"I'll just leave it in the corner until Kevin comes home. Once he sees it, he'll see why I would rather not hang it."

"You were wonderful, though," Norma said. "You handled her well."

"She's going to see her therapist, I gather."

"Yes. Paul's got his hands full. I feel sorry for him. We have tried to help, haven't we, Jean?"

"For weeks after Gloria's death, we called Helen and invited her to go places with us, but she locked herself up in the apartment and brooded. Finally, Mr. Milton got Paul to do something. If you think she's strange now, you should have seen her just after Gloria's death. She came to my apartment once and became hysterical, crying that we all had to move out of here, that we were all in danger . . . as if the building caused Gloria's death and Richard's suicide. I couldn't make any sense out of what she was babbling, and finally I called Dave. He got a hold of Paul, and Paul came to take her back to their place."

"They called a doctor who put her on sedatives," Norma continued. "Obviously, she's still somewhat sedated."

"She must have been very close to Gloria Jaffee."

"Not any closer than we were," Jean said sharply, a note of resentment in her voice.

"I just thought . . ."

"She's just . . . so sensitive," Norma explained, holding the back of her right hand against her forehead. "Because she's an artist and the artist's soul is in continual turmoil. After all," she went on, taking on the voice of a pedantic college professor, "she sees the tragic irony that lives beneath all things." She sighed.

"Still, I can't help but feel sorry for her," Miriam said, looking toward the front entrance as if Helen were still standing there.

"So do we," Jean said. "We're just getting a bit tired of it all. It's such a downer. All right, Gloria Jaffee had a tragic ending and Richard's suicide was horrible, but it's all over and there's nothing any of us can do to change what happened."

"We've got to go on with our lives," Norma added.

"The best thing we can do is be emotionally up whenever Helen's around," Jean said. "Mr. Milton told us that, remember, Norma?"

"Uh-huh. Well . . ." She looked at her watch. "I guess I'd better go shower and prepare dinner."

"Me too," Jean said.

"I don't know how I'll ever thank you two."

"Nonsense, you'll find a way," Norma said, and they all laughed again.

It was good to feel happy, Miriam thought, and these two could make anyone feel that way quickly. She hugged them both, and then they left.

As soon as they did, Miriam plopped down on the couch and closed her eyes. She must have fallen asleep because the next thing she knew, Kevin was standing before her, smiling and shaking his head. He still had his briefcase in his hand.

"Goofing off on the job, huh?"

"Oh, Kev." She scrubbed her face with her dry palms and looked around. "I must have dozed off. What time is it?"

"A little after six."

"Really? I did doze off. Norma and Jean left over an hour ago."

"See you guys did a lot, though," he said, looking around. "You deserve a wonderful dinner out. On the way back in the limo, Dave and Ted told me about a restaurant only two blocks west, a small Italian place run by a family. Everything has that home-cooked flavor and it's very informal. Sounds wonderfully relaxing, doesn't it?"

"Yes."

"Let's shower . . . together."

"If we do that, Kevin, we may not eat for hours."

"I'll gamble," he said, reaching down to pull her into a standing position. He embraced her, and they kissed. "After all, we have to break in our bedroom. First night here." She laughed and kissed him on the tip of his nose. They started away, arms around each other's waist.

"Whoa . . ." Kevin suddenly said. "What's that?"

He looked down at Helen Scholefield's painting. Miriam had placed it on the floor against the rear wall.

"Oh, Kevin . . . Paul's wife stopped by. It was . . . weird. She brought us that painting as a welcoming gift. I didn't know what to do about it."

"You didn't make her feel bad, did you?" he asked quickly.

"Of course not, Kevin, but look at that thing. It's ghastly."

"Well, we'll hang it for a while and eventually take it off."

"You're not serious, Kevin. I can't have that thing hanging on my walls. People will . . ."

"Just for a while, Miriam."

"But she will understand. She said so herself. She admitted it was special, different, and she said she would understand if someone didn't like it."

"You can't do that," he repeated, shaking his head.

"Why not? This is my house, Kevin. I should be able to decide what I put in it and what I don't."

"I'm not saying you shouldn't, Miriam." He thought for a moment. "I don't want to hurt Paul and Helen Scholefield any more than they have been."

"What? What do you mean?"

"On my way to the office, I met Helen in the hallway and realized she was having emotional problems. Paul stopped by and we talked, and he told me they got very depressing news yesterday. Seems she is incapable of having children."

"Oh."

"That, on top of their other problems . . ."

"Yes." She looked at the painting. "No wonder she's doing things like that. All right. For a while we'll hang it. I'll put it in that corner where it will be somewhat inconspicuous, not that anyone coming in here could ignore it long."

"That's my girl," Kevin said and kissed her. "Now, let's see about that shower, huh?"

She smiled, and they continued out. Miriam looked back once and shook her head. "Isn't it ironic, Kev? One woman's tragedy was she gave birth and another's is that she can't."

"Yeah. Well, the best thing we can do is be enthusiastic whenever we're around Helen," he said.

It sounded familiar, and Miriam remembered that was what Jean had said Mr. Milton had told them. "Did Mr. Milton tell you that?"

"Mr. Milton?" He laughed. "I know I've been raving about the guy, but really, Miriam, I can do some of my own thinking, too."

"Of course you can," she said quickly, but still, it did seem odd.

8

Stanley Rothberg sat back in the chair to the right of Mr. Milton. As soon as he entered the conference room, Kevin quickly scrutinized him. Rothberg looked considerably older than forty-one. He tried to hide the premature bald spot at the center of his head by brushing long strands of his thin, dirt-blond hair over the top. Although he was a tall man, standing at least six feet three, he had such an emphatic turn in his shoulders, he looked almost hunchbacked. The bags under his eyes, the deep creases in his face, and the black stubble beard gave him the crusty look of a late-night bartender.

So despite being dressed in a Pierre Cardin dark blue sports jacket and slacks, Rothberg had a seediness about him that triggered all sorts of alarms in Kevin's mind. He didn't like the sleepy look in Rothberg's eyes. He knew juries would interpret it as a

146

look of guilt, slyness, deceit. Even the man's smile left him cold. One corner lifted higher than the other, making it look more like a sneer.

Kevin's father used to tell him never to judge a book by its cover. He was referring to all the wealthy clients he had in his accounting firm who looked and dressed like paupers, but after Kevin had graduated from law school and his father used that expression again, Kevin had to disagree.

"I understand what you mean, Dad," he said, "but if I had to take one of those clients to court, I'd dress him so he looked distinguished. Juries do judge a book by its cover."

First impressions were too often final impressions, Kevin thought, and his first impression of Stanley Rothberg was that the man was guilty. He seemed capable of pushing his wife over the brink. He looked self-indulgent, disdainful, and boorish.

"Stanley," John Milton said, "this is Kevin Taylor."

"How do you do, Mr. Rothberg," Kevin said, extending his hand. Rothberg stared at it a moment and then widened his smile when he reached over the table to shake hands.

"Your boss says you're the whiz kid. Says I shouldn't worry about putting my life into your hands."

"I'll do my best, Mr. Rothberg."

"Question is," Rothberg replied quickly, "is your best going to be enough?" His smile faded.

Kevin looked at Mr. Milton, whose eyes were so intently focused on him, he felt as if they burned into his very soul. Kevin straightened up.

"More than enough," he said, unable to keep out a touch of arrogance, "and if you'll help me, we'll devastate the prosecution's case against you so completely, there'll be no question about your innocence."

Rothberg smiled and nodded. "That's good." He turned to John Milton. "That's good," he repeated, gesturing toward Kevin.

"I wouldn't put you in Kevin's hands if I didn't have complete confidence in his ability to win your vindication, Stanley. And you can be confident that you will have the full resources of my office at your disposal.

"Also, Kevin's youth will work to your favor. Everyone's expecting you to hire one of the more prestigious criminal attorneys in town, to use your wealth to buy yourself an established name and therefore gang up on the advocate of the people. But you're confident of your innocence. You don't need a high-priced attorney who has a media image. You need a competent attorney who can present the facts and counter any circumstantial evidence that suggests your guilt. People will be impressed."

"Yeah." Rothberg nodded. "Yeah, I see what you mean."

"What they don't know," John Milton said, smiling, "is that Kevin is more talented than most of the media-hyped attorneys in town. He has natural instincts when it comes to courtroom skill." Milton gazed up at Kevin with admiration. "He can be tenacious and ruthless when it comes to defending his clients. If I were on trial myself, I would want a man like him defending me."

Even though John Milton's adulation rang sincere, Kevin felt uncomfortable with it. It was almost as if he were being congratulated for being a good hit man. Rothberg, however, was very impressed.

"Oh, I see. Well, good, good. So then, what can I do to help myself?" Rothberg asked.

"That's the spirit," Mr. Milton said. He stood up. "I'll leave you in Kevin's competent hands. Kevin, you know where I am if you need me. I'd say good luck, Stanley," he said, looking down at Rothberg, "but this isn't a matter of luck. It's a matter of skill, and you're in the hands of a very skillful man." He patted Kevin on the shoulder. "Carry on," he said.

Kevin nodded, sat down, and opened his briefcase to begin doing just what Mr. Milton had wanted him to do: impress Stanley Rothberg with his grasp of the facts. He began by discussing Maxine's illness and then asked questions about the nurse. Kevin noticed that Rothberg's replies were tight, cautious. He was already behaving as though he were on the witness stand being cross-examined by the district attorney.

"I hope you understand, Mr. Rothberg . . ."

"Call me Stanley. We're going to be livin' pretty close to each other."

"Stanley. I hope you understand that for me to do the best job I can, there can't be any surprises."

"Surprises?"

"You can't hold back on anything the district attorney might use or know."

"Sure. No problem. If I can't be honest with my lawyer, I must be guilty, huh?"

"It's not always that guilt makes men secretive or tell only half the truth. Sometimes a person is afraid he might look guilty if a fact is known, so he or she keeps it from his or her own attorney. Let me be the judge of everything. I'll know what to hold back and what not to hold back," he added. Rothberg nodded, his eyes opening a little more. Kevin sensed he was impressing him.

"How long had you and your wife occupied separate bedrooms?"

"Oh, right after Maxine became seriously ill. I did that to make things more comfortable for her. Her room became a regular hospital room, especially after her leg had been amputated—medicines, equipment, a hospital bed. And as you know, she had a full-time nurse."

Kevin nodded and then sat back. "Perhaps the most damaging thing the district attorney is using against you is the fact that you kept a separate supply of insulin and needles in your room." He paused and looked at his notes. "At the bottom of a closet. Yet you were never required or asked to inject your wife, were you?"

"No. I couldn't even stand to see the nurse doin' it."

"Then why did you put the insulin in your closet? Why not in your wife's room?"

"I didn't put it there."

"But you don't deny it was there, do you? The investigating officers found it. Are you saying you never knew it was there?"

Rothberg hesitated for a moment. "Look, I did see it there the day before Maxine died, but I forgot all about it."

"You didn't put it there, but you saw it and forgot about it? Never questioned the nurse why it was there?"

"I've got a lot on my mind, Kevin. I'm running a major resort and a growing business with the raisin loaf. We're opening markets in Canada," he said proudly. "I just forgot."

"They've tracked down the prescription, and some of it is missing from what was in your closet, enough to provide the fatal dose. Obviously they'll develop the argument that that was the insulin used to bring about your wife's death. No syringe has been found with your prints on it, but if one should be . . ."

Rothberg just stared.

"The supply in your wife's room wasn't low. There was no reason for anyone to go to the supply in your closet and then to leave the remainder there," Kevin added to emphasize the importance of the point he was making. "Don't you realize what this suggests?"

Rothberg nodded.

"Well, what is your explanation, Stanley? I'm going to need some help on this one," Kevin added dryly.

"I've got to confess something," Rothberg finally said. "I didn't want it to come out during the trial, but I don't see how I can help it now."

"Go on."

"Maxine found out about me and . . . found out I was seeing someone else, a girl named Tracey Casewell. She works in the accounts office at the hotel."

"Yes, I don't think that's as much of a secret as you think it is. You have to understand that in the eyes of the prosecution and maybe in the eyes of the jury, it adds motive. I have it down to discuss your romantic affair with you and how we will handle it, but what has this to do with the insulin being in your room?"

"Maxine and I had an argument. It was terrible. I didn't want her to find out about Tracey. I thought she was suffering enough. It wasn't really an argument. She yelled and I just stood there, just took it. She threatened all sorts of things, you know. I thought she

151

was just hot and she wouldn't carry out a single threat, so I didn't pay any attention to them. I mean, she was a very sick woman by this time and it was affecting her mental condition."

"And?"

"One of those threats was she was going to kill herself and fix it so I would be blamed. Looks like she did." He sat back, contented with his own explanation.

Kevin heard a commotion down the hall after he had completed his interview with Stanley Rothberg and they had shaken hands and parted in the lobby.

"What's going on?" he asked Diane.

"Mr. McCarthy." She beamed. "He got them to drop the charges against his client."

"Really?" He hurried down the corridor to Ted's office. Dave, Paul, and Mr. Milton were standing in front of Ted's desk, and Ted was standing by his chair. They all held glasses in their hands, and there was an opened bottle of champagne on Ted's desk.

"Kevin, you finished just in time," John Milton said. "Join us in a toast. We always have a toast together after one of us does well with a case." John Milton poured him a glass and handed it to him. "To Ted," he said, raising his glass.

"To Ted," the others chanted, and everyone drank.

"What exactly happened?" Kevin inquired, swallowing quickly.

"The Blatts dropped the charges against Crowley. When they found out how promiscuous their little girl had been, and they realized it would all come out at the trial, they backpedaled," Ted said. Dave and Paul laughed. John Milton's smile widened. Kevin thought the revelry made him look younger, the lines in his face thinning, the light in his eyes brightening. Then his expression changed quickly.

"There's a lesson here," Mr. Milton said in a sober voice. "Not all legal maneuvering has to take place in court." He turned to Kevin. "Think of preparation for every court case the way you would think of two prize-fighters readying themselves for the bout. There are ways to psych out the opponent, shake him up before you actually face off so that he loses some confidence in himself and his case.

"Well," he said, smiling, "this adds another reason to have a celebration. First, we will celebrate Kevin's joining our firm and, second, Ted's success. Party in the penthouse this weekend." Kevin noted how the others brightened with excitement. "Is everyone free?"

"No problem for us," Dave said quickly.

"Nor us," Ted said.

"Fine," Paul said. They all looked at Kevin.

"And the guests of honor? It's time I met Miriam."

"We'll be there. Thank you."

"All right, gentlemen, let's go back to work."

Everyone congratulated Ted again and left the office. Dave and Paul went directly to their offices, both of them looking quite fired up by Ted's success and their short celebration. John Milton put his arm around Kevin's shoulders as they continued down the corridor.

"I didn't mean for it to seem as if I were deserting you back there with Rothberg, Kevin, but I wanted him to understand immediately that this is your case. You're in charge."

"Oh, there was no problem. Thanks for all the nice things you said about me."

"I meant every word of it. So. How did your meeting with Rothberg go?"

"His theory is that his wife killed herself and fixed it so he would take the fall. Claims she learned of his extramarital affair and put together a plan for vengeance and suicide by planting the fateful insulin in his room."

"Sounds plausible," John Milton said. "What's that line, 'Hell hath no fury like a woman scorned.'"

Kevin paused to look at him to see if he meant it. He couldn't help smirking.

"You have a problem with Rothberg's theory?"

"He claims he saw the insulin in the closet where she planted it but forgot about it because he was so busy running the hotel and business. Even after his wife threatened to frame him. I have some trouble believing that, yes."

"The question is, can you present it in a way so the jury will buy it? You've got to have confidence in your own case," John Milton warned.

Kevin realized that if he didn't say the right things now, John Milton might very well take the case from him and reassign it to Ted, who was now free.

"Well, it will help if Rothberg had nothing to do with picking up the insulin supply. I'll check that out. Most likely it was delivered to the hotel and the nurse signed for it. I'm going to see the nurse and find out what she knew about Maxine and Stanley's relationship. Perhaps Mrs. Rothberg confided in her, let her know how much she despised Stanley for what he was doing, or maybe she overheard the argument between Stanley and Maxine Rothberg. If she heard her say she would get even with him, kill herself and make it look as if he had done it . . ."

"That's good. I'm sure she will open up to you if you suggest that she could be blamed for Maxine's death. Let her know her drinking problem is well known," John Milton advised. "She will be more inclined to cooperate. Have we fixed Stanley Rothberg's whereabouts during the time the fatal insulin dosage was given?"

Kevin nodded but didn't look happy. John Milton understood.

"He was with his lover?"

"For a man who was too busy to remember that a supply of insulin was placed in his closet, he sure had a lot of time to mess around."

"I think we should follow your instincts on this, Kevin. Go with the honesty approach. Have Rothberg own up to his affair, place him with his girlfriend, have her testify to it. Allow the jury to convict him of adultery in their minds but not convict and punish him for murder just because he was an unfaithful husband. Besides, we can't show the wife as vengeful and suicidal if we don't first develop the premise of infidelity and give her the motive."

"I think I can get some help from her doctor on this, too," Kevin said. "In his reports he made mention of her depression."

"Yes, yes," John Milton said, a light coming into his face. "That's very good." It was as if the man's excitement could travel like electricity from his quickened heart down his arm and into Kevin's heart.

"Of course," he added, stopping at Kevin's office door, "it would help matters if he were remorseful, still blaming himself for his wife's death. Is he?"

"I didn't get that impression, no," Kevin said.

"Well, see to it that the jury does," Mr. Milton advised. He smiled, only his smile now was mischievous, almost impish. He looked more like a teenager who had come up with a clever Halloween prank than a masterful attorney developing a legal strategy.

"I hope I can do that," Kevin said, almost in a whisper. He was fascinated with John Milton's bright eyes.

John Milton patted Kevin on the shoulder. "You'll do fine, just fine. Keep me up to date," he said and continued on to his own office. Kevin watched him for a moment and then turned into his office.

After he sat down, he thought about John Milton's advice. "I think we should follow your instincts on this . . . go with the honesty approach," he had said. It was true, those were his instincts, but he didn't remember telling John Milton that. He remembered only thinking about it.

He shrugged. He must have mentioned it somehow. What other answer was there? he concluded. The man wasn't a mind reader.

Kevin turned back to his files and began to review his interview with Rothberg. The others looked in to see if he would join them for lunch, but Wendy had already inquired and at his request ordered in a sandwich. She volunteered to take notes and do research through her own lunch hour as well. He was impressed with the dedication and energy everyone at John Milton and Associates had. It stimulated him to push himself harder.

Because of the success Ted had had with his case, the ride back to the apartment house at the end of the day was quite jovial. Kevin noted that Paul and Dave were just as happy as Ted. They did seem more like a family than attorneys working at the same firm. Later, Kevin was sorry that he was the only one to introduce a dark note and interrupt their lighthearted mood, but he was interested in Ted's reaction to his success, so he could measure it against his own reaction at the end of the Lois Wilson case.

"Did you believe Crowley was guilty, though, Ted? I mean, even though the girl was promiscuous, did he rape her?" he asked.

Everyone stopped smiling, and for a moment the air was pregnant with tension.

"I didn't force the Blatts to drop the charges. That was their decision," he replied defensively.

"The district attorney should have convinced them to stay with the case," Paul added.

"Ted was just doing what he was paid to do and what he was trained to do," Dave said pointedly. "Just like you when you defended Lois Wilson."

"Oh, I didn't mean to imply anything otherwise. I was just curious about your feelings about the man, Ted."

"We have to put our feelings, morality, judgments aside to be advocates for the defense, Kevin. It's one of the first things I learned from Mr. Milton and it's worked well for me."

"For all of us," Paul said, nodding.

"It's like a doctor treating a patient," Dave explained. "Mr. Milton made this analogy for me when I first arrived. The doctor doesn't judge his patient's morality, politics, life-style. He treats the illness, reads the symptoms, and takes action. To be successful as a defense attorney, you have to separate the client from the case. Treat the accusations, read the facts, and take action. If you had to like and believe in everyone you defended, you'd starve to death."

Ted and Paul laughed. Kevin nodded. He remembered telling something similar to Miriam when she questioned his vigorous defense of Lois Wilson.

"If you can't live with that, you should probably go to work for the district attorney's office," Paul said. Then he smiled. "But you know what those guys make."

Everyone laughed once more, even Kevin. Paul poured each of them a cocktail and they sat back, the relaxed atmosphere quickly returning.

"By the way," Kevin asked, "how does Mr. Milton get back and forth?"

"In the limo. The man's a workaholic. He's in the office much earlier than we are and he often remains there well into the evening," Paul replied. "Charon brings him his dinner. But what a place he comes home to. Wait until you see the penthouse. Talk about luxury and hedonism."

"There are three bathrooms, each with its own whirlpool!" Dave said.

"And the view," Ted added. "It's like standing on top of the world. I always feel . . ."

"Like God," Paul said.

"Yeah." Ted smiled to himself. "I remember the first time I was up there. Milton put his arm around my shoulders and we both looked out over the city and he said, 'Ted, you're not just standing above it all; you are above it all and it will all be yours.' I was so excited, I couldn't speak, but he understood. He understood," Ted repeated. Kevin saw Paul and Dave nod, their faces sober.

There was something special about this, something

different and very unique, Kevin thought. Perhaps they would all be at the top of the world. He suddenly realized the three of them were staring at him.

"Think we're overdoing it?" Dave asked. "Making too much of the man?"

Kevin shrugged. "He's impressive. I got a bit carried away when I first described everything about the firm and Mr. Milton to Miriam."

"He's one in a million," Paul said. "We're all lucky to be with him."

"Here, here," Ted said and raised his glass. "To Mr. Milton."

"To Mr. Milton," Dave and Paul chanted. They all looked at Kevin again.

"To Mr. Milton," he said, and they drank. He couldn't help feeling as if he had just participated in a ritual of some sort. "So," he said, "he puts on a great party, huh?"

"The secretaries come, and he always invites interesting people," Dave said. "You and Miriam will have a great time. In fact, it will be so good, you won't realize how quickly the time passes."

"Sounds like fun," Kevin said. The three looked at him, all smiling the same way, their looks so similar, in fact, it was almost as if they were wearing identical masks.

By the time Charon stopped the limo in front of their apartment building and opened the door to let them out, they were all laughing again. Dave had just repeated a joke he had been told by Bob McKensie, an assistant district attorney. They carried their laughter into the lobby and Dave told the joke again, this time to Philip, the security man.

Kevin enjoyed the feeling of comradeship. They

carried it up the elevator, kidding each other about their college backgrounds. They were still joking when they parted to go to their respective apartments.

When Kevin entered his, he found Norma and Jean standing at opposite ends of the spinet listening to Miriam play. They looked up when he entered, both signaling him not to interrupt. Miriam was so intent on her playing, she didn't hear him enter anyway. She was playing Beethoven, and the girls looked thrilled. He tiptoed to the couch and sat down. When she finished, he joined the applause and she turned, beaming.

"Oh, Kev. I didn't even hear you come in. How long have you been here?"

"Two dozen bars." He shrugged.

"She's wonderful," Norma said. "I was telling her there's a grand piano in Mr. Milton's penthouse, and as soon as he has a party . . ."

"He's having one Saturday night."

"Oh, that's wonderful," Jean squealed. "You'll play for everyone this weekend!"

"I'm not that good," Miriam said.

"No false modesty. You're good and you know it," Norma said sternly. She turned to Kevin. "We're going to a concert at Lincoln Center tomorrow afternoon—Mahler, Symphony No. 2, 'Resurrection.'"

"Can you imagine, Kev? I finally found some people who like classical music, too."

"As well as rock," Jean added.

"And don't forget some country and western," Norma said. The three of them laughed. From the way they hugged and nudged each other, Kevin thought they really did look like lifelong friends. Miriam was really happy. It was going well.

"I better get my rear in gear," Norma said. "Kevin's home, that means Dave's home."

"And Ted."

"Oh," Kevin said as they started away. "Ted will be in a great mood, Jean. He scored a knockout without even going into battle."

"Pardon?" She grimaced as if he were going to tell her something terrible instead of something good. He looked to Miriam quickly and thought he saw her shake her head.

"His case, but I suppose I should let him tell you first."

"Oh. Ted never tells me the nitty-gritty details. He knows how much I hate to hear about those things. I don't even read about the cases when they make the papers."

"Nor do I," Norma said. "It's better to leave the unpleasant events in this world outside the door, like wiping your feet before entering," she said. She turned to Jean. "Wasn't that the way Mr. Milton put it?"

"Uh-huh."

They both turned back to him, smiling. Kevin widened his eyes with surprise. "Yeah, sure," he said quickly.

"'Bye, Miriam. Talk to you later," Jean sang.

"Me too," Norma chorused, and they left.

For a moment Kevin just stared at the closed door. Then he turned to Miriam.

"We had such a wonderful day," she began before he could say a word. "First we did the Museum of

Modern Art. There's a wonderful exhibition of paintings from Moscow, never before viewed in the West. We went to the Village for lunch. Norma knew this little place that had the most wonderful variety of quiche. Then we came back uptown and went to a matinee to catch that Australian film everyone's raving about. It had this great soundtrack taken from Beethoven, so when we came back I played a little of it for them.

"Oh," she said, barely stopping for a breath, "we knew we weren't going to be back in time to prepare dinner, so we stopped at this great take-out and I bought a lobster salad, some French bread, and a bottle of Chardonnay. Is that okay?"

"Sure." He shook his head.

"You're upset?"

"No." He laughed. "I'm just . . . happy you're happy."

"Did you have a good day, too?"

"Yes."

"Okay," she said quickly. "The girls tell me that's all I should ask you. I should work on getting you to put your work problems out of mind and really relax. So . . . you take a shower, get comfortable. I'll get the dinner ready and find some good dinner music." She started away before he could respond, leaving him with a smile of confusion on his face.

He was happy she was adapting so quickly, but there was something about it all that bothered him, like a sharp, short pain in the chest. It could be nothing, or, as was sometimes the case, it could be the first warning of something fatal.

He shrugged it off and headed for the shower.

* * *

Before the weekend arrived, John Milton and Associates had an additional reason for celebration. Dave Kotein was successful in getting the judge to throw out Karl Obermeister's confession on the basis that the arresting police officers and the assistant district attorney hadn't given him an opportunity to phone an attorney before they got him to make the confession. The judge also refused to permit the district attorney to use the evidence they found at Obermeister's apartment since a complete search of the apartment was made without a warrant and without any charges being lodged beforehand.

Without the confession and without the evidence they had taken from the apartment, the district attorney was seriously considering whether he should proceed with the case. Mr. Milton predicted the charges against Obermeister would be dropped by Monday.

"When that happens," Dave said, "Obermeister will leave the city."

"But Dave," Kevin asked after their staff conference. "Don't you think he will commit the same crime wherever he goes?"

"Kevin, are you going out there on the street and have everyone you think has the potential to commit a crime arrested? You'd stuff the jails until they burst. Besides, I'll be finished with Obermeister. And as for feelings of guilt later on, Bob McKensie blew this one, Kevin. Let him live with it," Dave emphasized.

Kevin nodded. It wasn't a point lost on him. He had made the same one himself when Miriam worried about his defense of Lois Wilson. His defense of her had laid more of a burden on his conscience than he would like to admit, but when he had these feelings, he went back to Mr. Milton's explanation of what the law was and what his responsibilities to it and to a client were. Those were the standards against which to measure action. Conscience, when it came to the law, was just excess baggage. He had worked under that philosophy; he was working that way now.

But did he believe it truly? He tried desperately to avoid that question. There was too much at stake. He wanted to succeed here and live up to Mr. Milton's expectations. This wasn't the time to question one's legal philosophy and get soft. He had a major case coming to trial.

And besides, with every passing day Miriam grew more and more enamored of the life they had chosen for themselves. Every day when he returned home from the office, he found her just as excited, as happy, and as full of energy as the day before. She rarely talked about Blithedale and her old friends and their old life. She stopped returning phone calls and wrote no letters. Whatever regrets she had voiced in the beginning were gone. Maybe it was still the honeymoon period, but he couldn't think of a dark moment between them since they had arrived.

Even so, he was astonished at the way she spoke to her mother on the phone, defending everything they had done, attacking her mother's views as silly prejudicial ideas, even calling her narrow-minded. And when her parents came to dinner on Thursday, she overwhelmed them by first cooking a wonderful gourmet meal. (Norma got her the recipe from a chef at the Four Seasons.) Then she brought out all the play and concert programs she had attended with her friends since moving to the city. She ranted on and on about her museum forays, the restaurants she had been to, the people she had met. Her conversation was full of references to Jean and Norma, the only downer being a short discussion of Helen Scholefield.

Kevin was surprised at how Miriam had avoided telling her parents the reason for Helen's depression, blaming it all on their discovery that she was unable to have children.

"That's why we still have that horrible painting hanging there, Mom. Actually, Kevin suggested we keep it for a while, so the woman's feelings wouldn't be hurt." She turned to him. "Isn't he just a big softy when it comes right down to it? But I love him for being so thoughtful."

"Well, it is thoughtful of you, Kevin," Miriam's mother said, "but that painting is so ghastly, I just can't look at it. It gives me the chills."

"Oh, let's not think about it. Here," Miriam said, getting up and taking the picture down. "I'll keep it on the floor facing the wall until you leave. Daddy," she said, "I'm going to play your favorite piece."

She went to the piano and played, more beautifully, with more feeling than Kevin could remember. When he looked at her parents, he saw amazement in their faces, too.

On the way out at the end of the evening, her mother pulled him aside while Miriam was saying goodbye to her father.

"She really is happy here, Kevin. I didn't think she would be when I first heard about all this, but it looks as if you've made a wonderful move. I'm happy for both of you."

"Thanks, Mom."

"I'll be calling your parents and giving them my reviews," she whispered.

"They'll be here next week, but I'm sure Mom's waiting to hear from you."

"She is. Five stars," she added and kissed him on the cheek.

After they left, Miriam went into the kitchen to clean up, and Kevin returned to the living room. His gaze drifted to Helen Scholefield's painting on the floor. He picked it up and rehung it and then stepped back. For a long moment, he stared at it. He felt himself drawn to the woman's face. He could almost hear her cries as she was poured over the edge into the boiling red sea below. As he stared, her facial characteristics took more shape, and for an instant it looked like Miriam's face. Kevin felt a wave of heat and then a chill race up and down his spine, and he had to close his eyes. When he opened them again the painting was the way it had always been—abstract. Miriam's face was gone. But what an illusion, even for a moment, he thought.

Kevin walked into the kitchen to find Miriam and took her in his arms. He turned her to him and kissed her as if he were kissing her for the last time.

"Kev," she said, catching her breath. "What is it?"

"Nothing . . . you made a great meal. It was a great evening, and I wanted you to know just how much I love you. I'm going to do all I can to make you happy, Miriam."

"Oh, Kev, I know that. Look at all you've done already. I don't mind putting my future in your hands." She kissed him on the cheek and turned back to the dishes and silverware. He watched her for a moment and then wandered out to the patio. Despite the cold November night air, he stepped out and peered over the edge. The world below looked unreal.

He tried to imagine what it would be like falling from such a height.

Was it only his wife's tragic death that had made Richard Jaffee do it? Why wouldn't he be thinking about his infant son and his responsibility to him?

Suddenly a sheet of light fell over him. He shaded his eyes with his forehead and looked up. He realized John Milton had come home and put on his rooftop lights and patio lights. Most of the small spotlights were directed so that their illumination would shine downward, the light blanketing the building from the fifteenth floor up. It was as if the associates and their wives were under his protection.

Or under his spell, Kevin thought. It was the first time he had thought such a thing, but he blamed it on the melancholy mood he had put himself into by coming out on the patio and thinking of Richard Jaffee's suicide. The cold night air drove him back inside. He heard Miriam singing in the kitchen. That and the warmth of his apartment put an end to his maudlin thoughts.

9

"Charon brought us our very own key," Miriam said, making no attempt to hide how impressed she was. "I called Norma and she told me all the associates have a key. Anyone else, guests and the like, has to have the security guard insert his key," she added, a distinctly arrogant tone in her voice.

I thought I was the one with all the arrogance, Kevin thought. He nodded and looked at the gold key in Miriam's palm. It looked like solid gold. She read his thoughts.

"It's solid gold. I asked Charon if it was, and he said of course. He almost smiled."

Kevin took the key and turned it over and then felt the weight of it in his palm. "Rather extravagant, don't you think?"

She plucked it from his open hand. "Oh, I don't know." She shrugged and turned to look at herself one more time in the hallway mirror. She had gone shopping with Norma and Jean to buy something special for the occasion. Kevin was surprised at what she had chosen: a tight, black knit dress that fit so snugly to her body, one could actually see the imprint of her ribs in the material. It didn't come off her shoulders, but the bodice was cut so low that more than half her bosom was visible. And she wasn't wearing a regular bra. Instead, she wore a push-up bra, something Norma and Jean had talked her into wearing. It fit under her breasts, lifting and shaping them. There was an enticing splash of crimson along the top edges of her cleavage.

It wasn't Miriam, he thought. She could dress sexy and be alluring, but never in so obvious a way. She had more class, was more reserved, and cared more about being stylish and elegant than being seductive.

And she never wore this much makeup. Both the eyeliner and the eyeshadow were far too heavy. She had blended some rouge into her cheeks and had used a cardinal-red wet-look lipstick on her lips.

He saw she had decided against wearing the necklace that matched the gold and pearl earrings, a set he had bought her for her last birthday. Not that he thought she needed the added adornment. Miriam did have a graceful neck, the lines turning softly into her small, feminine shoulders, shoulders that fit so neatly into Kevin's palms when he brought her to him to kiss. It was just that the absence of jewelry around her neck added to the nude look, making her appear even more provocative.

She had done her hair quite differently, teasing and blowing it out. It gave her a wild, tempestuous appearance. He wasn't against that per se, but wearing that dress and all that makeup, combined with this coiffure, made her appear cheap, more like a street prostitute. Yes, there was a new sensuality about her, and it stirred him; but he was upset about it, too.

"What's the matter? Don't you like the way I look?"

"It's . . . different," he said as diplomatically as he could.

She turned back to her image in the mirror. "Yes, isn't it? I thought I should change my appearance a bit. Both Norma and Jean thought I was too conservative." She laughed. "You should have seen their imitation of an upper-middle-class Long Island type —you know, the steel jaw, tight vowels, nasal sounds. May I see that fox wrap?" she added, imitating the imitators and pretending to be in a fur coat store.

"I never thought you were a type, honey. And I never thought you were too conservative. You've always been quite fashionable. Is this really what women your age are wearing now?"

"Women my age? Really, Kevin." She put her hands on her hips and scowled.

"Just asking. Maybe I've had my nose in law books and missed what's happening."

"I think we both have, more than we realized."

"Really?" How remarkable, he thought. Just a short while ago, he was trying to convince her of that, and now she was making it sound as if he were the one who had wanted to remain in their safe haven on Long Island.

"You don't like how I look, do you?" She began to pout.

"I'm not saying I don't like it. It's very nice. I just don't know if I can let you out of the house. I'll have to fight them off you all night."

"Oh, Kevin." She looked at her watch. "We'd better go up. It's fashionably late."

"Uh-huh." He nodded, opening the door. As she passed him, he pecked the side of her neck.

"Kevin! You'll mess up my makeup."

"All right, all right." He lifted his hands. Then he leaned into her, leering. "Only, I think this is the night we make the baby."

"Later."

"I can wait . . . a little." He laughed as they went to the elevator. After the door opened and they stepped in, Miriam inserted the gold key under the letter "P" and turned it, smiling up at him as the doors closed. He shook his head. She dropped the key into her small, matching black handbag.

"It opens to his living room," she whispered as the elevator climbed.

"I know. The boys told me."

When the doors parted, however, they both stood there for a moment, awestruck. Mr. Milton's living room was as wide and as long as a converted warehouse loft. There was a fountain at the center, surrounded by a circular burgundy couch done in velvet with large cushions and throw pillows. Small spotlights painted the colors of the rainbow over the sparkling water that rose from a giant white marble lily in the center.

The floor was covered with a thick, fluffy milk-white carpet, the kind, Kevin thought, that makes you want to get down on your knees and run your hands over it. Ruby-red drapes were hung on the walls, interspersed here and there with paintings, most of them modern, and nearly all were originals. Some even looked as if they had been painted by Helen Scholefield. Along the walls and placed between various pieces of furniture were pedestals with stone and wood sculpture.

The far wall consisted of the large windows Dave, Ted, and Paul had described so passionately in the limo. The long drapes had been pulled completely open to provide a breathtaking view of the New York skyline. Off to the far right was the grand piano, with a gold candelabra—solid gold, Kevin conjectured—placed on it. In the left corner, built into the wall, was a large stereo unit, its quadraphonic speakers also embedded in the walls and even the ceiling. A tall, very thin black disc jockey had a turntable set up in front and provided commentary along with the music. His black silk shirt was opened to his navel, and a gold medallion on a thick gold chain glittered against his ebony skin.

The room was illuminated by rows of recessed lights along the ceiling, and some Tiffany and Waterford crystal lamps in a variety of shapes and sizes were lit next to the settees and lounge chairs. On the immediate right was the bar, its facing constructed with polished fieldstone, its long, narrow top built from oak. There were black-cushioned bar stools with high backs lined up against it. Behind the bar, two bartenders shook and mixed cocktails, their mirrored twin images giving the illusion of being just a split second late no matter how they twisted or turned. Wineglasses glittering like dangling diamonds hung in a hickory rack above them.

On the immediate left, Mr. Milton had created a small dance floor of crimson tile. The strobe light spinning above it rained down a mixture of blues and greens and reds over the guests turning and twisting to the music. The dance floor was boxed in a wall of mirrors so that the light reflected everywhere and the dancers saw themselves move. Some looked mesmerized by their own kinetic images.

There were at least three dozen people already at the party. Kevin saw that each of the secretaries had an escort. Wendy waved from the dance floor. Diane, who was sitting on the couch with her date, waved, too.

"Those are two of our secretaries," Kevin explained quickly.

"Secretaries?" Miriam looked from Wendy to Diane. Wendy wore a backless bright blue pants suit, the sides cut so sharply that half her bosom was visible from behind. Diane was in a black body suit and jeans, her braless breasts pressing against the thin material.

"No wonder you're so eager to go to work every day," Miriam complained. Kevin responded with a wicked smile.

But there were good-looking women everywhere, flanked by men dressed in sports jackets and suits. It had the look of an opulent affair—waiters in white jackets and black tie; waitresses in black skirts and white blouses moving through the room, carrying trays of delicious-looking hot hors d'oeuvres, cocktails, glasses of champagne.

Diane leaned back on the couch, and two men began feeding her grapes, teasing her and then touching her lips, until she took one man's fingers into her mouth along with the grape. Just then Kevin heard a peal of feminine laughter to his left and turned to see men and women dancing so closely, they looked like they were in the throes of sexual ecstasy. In the center of the large room, a buxom redhead, barefoot and wearing something that looked more like a slip, seemed to float to the bar. Even women looked at her appreciatively. In the brighter light, the redhead's bosom was completely revealed. She might as well have gone topless, Kevin thought. She joined two men at the bar who drew close to her as if she were a magnet and they were made of iron.

Kevin began to feel he and Miriam had entered a modern-day Roman orgy. He was fascinated, titillated, and amused. No wonder the associates were so excited about attending another party in the penthouse.

In the background, close to the windows, stood Mr. Milton and the associates, each holding a glass of champagne. Mr. Milton was wearing what looked to be a scarlet smoking jacket and a pair of matching slacks. As soon as he saw Kevin and Miriam in the open elevator, he said something to Paul Scholefield. Paul nodded at the disc jockey working the turntable, and the music was stopped.

Everyone quieted down. Mr. Milton stepped forward. "Ladies and gentlemen, may I present our newest associate and his wife, Kevin and Miriam Taylor."

The gathering broke into applause. Kevin looked at Miriam and saw she was beaming. Her eyes sparkled with excitement. He couldn't remember her looking more radiant, her natural look burning through the makeup. She squeezed his hand in hers.

"Thank you," Kevin said, nodding from left to right. Mr. Milton proceeded toward them, and the music continued. Everyone went back to what he or she was doing. Miriam looked about for Norma and Jean and saw them waving at her from the other side of the dance floor. About halfway across the room, on the left side, Helen Scholefield sat complacently, staring out at the gathering, a goblet of white wine in her hand. She sat so still, she looked like one of the alabaster statues.

"Welcome," Mr. Milton said.

"Miriam, may I present Mr. Milton," Kevin said. John Milton took Miriam's extended hand into his right hand and then placed his left over it. He smiled.

"They told me you were a very attractive woman, Miriam. I can see that was a gross understatement."

Miriam blushed. "Thank you. I don't have to tell you that I feel I know you already. Everyone I meet talks so much about you."

"All good, I hope." He pretended to scowl at Kevin.

"Nothing you could even question," Kevin said, raising his right hand. John Milton laughed.

"Let me get you two something to drink and then introduce you to some of my guests. And, not long after that," he said, still holding Miriam's hand, "we'll see if we can talk Miriam into playing the piano for us."

"Oh no. They told you." She shot a chastising look toward Norma and Jean, who were both watching and smiling widely.

"They didn't have to. I knew. Your reputation preceded you," he added quickly, and Miriam laughed.

"I think I'm going to need that drink," she said. Kevin laughed, and the three of them started across the room, stopping by a waiter so that John Milton could get them a cocktail before proceeding with introductions.

Kevin was impressed with the variety of professionals attending Mr. Milton's party. There were lawyers from other firms, many of which Kevin had heard of or remembered from his college days when the law students would discuss ideal places to work. He and Miriam were introduced to two doctors, both heart specialists. He recognized a rather famous Broadway actor, known for his character roles. They met a well-known *New York Post* columnist and were eventually introduced to Bob McKensie, an assistant district attorney.

"Bob likes to visit the enemy camp once in a while," Mr. Milton joked, and then added in a mock-serious tone, "especially when we have a new star."

"I'm not a star yet," Kevin said and shook McKensie's long hand. To Kevin, McKensie looked Lincolnesque, standing at least six feet five, lanky but firm, something he could tell from the man's grip. McKensie had a narrow, dark face with deep, sad eyes and sharply cut features.

"Trouble is," McKensie said, "everyone who works for John Milton becomes a star sooner or later. Which makes work for the prosecutor's office that much harder."

John Milton laughed. "Listen, Bob," he said, "we don't make your job harder; we make you strive to be the best you can be. You should be thanking us."

"Listen to that logic," McKensie said, shaking his head. "See why he and all his associates are so formidable in court? Nice to meet you, Kevin. I understand you're going to handle the Rothberg case."

"Yes."

"As they say, see you in court." McKensie nodded to Miriam and went off to talk to other people.

"Rather serious fellow," Kevin said. "Doesn't he ever smile?"

"Hasn't got all that much to smile about these days," Mr. Milton replied, his eyes twinkling. "Now let me show you the rest of the penthouse." John Milton took Miriam's arm. He led them to the left, where the doorway opened to a corridor, off of which were three guest bedrooms, a study, three bathrooms, and John Milton's bedroom.

All the rooms were large. The bathrooms were tiled and plush, each with its own whirlpool, just as the associates had described.

"I don't like this railroad car arrangement," John Milton said as they walked down the corridor, "but I didn't feel like ripping everything out to start all over."

"Oh, it's beautiful!" Miriam exclaimed, especially when they stopped at one of the bathrooms.

John Milton gazed at her a moment and then winked at Kevin. "Later, if you want, feel free to use a whirlpool. It's first come, first served."

When they reached John Milton's bedroom and looked in, Kevin understood why Paul and the others talked about the luxury and hedonism of the penthouse. The heavy oak bed at the center of the room was enormous. The mattress, box spring, and bedding all had to be custom-made. It looked like a bed Henry VIII might have had constructed. The posts were large and tall. An artisan had carved mythological figures into them—unicorns, satyrs, cyclops. Kevin was reminded of some of the furniture in John Milton's office. Perhaps the same craftsman had built this bed.

The bedspread and oversized pillows were done in a pattern of scarlet and white, which matched the room's decor—scarlet and white drapes, ruby lamp shades, and white walls with spiraling bursts of red that looked like explosions of stars. The same white rug covering the floor in the large room covered the floor here.

Above the bed was a ceiling of mirrors. When they gazed up, it looked as if they were liquefied and spilling down toward the center of the room. The distortions must make for interesting erotic pictures, Kevin mused.

"I gather red's your favorite color," he said when he saw how John Milton was smiling at him.

"Yes. I like sharp, clean colors—reds, whites, stark black. I suppose it's my leaning toward clear and unclouded things. I hate it when people say someone or something is neither good nor bad. Life is much simpler when we identify everything for what it is, don't you think?" he asked Miriam.

"Oh yes, yes," she said, still intrigued with the furniture, the closets, the artwork, and the great bed. In the wall directly across from it was a built-in giant television screen.

"Well, I've kept you two from the party long enough. Let's go back and have some fun, eh?" He snapped off the bedroom lights, and they returned to the gathering.

Both Kevin and Miriam thought it was a wonderful party. Conversations were stimulating and interesting. People were discussing the new shows on Broadway and off-Broadway. Kevin got into a heated political discussion with some lawyers and a state supreme court judge. He and Miriam danced with each other and with other people, especially Ted and Dave and their wives.

But Helen Scholefield never moved from her chair. Whenever Kevin looked over, he found her looking at him. Finally, he made his way across the room and said hello. He noticed Paul standing beside Mr. Milton. They were both watching him closely. Probably worrying about her, Kevin thought.

"You don't look like you're having a good time," he said. "Can I get you something to eat or drink, ask you to dance . . ."

"No, I'm fine. You should worry about yourself . . . and your wife," she replied, without any sarcasm or anger.

"Pardon?"

"Are you having a good time, Kevin Taylor?"

He laughed. "You can just call me Kevin. Yes, as a matter of fact. This is quite a party."

"It's only the beginning. The party hasn't even begun yet."

"No?" He looked around. She was staring up at him, glaring at him the way she had at the elevator the day he met her. It made him nervous, self-conscious. "So . . . tell me, are any of these paintings yours?"

"Yes, some of mine are here. They're from my early days, though. I was painting only what Mr. Milton wanted me to paint then. You can be sure he didn't want me to do the painting that's in your apartment. Is it still there?"

"Oh yeah, sure. I find it . . . interesting."

"Keep looking at it, Kevin Taylor. It's the only hope

you have," she said just before Paul stepped up to them.

"Helen, how are you doing, honey?"

"I'm tired, Paul. Would you mind very much if I slipped away?"

Paul turned instinctively in Mr. Milton's direction.

"Mr. Milton shouldn't care," she added quickly. "He has new entertainment." She turned to Kevin and looked at him pointedly.

Kevin glanced at Paul with confusion, but Paul only shook his head. "No problem, honey. You go on down to our apartment. I won't stay late."

"No later than you usually stay, I'm sure," she replied dryly. She stood up. "Good night, Kevin Taylor," she said and started away. Then she stopped and turned back, tilting her head to one side before speaking. "You do like all this, don't you?"

Kevin smiled and lifted his arms a bit.

"How can anyone not help but like it?" he replied.

She nodded, confirming a thought. "He chooses well," she said.

"Go on down, Helen," Paul snapped. She turned obediently and continued toward the elevator. "I'm sorry," Paul muttered, looking after her. "I thought bringing her to the party might help cheer her up a bit, but she's just so depressed. She's taking something the doctor prescribed, but it's not helping. I'll have to speak to him tomorrow."

"It's too bad. If there is anything Miriam and I can do . . ."

"Thanks. You guys just have a good time. It's your night. Don't let this put a damper on anything. Come on, let's go into Mr. Milton's study. Ted and Dave are in there." Paul glared in his wife's direction, scowling and shaking his head as she got into the elevator. She stood like a statue, with a puzzling Mona Lisa smile on her face as the doors closed.

Kevin looked for Miriam and saw her moving toward the dance floor with Mr. Milton. He waited for them to start.

"Look at the boss. From here he looks twenty years younger."

"Yeah," Paul said, his face returning to a relaxed smile. "What a guy. Come on."

Paul followed him across the room. Just before they stepped into the corridor, he glanced back and saw Miriam turning and twisting her body more suggestively than he had ever seen her do in public before.

"Come on," Paul repeated, and Kevin continued down the corridor to the den where the other associates waited.

From the smiles on Ted's, Dave's, and Paul's faces, Kevin realized the gathering in the study was not spontaneous. After Ted poured him another glass of champagne, this time from a bottle of Dom Perignon, Dave cleared his throat.

"We wanted to get away from the crowd for a few private moments with you, Kevin," he said. "But first things first." He raised his glass. "We three would like to take this opportunity to welcome a new member to our legal family. May his talents, wit, and knowledge reach their full strength in the courtroom battles yet to come."

"Here, here," Ted and Paul added.

"To Kevin," Dave said.

"To Kevin," they repeated, and everyone drank.

"Thank you, guys. I want to say how much I

appreciate the way you and your wives have made things easier for me and for Miriam. I really want to be a part of this. My only fear is that I won't live up to your and Mr. Milton's high expectations."

"Oh, yes you will, buddy," Paul said.

"We all started with that feeling," Ted said. "You'll be surprised how quickly it passes."

They sat down because Dave had a new joke to tell. When he was finished, their laughter spilled out and into the corridor. More champagne was poured, more stories related. Kevin had no idea how much time had passed, but suddenly they all stopped talking because they heard the sounds of the piano.

"That must be your wife," Dave said. "We heard she can play well."

They got up quickly and joined the crowd that had surrounded Miriam and the piano. Mr. Milton was standing on her left side, his hand on the piano top, looking out at the audience. He wore a look of pride, as if Miriam were his daughter or even . . . his wife.

Kevin drew closer. Miriam's fingers were flying over the keys with a movement and a grace he had never seen before. The expression on her face was somber, and she sat firmly, with a demeanor of confidence. There was no hesitation, no tentativeness, no uncertainty. She looked like a professional pianist.

And the music. It was wonderful. Kevin didn't recognize the piece and wondered if it were something she had prepared just in case she was talked into doing this. Only she didn't look like someone who had had to be talked into it. She looked like someone hired to play. When he looked at the faces in the crowd, he saw expressions of deep appreciation and awe. People nodded to each other, their eyes widening. It was as if Miriam were another one of Mr. Milton's finds.

But she wasn't, Kevin thought. This was strange. He began to feel a bit overwhelmed and regretted drinking so much champagne. He had lost track of how many glasses he had drunk, yet, when he looked at the champagne in his glass now, he felt an irresistible urge to sip it. It seemed to turn from a blush to blood-red right before his eyes.

He saw Diane staring at him and smiled at her. She nodded toward Miriam and raised her eyebrows. Suddenly the room took a spin. He staggered but kept his balance by taking hold of a high-back chair to his right. He closed his eyes and shook his head. When he opened his eyes again, he felt as if he were an inch or two above a treadmill. The floor seemed to be flowing under him. He shook his head again and closed his eyes. When he opened them a second time, he found Diane at his side.

"You all right?" she whispered.

"Just a little dizzy. Too much champagne, I think."

"It's okay. No one's paying any attention to you. They're all infatuated with Miriam. Lean on me, and I'll help you back to the study where you can rest up a bit. I'll get you a wet washcloth, too."

"Yeah, maybe you're right."

He let her lead him away, keeping his eyes closed most of the time, because every time he opened them the room spun. She guided him back onto the soft leather couch in the study and then went out to get him a washcloth. Kevin lay back, resting his head against the top of the couch, and tried to open his eyes. The ceiling looked like a whirlpool, and he had the horrible feeling he was falling into it, so he closed his eyes again and kept them closed until he felt the cold cloth on his forehead.

"You'll be all right in a few minutes," Diane said.

"Thank you."

"Do you want me to stay with you?"

"No, that's all right. I'll just rest a bit. As soon as Miriam's finished playing, tell her where I am and that I'm all right."

"Sure."

"Thanks," he said and closed his eyes. In moments he was asleep. He had no idea how long he was there. When he awoke, he was confused at first. Where was he? How did he get there? He scrubbed his face with his dry palms and looked around the study. It all came back to him in a moment, and he realized it was very, very quiet. There was no music, no sounds of the party.

Kevin got to his feet, a little unsteady at first, but quickly regained his composure. Then he went to the doorway and stepped out. The hallway was brightly lit, but the party room was only dimly illuminated. Confused, he moved down the hallway as quickly as he could until he reached the loft. The fountain was going, but all the colorful lights had been turned off. A small light was burning behind the bar. The curtains had been drawn over the large windows. The stereo was off, the disco removed. Most of the light in the room spilled out from the elevator, its door open.

"What the . . . where the hell . . ."

He rubbed his face vigorously, as if doing so would restore the evening, but nothing changed.

"Hello?" His voice echoed in the great room. "Mr. Milton?"

184

He turned and looked down the corridor.

"Miriam?"

He heard nothing but the monotonous soft sound of the fountain.

Miriam certainly wouldn't have left without me, he thought. *That's insane. Where the hell is everyone? What is this, some kind of practical joke being played on me for passing out from too much champagne?* Sure, what else could it be? Everyone, at least the associates, was probably hiding in these rooms. He laughed to himself and shook his head. What a bunch of guys.

He started down the corridor, moving as quietly as he could, expecting Dave or Ted to burst out of a room. But when he paused at the first door and looked in, he saw nothing but darkness. It was the same at the second bedroom doorway and the third, and no one was in any of the large bathrooms. He already knew no one was in the study.

He stopped at Mr. Milton's bedroom door and listened. All was quiet. He knocked gently and waited.

"Mr. Milton?"

There was no response. Should he knock louder? *He must have gone to sleep,* Kevin thought. *The party ended, everyone left, and he went to bed. Miriam did leave me. Maybe she was angry and left in a huff. Diane told her where I was and what had happened. She came to get me, couldn't wake me, and was embarrassed. Mr. Milton probably told her to let me sleep it off. If I woke up, he'd send me down. That had to be it. What else could it be?* he wondered.

He listened at the doorway a few more moments and then turned and went back through the corridor to the loft and to the elevator. "What a night," he muttered to himself after he pushed the button and the elevator doors began to close.

They opened again on a deadly quiet corridor. He stepped out and quickly made his way to his apartment door, fumbling for his key. He was surprised that all the lights in the apartment were off. Didn't she think he'd come home? *Damn, she must be angry,* he thought. It was the first time he could ever remember being so dead drunk.

He made his way through the apartment and stopped when he saw that their bedroom door was closed. There was some light leaking under it. At least she had left a lamp on for him in there, he thought. He began to frame his apologies. But when he reached for the doorknob, he stopped, because he heard something that sounded like muffled moans. He listened for a moment. The moaning grew louder. It was an erotic moan, and it cut through him like a sword of ice. He reached for the doorknob again, but the moment he touched it his fingers grew numb, frozen. The doorknob burned the tips of his fingers as if it were made of dry ice. He tried pulling his hand away, but his skin was stuck to the metal. His fingers were no longer under his control. They turned the knob, and his arm pushed the door forward, inches at a time until it was open wide enough for him to see clearly.

There was a naked couple on the bed. Something about the man's head seemed terribly familiar. He stepped into the room. Was that Miriam? He moved to the foot of the bed. The man's body paused, his thrusting halted. The woman beneath him shifted to her right and then sat up enough for him to see her clearly. It was Miriam!

"No!" he screamed.

The man lifted his lips from Miriam's but held himself frozen in position, looking down at her. Miriam reached up to draw the man back to her and pulled him down so she could kiss his lips. In a moment they were back at it, moving in rhythm, Miriam moaning, her fingers pressed firmly into his buttocks, pulling him into her, demanding longer, deeper thrusts. She lifted her legs and wrapped them tightly around his waist. The energy and force of their lovemaking was so great that the bed shook and the mattress springs squeaked.

"No!" Kevin screamed.

He moved quickly around the side of the bed and reached forward to take hold of the man's shoulders, pulling him away, pulling him up. The man seemed glued to her, firmly attached. Kevin pounded him on the back, putting the full weight of his body behind each blow, but the man seemed not to feel it. On and on the man went, thrusting, driving. Kevin seized him at the waist, but instead of pulling him off Miriam, he was drawn into the man's movement, and he found he was pushing the man downward with each thrust and pulling him back with each return. He struggled to free himself from the man's body, but his hands were stuck. Miriam's moans grew louder. She peaked and screamed with ecstasy.

"Miriam!" His hands broke free.

Desperate now, Kevin took hold of the man's hair and pulled the strands back, nearly tearing them from their roots. Finally, the man lifted himself off Miriam's body and began a slow and deliberate turn. Kevin released his grip and poised himself to drive his fist into the man's face. But when the man turned completely, Kevin opened his fist and pressed both hands against his own head.

"No!" he screamed. "What . . ."

He was looking at himself. And the shock of it sent him reeling back into darkness.

10

No!" Kevin screamed. He sat up in the darkness.

"Kevin?" Miriam leaned over to turn on the night lamp on the end table. As soon as the bedroom was light, Kevin spun around, a mixture of fear and confusion in his face.

"What? Where . . ." He glared down at Miriam, who had fallen back to the pillow and stared up at him in astonishment. "Miriam . . . I . . . how did I get into bed? Where is . . ." He spun around, searching the room for signs of . . . of whom? Himself?

Miriam shook her head and drew herself into a sitting position.

"Where is who?"

He stared at her. She looked genuinely confused.

"How did I get into bed?" he muttered.

"Kevin Taylor, don't you remember anything?"

"I . . ." He took a deep breath and then pressed his

189

palms against his eyes. "The last thing I remember, I was in the study and I awoke to find everyone gone, so I came down here and . . ."

"You didn't come down here. You were brought down here."

"I was?"

"The boys found you drunk and babbling on the floor in Mr. Milton's study. One of the secretaries told them what had happened to you. They got you out and brought you down here discreetly. Paul Scholefield came up to me after I played another piece on the piano and told me where you were. He said you were out like a light, so I didn't come right down. I stayed until people started to leave. Then I said good night to Mr. Milton and came down myself. Not long after I got into bed, you woke up and we . . ."

"What?"

"Some lover. I thought you were wonderful, I thought it was one of the best times, and all the time you were so drunk you didn't know what you were doing? You don't remember any of it?"

"We made love?" He considered what she was saying and what he had thought. "Then it was just a dream." He laughed a laugh of relief. "It was just a dream," he repeated.

"What was just a dream?"

"Nothing. I . . . oh, Miriam, I'm sorry. I guess I just didn't realize how much I had drunk. I missed the rest of the party?"

"It's all right. Nobody really noticed. As I said, the boys handled it well."

"And Mr. Milton?"

"No problem. He really likes you. I had a wonderful time, especially afterward, whether you remember it or not. Maybe you should get drunk more often," she added.

He thought for a moment. Not to be able to remember making love?

"I was good?"

"All I can say is you touched me where I had never been touched before. It was like you . . ."

"What?" He saw her redden with the thought. "Come on, tell me."

"Like you grew larger and larger in me until I was filled with you. If we didn't make the baby tonight, I don't know when we will." She leaned over and kissed him softly on the lips. "I'm sorry if I got a little wild," she whispered. The blanket fell away from her breasts.

"Wild?"

"And dug my fingernails in too deeply. I know I scratched you, but that's the price you pay for getting so passionate." She kissed him again, working her tongue into his mouth, nearly gagging him. "I'll never forget it," she whispered after the kiss. "Even if you already have."

"Well, I . . . I've never been so drunk that I forgot where I was and what I had done, much less forgot making love. Sorry. But I'll make it up to you."

"You'd better," she whispered. Then she lay back. She smiled up at him, and images of what he remembered from his dream returned. He shook his head to drive them away.

"What's wrong?"

"Nothing, just a little dizzy. I think I'd better go splash some cold water on my face. Wow, what a night." He slipped off the bed to go into the bathroom. When he looked at himself in the mirror, he saw that his eyes were somewhat bloodshot. He splashed some cold water on his face and then took a leak. Before he left the bathroom, he turned around and looked at his naked buttocks in the mirror. There wasn't a mark on them.

Scratched me? He shrugged. *She probably got so excited, she thought she scratched me. Oh well, thank God what I saw was just a nightmare. Too bad I didn't enjoy the sex, though. From the way she described it,* he thought, *I must have been wonderful.*

Kevin laughed to himself and went back to bed. Miriam embraced him, and they made love, but when it was over, she looked disappointed.

"What's wrong? Wasn't I as good as before?"

"You're probably tired," she said. "It was good," she added when his look of disappointment came, "but it wasn't like before. I'm sure it will be again."

"Well, I'm not going to get drunk like that again. You can bet your ass on that."

She looked at him suspiciously. "When did you leave the party and go into the den?"

"You were playing the piano . . . beautifully. I never heard you play like that, Miriam. And that piece. When did you learn a new piece?"

"It wasn't a new piece, Kevin. I've played it often."

"You have? Funny, I can't remember that, either," he said, shaking his head.

"Maybe the champagne burned out some of your memory," she said sarcastically.

"I'm sorry. I just . . . I guess I'll just go to sleep."

"Good idea, Kev." She turned over.

He lay back and thought about it. How can something as dramatic and as involving as making love passionately be beyond recall? It didn't make sense.

Nor did my nightmare, he thought. For now, the two

seemed to cancel each other out. He closed his eyes, and in moments he was asleep.

In the morning both Ted and Dave called to ask how he was. Paul actually came around to see him.

"I guess I should thank you guys," Kevin said, "but I can't remember a damn thing about it."

"Well, you were really more asleep than awake when we brought you down . . . carried you down, I should say." He winked at Miriam. "You played beautifully, Miriam."

"Thank you," she said and gave Kevin a look of self-satisfaction that made his eyebrows rise.

The rest of the weekend proved to be wonderful. Dave and Ted, Norma and Jean, and he and Miriam went to a Broadway matinee on Saturday. They had highly sought-after front-row tickets provided for them through a connection Mr. Milton had with the theater. Paul begged out, telling them he wanted to take Helen back to their doctor. He said he would try to join them for dinner afterward, but he never showed. Later he told them Helen wasn't up to going anywhere and he didn't want to leave her alone.

On Sunday, they all went up to the penthouse to watch the football game. Paul joined them, but Helen remained in their apartment, resting. He said she had been placed on newer, stronger medication.

"I had to hire a nurse to stay with her," he told them. "Lucky for me, the nurse Richard Jaffee had was available, Mrs. Longchamp, so if you see her around, you'll know why. If there's no improvement soon," he told everyone, "I'll have to put her in the sanitarium."

"You'll do what's best for her, Paul," Mr. Milton told him and then took him aside to talk with him.

Norma and Jean brought out some hot buttered popcorn they had prepared in Mr. Milton's kitchen, and everyone's attention returned to the game.

The following week at the firm was very busy. Paul's case came to trial, and Dave and Ted picked up new clients. Dave was defending a doctor's son who had been allegedly pilfering drugs from his father and peddling them at college. Ted was handling a routine breaking and entering; the burglar was someone he had defended once before and gotten acquitted. He said his best hope was to get a deal, and sure enough, before the week was out, he had negotiated a settlement providing for less than a quarter of what the client would have been sentenced to had the case gone to trial.

Paul's case went according to plan, too. The district attorney's decision to prove that Philip Galan was guilty of murdering his little brother proved to be a mistake in strategy. Despite Philip's lack of remorse, Paul was able to get expert psychiatrists to testify that Philip had a history of impulsive behavior and was an emotionally disturbed youngster. Just as Paul intended, he was able to show how the parents were more guilty in many ways. The trial resulted in Philip being remanded to psychiatric care.

On Thursday, Kevin had his meeting with Beverly Morgan, Maxine Rothberg's nurse. She had left the hotel after Maxine's death and was living with a sister in Middletown, New York, a small city approximately an hour and a half from Manhattan. Kevin made arrangements for Charon to drive him upstate.

Beverly Morgan's sister owned a small, Cape Cod–style house on a side street. It was a low-income neighborhood; the street was narrow, the houses old and run-down, their small porch fronts sagging, their sidewalks chipped and cracked and pitted. It had snowed much more frequently and more heavily in the upstate New York area, so the narrow street was cramped by the slush and the residue of the last storm. Kevin found it a depressing area, everything dull, faded, worn.

Beverly Morgan was home alone. The stocky fifty-eight-year-old black woman had a head of dull black hair with snowy white strands streaked through the center. Her hair had been cut unevenly, probably by her sister, Kevin thought, or some nonprofessional.

She gazed out at him with large black eyes, the whites bright, her look fearful, distrusting. She wore a kelly green sweater over a light green one-piece dress that looked like a nurse's uniform that had been dyed. Before she greeted him, she glanced quickly at the limo. Charon stood by the driver's side looking back at her.

"You're the lawyer?" she asked, still looking Charon's way.

"Yes, ma'am. Kevin Taylor."

She nodded and stepped back to let him enter, pausing to look once more at Charon before closing the door. The small entryway was covered with a narrow throw rug, stained and faded. There was a dark pine coat- and hatrack on the right and a square two-foot mirror in a matching pine frame on the wall beside it.

"You can put your coat there," Beverly said and nodded at the rack.

"Thank you." Kevin slipped out of his suede and wool topcoat and hung it quickly. There was a delicious aroma throughout the house, the scent of chicken being fried. It made his mouth water. "Something smells good."

"Um," she said and turned to lead him into the living room, a small room overly heated by a coal stove. Kevin loosened his tie and looked about. The furniture was of discount department store quality, the cushions on the couch showing their wear. The one attractive piece was a vintage dark pine grandfather clock, its face reporting accurate time.

"Beautiful clock," he remarked.

"Was my father's. Held on to it no matter how bad times got. Sit down. You want some tea?"

"No, no thanks."

"Well, let's get to it. I had some experience with lawyers before," she said, dropping herself into a light brown easy chair across from the couch. It seemed to close itself snugly around her. She crossed her legs and smirked.

"Well, this is quite an important case."

"Rich people's cases always are."

Kevin tried to smile. He saw a bottle of bourbon on the bottom bookshelf with a tumbler beside it. The glass had some whiskey in it. He opened his briefcase and took out a long notepad. Then he sat back.

"What can you tell me about the way Mrs. Rothberg died?"

"Same as I told the district attorney," she began with mechanical swiftness. "I came into the room and found her sprawled out on the bed. I thought she had had a heart attack at first. I called the doctor right away, tried CPR, and called the hotel to have Mr. Rothberg paged."

"When was the last time you had seen her conscious?"

"Right after dinner. I sat with her for a while, and then she said she was tired, but she wanted me to leave the television set on. So I went to my own room to watch television. When I came back, she was dead."

"And you had given her the usual dosage of insulin that day?"

"Uh-huh."

"Now are you confident that you gave her the correct amount?"

"Yes, I am," she said firmly.

"I see." Kevin pretended to write some notes. He did write "Appears defensive," but he realized anyone in her position had a right to be.

"Let me get right to it, Beverly. Is it all right if I call you Beverly?"

"It's my name."

"Yes. Let me get to the heart of the thing so I don't waste any of your time." She nodded, her eyes narrowing suspiciously. "Do you know anything that would incriminate Mr. Rothberg? Did you see him go into his wife's bedroom after you had left, for instance?"

"No. I went right to my room. I told you."

"Uh-huh. You know about the supply of insulin that was found in Mr. Rothberg's room. Do you have any explanation for why it was there?"

She shook her head.

"Beverly, you must know that Mr. Rothberg was seeing someone on the side."

"Sure do."

"Did Mrs. Rothberg know it, too?"

"Uh-huh."

"She ever talk to you about it?"

"No. She was a lady, right to the end."

"Then how did you know she knew?" he asked quickly, falling into his cross-examination tone of voice and demeanor.

"She had to know. Other people came to see her."

"Then you overheard someone tell her, talk to her about it?"

She hesitated.

"Not that you were spying, but I'm sure while you were working nearby . . ."

"Yeah, I heard some talk sometimes."

"I see. Did you happen, by accident, of course, to ever overhear an exchange between Mr. and Mrs. Rothberg concerning this matter?"

"You mean, did they have an argument about it? Not that I heard, no, but I came into her room many a time just after he had left and found her looking upset."

"Uh-huh." Kevin sat for a moment staring at her. "Mrs. Rothberg was quite depressed then, you would say?"

"Well she didn't have a helluva lot to be happy about. She was an invalid and her husband was screwin' around. But even though she had a rough time of it, she managed to be in good spirits most of the time. She was quite a woman. I thought she was a real lady, understand?" she repeated with emphasis.

"Yes, I do." He sat back, taking a relaxed posture. "You've had a pretty rough time of it yourself, haven't you, Beverly?" he asked in his most sympathetic tone of voice.

"Rough time?"

"With your own life, your own family."

"Yes, I have."

Kevin shifted his eyes obviously and clearly toward

the bottle of bourbon. "You do some drinking, Beverly?" She straightened up quickly. "Even at the hotel?"

"I have a drink once in a while. Helps me get through the day."

"More than once in a while, perhaps? People know about that, too, Beverly," he said quickly, sitting forward.

"I never got so I couldn't do my job, Mr. Taylor."

"As a nurse, you know that people who drink often don't face up to how much they drink or how it affects them."

"I'm no alcoholic. It ain't goin' to do you any good to try to say I am and that I accidentally killed Mrs. Rothberg."

"I read Mr. and Mrs. Rothberg's doctor's reports. He had some critical things to say about you, Beverly."

"He never liked me. He was Mr. Rothberg's doctor," she added. "He wasn't the doctor Mrs. Rothberg's mother had."

"You were in charge of giving Mrs. Rothberg her insulin, you drank, the doctor knew it and wasn't pleased," Kevin said, ignoring her implications.

"I didn't accidentally kill Mrs. Rothberg."

"I see. Mr. Rothberg tells me he and his wife did have an argument about his affair and that she threatened to commit suicide and make it look as if he had killed her. He thinks that's why the insulin was placed in his closet. There is a strong suggestion that the fatal dosage came from that supply. Do you think you can search your memory for any possible recollection of how that insulin got into Mr. Rothberg's closet?"

She stared at him.

"Did you put it there?"

"No."

"Your fingerprints were found on it."

"So? My fingerprints are on everything in Mrs. Rothberg's room. Look, why the hell would I put it in there?" she asked, her voice rising in pitch.

"Maybe Mrs. Rothberg asked you to do so."

"She didn't and I didn't."

"Did you see her wheel herself into Mr. Rothberg's room?"

"When?"

"Ever?"

"Maybe . . . yes, I guess."

"With the box of insulin in her lap, perhaps?"

"No, never. And if she did, why ain't her fingerprints on the box?"

"She could have worn plastic gloves."

"Oh, what a load a garbage. Mr. Rothberg coulda worn plastic gloves, too!"

He smiled to himself. She wasn't dumb. She imbibed and might have been less efficient than the doctor would have liked, he thought, but she wasn't stupid. He decided to try another tact.

"You liked Mrs. Rothberg, didn't you, Beverly?"

"Of course. She was a real lady, I told you."

"And you didn't like what Mr. Rothberg was doing, seeing another woman while his devoted wife was so sick, right?"

"He is a selfish person. He didn't even visit her all that much. She was always asking me to call him or get him."

"So maybe you would understand why she would want to blame him for her death."

"She wouldn't kill herself. I just can't believe that."

"You always felt sorry for her . . . you had a drink

or two beforehand, she asked you to put the insulin in his room . . ."

"No. Look here, I don't like what you're trying to say, Mr. Taylor, and I don't think I should talk to you anymore." She folded her arms over her bosom and glared at him.

"All right, I'll save my other questions for the trial when you have to answer under oath," he said. He was sorry he was taking such a hard stance with her, but he wanted to shake her loose. What if there was nothing to shake loose? he asked himself. But he let the question pass quickly. He put his notepad back into the briefcase.

"If you did do it and it comes out in court, you'll be considered an accessory to a crime, a serious crime."

"I didn't do it."

"And then, of course," he said, standing, "if you did it not knowing what her intentions were, no one can blame you for anything."

"I didn't put any insulin in Mr. Rothberg's room," she repeated.

Kevin nodded. "Okay. There are other people to see, other facts to check." He started out of the room. Beverly got up and followed him to the entryway and watched him put on his coat. He looked back at her.

Here she was, a black woman who was reaching the autumn of her life. She had little to look back on with happiness. She had become a professional and tried to bring up her sons without a husband. Much of it had resulted in disaster. She drank but held on to her job. And now it was over, and over in a terrible way. Surely she must look at the world with jaundiced eyes and see less sunlight with each and every passing day. It was as if she had been born on a bright day and gradually the world had closed in on her until she was looking through a tunnel. Kevin regretted the harsh tone he had taken. Rothberg certainly wasn't worth it.

"Must say, what you're cooking smells wonderful."

Beverly's face didn't soften. She looked at him fearfully, her eyes filled with distrust. He couldn't blame her. Lately, everything he said and did was contrived, planned for a purpose. Why should she think he was sincere? Yet his stomach did churn with covetousness.

"So long and thank you," he said, opening the door. She came to it and stood there looking out as he walked down the small walkway to the limo. Charon opened the door for him and then turned around and gazed at her. Kevin watched her face change from anger and distrust to downright terror and fear. She closed the door quickly, and moments later he was on his way back.

As soon as Kevin was within mobile phone range of the city, he called the office to see if he had any messages. He realized all the secretaries would be going home before he could arrive.

"You have an appointment with Tracey Casewell, Mr. Rothberg's 'friend,' tomorrow at two," Wendy told him. "Other than that, things have been quiet."

"Okay, I'll be going straight home, then."

"Oh, Mr. Taylor, Mr. Milton wants to speak to you. Just one moment."

Kevin had hoped he could put off speaking with John Milton until tomorrow. He was depressed about the interview with Beverly Morgan and couldn't help feeling he had let Mr. Milton down. It wasn't a rational reaction. There was no reason for him to blame himself, but there was just something about working for Mr. Milton that made him want to succeed.

"Kevin?"

"Yes, sir."

"How did it go?"

"It didn't go well," he said. Even though he knew Charon couldn't hear the conversation, he saw the man look up in his rearview mirror at those words.

"Oh?"

"She doesn't like Rothberg, says he's self-centered, and couldn't explain how the insulin got into his closet. I asked her if she had overheard an argument between them described the way Rothberg described it, and she said no. It was a definite no."

"I see. Well, don't be discouraged. We'll talk tomorrow and see what we can make of it. Just relax tonight. Put it out of mind. Enjoy your wonderful wife."

"Thank you. Sorry."

"Nothing to be sorry about, Kevin. It'll be all right. I'm sure."

"Right. Goodbye."

He flipped the switch on the phone, putting it into the intercom mode, and told Charon to take him directly to the apartment. The chauffeur barely acknowledged the order with a slight nod. Kevin recalled how Miriam thought it funny that Charon had almost smiled when she questioned him about the gold elevator key. He could sympathize with her reaction to him. The man rarely spoke. He never asked questions, and whenever he was told where to take him or the others, he seemed to already know.

The glass between the rear seat and the front seat was always up. If any communicating had to be done with him, it was done through the intercom.

Kevin couldn't help wondering about Charon. Where was he from? Where did he live? How long had he been working as John Milton's chauffeur? Kevin was positive the man hadn't been a chauffeur all his mature life. He had an interesting face. He must have traveled a great deal and done some interesting things. Why didn't any of the others talk about him? They acted as if he weren't even there half the time. It was just "Charon, take us here" or "Charon, take us there." They didn't even pass small talk. Did the man have a family? Was he married?

When they pulled up in front of the apartment house and Charon opened the door this time, Kevin got out very slowly.

"So, Charon," he said, "your day's almost over, too, eh?"

"Yes, sir."

"You have to go back and hang around to bring Mr. Milton home, though, don't you?"

"It's no problem."

"Oh. You live in the city, too?"

"I live here, Mr. Taylor," he said.

"You do? In one of these apartments?"

"Yes. In an apartment off the garage."

"I never knew that. Are you married, Charon?"

"No, sir."

"Well, I'm sure you're not a native New Yorker. Where are you from? You have such a beautiful speaking voice, it's hard to pinpoint any dialect."

"I'm from here, Mr. Taylor."

"You are a New Yorker?" Kevin smiled, but Charon didn't relax or smile back.

"Will there be anything else, Mr. Taylor?"

The man doesn't show any emotion. He's like a cyborg, Kevin thought.

"Oh no, Charon. Have a good night."

"You too, Mr. Taylor."

He watched him get back in the limo and start off. Then he entered the apartment building.

"Have a good day, did you, Mr. Taylor?" Philip asked, looking up from the small television set he had just under the counter. He got up and came around the desk.

"A hard day, Philip. It remains to be seen whether or not it was a good one."

"Know what you mean, sir." He pushed the elevator call button for Kevin.

"You been here a long time, Philip?"

"Came right after Mr. Milton took over the building, Mr. Taylor."

"I just found out Charon lives in an apartment downstairs. Never knew it. He doesn't talk much," Kevin whispered and smiled.

"No, sir, but he's devoted to Mr. Milton. He owes him his life, you might say."

"Oh?" The elevator door opened. "Why is that?"

"Mr. Milton defended him and got him acquitted."

"Really? I never knew that. What had he been accused of doing?"

"Murdering his family, Mr. Taylor. Of course, he was so depressed by the death of his loved ones, he didn't care much what happened to him, but Mr. Milton pumped the life back into him."

"I see."

"Might say he did the same for me."

"Oh?"

"I was accused of being on the take from drug pushers. They tried to set me up. Mr. Milton got me off when he proved it to be entrapment. Yes, sir, you're working for one helluva guy," Philip said. "Have a good night, Mr. Taylor."

"You too, Philip," Kevin said and backed into the elevator. Philip smiled at him as the doors closed.

He was in such deep thought when he first entered his apartment that he didn't notice Miriam was not there. He put down his briefcase, took off his overcoat, went into the living room, and poured himself a scotch and soda.

"Miriam?"

Kevin went through the apartment. She hadn't left a note. She should have been home long ago, he thought. He went back into the living room and waited. Nearly twenty minutes went by before the front door opened and Miriam stepped in, dressed in his blue terry-cloth robe with a bath towel around her neck.

"Where the hell were you?" he asked.

"Oh, Kev. I thought you wouldn't be home for another hour at least."

"I had an aborted interview, otherwise it might have been closer to that. But where were you dressed like that?"

"In the penthouse . . . in the whirlpool," she sang and continued through the hallway toward the bedroom.

"What?" He followed along, drink still in hand.

"You went up to Mr. Milton's apartment and used his whirlpool?"

"It's not the first time, Kev," she said, taking off his robe and letting it drop to her feet. She was completely naked underneath, and her skin was still bright red from the heat of the water. She turned about, studying herself in the mirror. Then she pulled her shoulders back to lift her breasts. "Do you think the aerobics classes are making a difference? Doesn't the back of my thigh look leaner?"

"What did you mean, it isn't the first time you've gone up there, Miriam? You never told me about this before."

"I didn't?" She turned to him. "Yes I did." She smiled. "Morning before last, but I guess you were too overwhelmed with yourself to remember." She started for the shower.

"What? Wait a minute." He reached out and seized her arm. He wasn't rough about it, but she screamed as if he had closed a vise around her elbow. "I'm sorry."

"What's wrong with you?" she asked, tears coming into her eyes as she rubbed her arm. "I'm sure to have another black and blue mark now."

"I didn't squeeze that hard, Miriam."

"Well, I'm not one of the boys, Kevin. Why is it you can be so tender and romantic sometimes and then get like this? What are you, Jekyll and Hyde?" She continued into the bathroom. He followed.

"Miriam, what did you mean by morning before last?"

"Morning before last means two days ago, Kevin," she said and turned on the water.

"I know that. Don't be so smug. It's not like you. You said you told me about your going up to the penthouse."

"We all have the gold keys, and Mr. Milton said we should use them whenever we like. Enjoy the penthouse, he said. Use the whirlpools, use his stereo. We're up there often."

"Who's we?"

"Norma, Jean, and I. Now can I take a quick shower so I can make us some supper? I'm hungry, too."

"I'm not hungry. I'm confused. You implied that we made love morning before last."

She stared at him and then shook her head. Then she stepped into the shower stall. He pursued.

"Miriam?" He pulled the door open.

"What?"

"Did we?"

"Did we what?"

"Make love?"

"I didn't know you make love so often that you forget with whom and when you do it," she snapped and pulled the shower door closed again. He stood there staring through the glass at her. Then he looked down at the glass of scotch in his hand and quickly downed it.

What the hell was she talking about?

Really, what the hell was she talking about?

11

Miriam did develop a black-and-blue mark on her arm, one so large and vivid it made him feel very guilty. He had gone back to the living room to make himself another drink and sit and think when he heard her in the kitchen. She was wearing his robe again, but when she reached up for a dish in the cabinet, the sleeve fell back and he saw the injury.

"Jeez, I didn't think I squeezed you that hard, Miriam."

"Well, you must have," she replied without turning to him. She started to set the table.

"Maybe you have a vitamin C deficiency or something. Makes your capillaries weak."

She didn't reply.

"I'm sorry, Miriam. Really."

"It's all right." She paused and looked at him. "I forgot to ask, how did your day go?"

He didn't reply immediately. Ever since he had begun working at John Milton and Associates, she would greet him with that question, and then, before he could elaborate, she would cut him off and tell him it wasn't necessary to relive the nitty-gritty details. But in Blithedale, she had loved hearing about his work. She had apparently adopted Norma and Jean's attitude wholeheartedly when it came to this, and he wasn't happy about it. It was as if they weren't sharing anymore, as if they were off on two different courses, coming together only to participate in pleasurable activities.

"Do you really want to know? Can I tell you without your running away from it?"

"Kevin, I'm only trying to . . ."

"I know, help me relax. But you're not some geisha girl, Miriam. You're my wife. I want to share my frustrations as well as my successes with you. I want you to be part of what I do and what I am, just as I will be part of whatever you do and what you are."

"I don't want to hear unpleasant things, Kevin," she said firmly. "I just don't. Mr. Milton's right. You should take your shoes off before you come in the door and leave the mud outside. A man's home should be his private piece of heaven."

"Oh, brother."

"Well, it's worked for Norma and Jean. Look how happy they are and how wonderful their marriages are. Don't you want that for us? Isn't that why you brought me here—to have a better, happier life?"

"All right, all right. It's just that sometimes I like to confide in you, to look to you for support and get your impression of things, too."

"Like you did in the Lois Wilson case?" she snapped.

He stared at her a moment. "I was wrong then. I admit it. I could have considered your viewpoint, too, and taken more time to explain my own, instead of going bull-headed into the melee, but . . ."

"Just drop it, Kevin. Please. You're doing well. Everyone likes you. You have an important case to try. We're making a lot of money and living comfortably. We have great new friends. I don't feel like being depressed by someone else's hard luck or by the ugly crimes that go on every day out there." She grimaced.

"Now," she continued, smiling so quickly and so mechanically it was as if she had become robotic. "I picked up this gourmet chicken Kiev prepared by the chef at the Russian Tea Room. There's this store on Sixth that sells it in the frozen food section. Norma found it. I'll put it in the microwave and we'll have it in minutes," she sang. "So get ready to eat."

Kevin pressed his lips together and nodded. "Okay," he whispered. "Okay."

He did what she said, but he couldn't help feeling frustrated, even though the food was delicious and the wine was wonderful. Miriam babbled on about her day, the shopping, the exercise classes, things Norma and Jean had said, rumors about Helen Scholefield getting worse, Mr. Milton's wonderful penthouse. She talked on and on, around him, around any attempt he might make to bring up the details of his case.

Maybe because he was frustrated and confused, or maybe because he was more tired than he thought, whatever the reason, the scotch and the wine hit him, and he fell asleep on the couch in the living room watching television. He woke abruptly when Miriam turned off the set.

"I'm tired, Kev."

"What? Oh, sure." He got himself up and followed her into the bedroom. Moments after he slipped into the bed beside her, he was asleep, and again he was haunted by an erotic dream. In it, he awoke in the bed and turned his head slightly because he felt movement beside him.

Miriam was set upon a man, the man's legs bent at the knees to position his hardness. The man gripped her just an inch or so above her knees. Her breasts shook emphatically as she pressed herself up and down with a vigor that was almost comical because of its intensity. She moaned and threw her head back. Then she leaned forward so the man could reach up and run his fingers under her breasts and around her nipples, holding them gently between two fingers.

Kevin couldn't move. The sight gave him an erection, but he was unable to turn his body or lift it from the bed. All efforts were in vain. It was as if he were glued to the sheets, his arms locked at his sides.

On and on they went, Miriam reaching climax after climax, moaning, screaming with ecstatic pleasure, and then finally throwing herself over the naked man beneath her as she caught her breath. The man's hand slipped up around her shoulders, and Kevin could see the fingers. On the pinky finger was his gold ring with the letter "K." He struggled to turn his head farther, and finally, gradually, his head was completely turned and he was looking into the eyes of Miriam's lover.

Once again, he was looking into his own eyes, only this time his duplicated face was smiling arrogantly. He closed his eyes and wished with all his might that the dream would end. It finally did, and he fell back into a restless sleep. When he woke in the morning and turned to Miriam, he found her facedown, out of the blanket, sprawled naked the way she had been over his duplicate in the dream.

Kevin stared at her until her eyes opened, too.

"Good morning," she said. She smiled at him. He didn't say anything. Then she turned over on her back and rubbed her eyes. "I slept so well afterward," she said. She turned back to him and kissed him on the cheek.

He wanted to say, "Afterward?" But he held back. She sat up and then moaned.

"What is it?"

"You're an animal," she said.

"What?"

"Look."

He sat up beside her and gazed down at her legs. Just above her knees were two small black and blue marks, made by fingers squeezing too hard.

"And don't tell me it's because I lack vitamin C, Kevin Taylor. You devil, you."

He said nothing. He stared incredulously. Miriam got up and went into the bathroom, and Kevin fell back against the pillow, feeling as exhausted as he might be after making love passionately all night. But why did it all seem like a nightmare? Why was he out of his own body observing? Was he having some sort of paraphysical experience? If it continued, he would have to talk to someone, perhaps a psychiatrist.

Kevin got up, took his shower, got dressed, and had breakfast, listening to Miriam outline her activities for the day. He couldn't remember her ever being so absorbed in herself. Like anyone, she had her share of vanity, but she had always been modest and always conscious of when the conversation was leaning too heavily on her. But as Kevin left the apartment that morning, he realized she had not mentioned one thing that didn't have to do with her, whether it was how she was going to improve her knowledge of art, improve her thighs at exercise class, or look for something new to wear. He might as well have been a mirror set in the chair across from her.

That afternoon he interviewed Tracey Casewell. Rothberg had sent her to the city to come to his office. She wasn't a particularly pretty woman, but she had a very nice figure and she was only twenty-four. She had been working at the hotel for a little more than three years. She confirmed Rothberg's tale, describing how he had come to her directly after the argument with his wife to relate the details. Her repetition of his story was too exact to be anything but memorized, Kevin thought, and anyway, the prosecution would easily get the jury to think she was part of a murder conspiracy.

Kevin questioned her quickly and as directly as he could, assuming the prosecutor's role and trying to show that she was lying to protect her lover. He caught her in two minor contradictions, one relating to the time when Rothberg was supposed to have told her about the argument. She immediately corrected herself after he pointed it out.

She appeared sincerely remorseful about the situation and confessed being uncomfortable about having an affair with Rothberg while his wife was an invalid. She had known Maxine Rothberg before her affair with Stanley and actually liked her. If he could get the jury to buy this part of her testimony, she might help, Kevin thought, but he wasn't feeling very confident about it.

In fact, as the trial date drew closer, Kevin began to

grow even more pessimistic. He put on a good face with reporters and promised that he would prove Mr. Rothberg innocent beyond a doubt, but personally he felt the best he could do was confuse the jury and keep them from feeling certain beyond a doubt, and thus find him not guilty. Rothberg would always be suspected of murdering his wife, as far as the public was concerned, but at least he would win the case.

Although he was surprised at Miriam's disinterest about the progress of the case, Kevin gradually conceded that he should probably follow Mr. Milton's advice. The associates talked their cases to death riding back and forth to work in the limo, anyway. It *was* good to come through the door knowing he could leave his worries and tensions outside.

They went out to dinner with Dave and Norma and Ted and Jean at least twice during the week. Paul joined them on the weekend and told them Helen was almost catatonic. He had been resisting putting her in the sanitarium, but even with a live-in nurse he didn't know how much longer he could wait.

"She won't even pick up a paint brush anymore," he told them.

Miriam wondered aloud if she and the girls should visit her, but Paul thought it would be fruitless and quite depressing for them. Kevin noticed how the mere mention of the word *depressing* put an immediate end to the idea. Miriam's tolerance of anything gray or bleak had dropped considerably since their move to the city. She didn't seem to want to do anything that involved even the slightest effort or compromise. Meeting her parents for dinner, for example, was suddenly an ordeal.

"Who wants to buck that traffic going to and from

215

the Island?" she said. "Let them come into the city. It's so much easier."

"For us, maybe. Not for them," Kevin pointed out, but she didn't care.

Kevin noticed now that whenever they did eat at home, they usually ate microwave frozen foods. Most of the time, Miriam picked up prepared things and merely served them. Her own cooking, something she once took great pride in, disappeared. She was too busy for any of that. If Kevin wondered aloud about what made her so busy, she was more than eager to run off a list: exercise classes, shopping, shows and museums, lunch every day at a different bistro, and now vocal lessons. All of the girls were doing it, except Helen, of course.

Miriam was rarely at home if he called from the office. Instead he would get her answering service. Why did she need an answering service? he wondered. She never returned any of the calls her old friends on the Island made, and she often didn't even call her parents or his parents back. They would call later at night and complain, and when he would ask her about it, she would laugh and say something like, "Oh, I'm just so distracted these days. But I'll get organized soon."

Whenever he complained, she'd reply, "But this is the life you wanted for us, isn't it, Kevin? Now that I'm busy and we're doing things, you complain. Do you know what you want?"

He began to question himself. Sometimes, when he came home and she wasn't back yet from one of her activities, he would pour himself a scotch and soda and look out at the Hudson River and wonder. Could it be that he was indeed happier back on the Island?

What was it going to be like when they had their children? Miriam was already talking about moving to a bigger apartment in the building and hiring a live-in mother's helper for their first baby.

"Norma and Jean will be doing that," she told him. "Children shouldn't cramp your style in this day and age."

"But you always hated that idea," he reminded her. "Remember how you complained about the Rosenblatts and the way they brought up their children? The kids practically had to make appointments to see their own parents."

"They're different. Phyllis Rosenblatt is a . . . a vapid person. She couldn't tell the difference between a Jackson Pollock and a wallpaper sample."

He didn't see her point, but if he pursued the topic, Miriam would walk away. He was getting more and more upset with her behavior, but the night before the start of the Rothberg trial, she suddenly did an about-face.

When he came home from the office that night, he found she had prepared a home-cooked meal. She had her hair brushed back and straight the way he liked it, instead of wearing it in that new crimped style. She wore little makeup, and she had put on one of her older dresses. The table was set; they would eat by candlelight.

"I thought you might be a little tense and would want to relax at home," she told him.

"Great. What smells so good?"

"Chicken in wine sauce, just the way you like it."

"The way you make it?"

"Uh-huh. I did make it, and I made an apple pie, too. From scratch," she added. "I didn't go anywhere with the girls today. I just stayed here and slaved away for you like a devoted little housewife."

He laughed, even though he thought he detected a slight undercurrent of sarcasm. There's more Norma and Jean in that sarcasm than there is Miriam, he thought.

"I love you for it, honey," he told her and then kissed her.

"After dinner," she told him, pushing him back gently. "First things first. Get comfortable."

After he showered and changed, he found she had made a fire in the fireplace and set out cocktails and hors d'oeuvres. The warm fire, the good food, the whiskey, and the wine relaxed him. He told Miriam he felt he had been returned to the womb.

After dinner, they had a cognac and she played their wedding song on the piano. It was an old song, a song his parents loved and she had loved from the first moment she had heard it.

"I'll show you the result of my singing lessons, too," she said and began. "I'm stuck on lovin' you. Won't you say you love me too? I'm stuck on needin' you . . . honest I am . . ."

It brought tears to his eyes.

"Oh, Miriam, I've been working so hard, I almost forgot what it's all for. It is for you. None of this would have any meaning without you."

He kissed her and lifted her into his arms and then carried her to the bedroom. It was all so wonderful. All the doubts, all the questions died away. They were going to be all right. Things would be as wonderful as he had hoped and expected they would be. Miriam was still Miriam, and they were still in love. He started to undress.

"No, wait," she said, sitting up and leaning toward him. "Let's do it the way we did it Wednesday night."

"Wednesday night?"

"After we came home from dinner with Ted and Jean. Don't tell me again that you forgot?"

He kept a smile. She started to unbutton his shirt.

"I undressed you and then you undressed me," she whispered, and continued to replay an event he couldn't, for the life of him, remember.

Everyone at the firm attended the Rothberg trial at one time or another during the proceedings. Even the secretaries were permitted a few hours off to watch the court battle unfold. Oddly, though, Mr. Milton didn't attend. He seemed contented with the reports brought back to him. What bothered Kevin the most was Miriam's refusal to attend. She surprised him the morning of the first day after breakfast, when she announced she wouldn't be in court. He hoped she would change her mind before the trial ended.

Bob McKensie began the prosecution's case in a slow, methodical manner, structuring his theories, arguments, and facts on what he saw as a firm foundation of guilt. Kevin thought it was very clever of him to organize his case with a definite beginning, middle, and end, holding back the clinical and forensic evidence until the last chapter. He worked carefully and confidently and had the look of a mature, experienced attorney. It made Kevin more self-conscious of his youth and relative inexperience.

Why, he wondered, before he even began his statements, was John Milton so confident of his abilities, and why was he so determined that Kevin defend Rothberg? He began to grow paranoid about Mr.

Milton's true motives for assigning him the Rothberg case. Perhaps he knew they were going to lose all along, and he wanted Kevin to take the fall, blaming it on his youth and inexperience.

"You will see, ladies and gentlemen of the jury," McKensie began, "how the seeds of this cunning murder were planted years before it occurred; how the defendant developed motive, had opportunity, and committed the unconscionable act in a cold and calculated manner, confident that his guilt would be clouded by confusion or supposed negligence." He turned toward Rothberg and pointed.

"He is depending on one word, *doubt,* and hoping that his lawyer will keep that doubt alive to prevent you, in your good conscience, from convicting him of the heinous crime."

McKensie's deliberate speech and slow movement added a somber mood to a case fraught with electricity. Newspaper and television people scribbled notes quickly. Artists began capturing the faces of jury members, as well as Rothberg's pedestrian expression. The man actually yawned at one point during the prosecutor's opening remarks.

During the first two days, McKensie brought forth witnesses to show Rothberg's despicable character. They revealed that he was a gambler who had lost a great deal of the Shapiro family's wealth and had even put the hotel into a second mortgage, this despite its national reputation and the success of the raisin bread bakery. Much of this occurred after Maxine became too sick to take an active role in the management of the hotel and the business.

McKensie went as far back as Rothberg's days working in the dining room, when at night he would play cards and gamble away the tips he had made. He worked Rothberg's history up carefully, depicting him as a lowlife, but showing him as a conniver who worked his way into Maxine Shapiro's heart. It was, he concluded, a marriage of convenience. Obviously, he married her for her money. When Kevin objected to the characterization as unfounded, McKensie called a witness to support the accusation: a retired chef who swore Rothberg told him he would own Shapiro's Lake House one day by seducing Maxine.

Then, after a smooth transition demonstrating that Rothberg had a history of extramarital relationships, McKensie introduced Tracey Casewell. He called her to the stand and quickly got her to admit she was having an affair with Stanley Rothberg during the time his wife had been ill.

The following day McKensie moved to Maxine Rothberg's illness. He called the doctor to the stand and got a clear description of her problems and the dangers. McKensie didn't take him through his criticism of Beverly Morgan. He obviously didn't want to plant the possibility in the minds of the jury that Beverly Morgan could have accidentally killed Maxine Rothberg because she was a drinker. Kevin's main point in his cross-examination was to get the doctor to admit that Maxine was capable of giving herself the insulin shot.

At this point, McKensie went to the police evidence, revealing the supply of insulin hidden in Stanley's closet. The pathologist brought in the autopsy report, and the implications were clearly made. To help support the contention, Beverly Morgan was finally called to the stand. McKensie got her to describe Rothberg's relationship with his wife, how infrequently he visited and asked after her. She narrated the events of the day of Maxine Rothberg's death, much the same way she had first related it to Kevin. And then it was Kevin's turn.

Before he got up to cross-examine Beverly Morgan, he felt someone tap him on the shoulder and turned to find Ted standing behind him. "This is from Mr. Milton," he whispered and nodded toward the section where Dave, Ted, and Paul usually sat whenever they attended the trial. Dave and Paul were there, only this time Mr. Milton was sitting between them as well. He smiled and nodded.

"What?" Kevin opened the slip of paper and read the note. Then he looked back again. Mr. Milton nodded again, but more firmly. Ted patted Kevin on the shoulder and returned to his seat. Kevin stood up and faced Beverly Morgan. He glanced down at the note once again to be sure he was reading it correctly. Then he began, just as surprised himself at Beverly Morgan's responses as was the prosecution.

"Mrs. Morgan, you just testified that on occasion, after Mr. Rothberg visited with Mrs. Rothberg, she was left very unhappy. Is there one time that stands out in your mind, perhaps a more recent one?"

"There is," Beverly Morgan said, and then she related the events and the argument that Stanley Rothberg claimed occurred between his wife and him. Without batting an eyelash or changing expression, she described seeing Maxine Rothberg wheel herself into Stanley's room.

"The insulin was in her lap." She paused and looked out at the audience. "And she was wearing a pair of my plastic gloves," she concluded.

For a moment there was a heavy silence, the silence

before a storm, and then pandemonium broke out in the courtroom as reporters rushed to make phone calls and people expressed their amazement. The judge batted his gavel to silence the crowd and threatened to remove everyone except the participants. Kevin looked back and saw that, although the other associates were there, John Milton was gone. When order was restored, Kevin told the judge he had no further questions.

McKensie reexamined Beverly Morgan, demanding to know why she hadn't told this story before. She calmly responded that no one had asked her the question. Kevin wondered if McKensie would then bring up the doctor's criticism of her and her drinking problem to discredit what she had said. If he did so, Kevin was ready to illustrate how she could then have been negligent and caused the death of Maxine Rothberg. In either case, he could confuse the jury and put serious doubts in their minds about Stanley Rothberg's guilt.

McKensie decided instead to end the prosecution's case. The judge called a recess, and Kevin asked Paul where Mr. Milton was. He wanted to ask him how he knew Beverly Morgan would change her story.

"He had to rush off to meet with a new client," Paul told him. "He said he'll speak to you later, but he wanted me to tell you that he thinks you're doing a great job."

"Up until now, I thought I was losing it."

Paul smiled and looked at Ted and Dave. They wore the same look of arrogance.

"We don't lose," Paul said.

Kevin nodded. "I'm beginning to believe it," he replied, looking from one to the other. When Kevin entered the courtroom after the recess, there was an air of expectancy. Looking around at the audience, the reporters, and other media people, he suddenly felt the same sense of power and elation he had felt defending Lois Wilson. It was all in his hands. How he wished Miriam had decided to come, at least today.

Kevin began by calling up Stanley Rothberg. After Rothberg was sworn in, Kevin sat back on the table and folded his arms.

"Mr. Rothberg, you have heard a line of witnesses testify to your character. You have been described first as a gambler, often losing large sums of money and often in debt. Is there any truth to that?"

"Yes, there is," Rothberg said. "I've been a gambler all my mature life. It's a sickness, and I don't deny suffering from it." He turned directly to the audience on the word *sickness,* just as Kevin had advised him.

"You have also been charged with being an adulterer, and that charge has been corroborated by the woman who claims to be your lover, Tracey Casewell. Do you deny that charge?"

"No. I've been in love with and seeing Tracey Casewell for nearly three years."

"Why didn't you get a divorce?"

"I wanted to, but I couldn't make myself do it while Maxine was suffering, and Tracey wouldn't let me do it. I tried to be as discreet as I could."

"Apparently, you weren't successful," Kevin snapped. It was a brilliant tactic. He was treating his client as if he were the prosecutor and not the defense attorney. It gave his line of questioning a certain validity in the eyes of the jury and the audience. He didn't look like he liked Stanley Rothberg, and that gave the impression that he wouldn't help him lie.

"No, I guess not."

"And is it true, as was testified, that news of this affair eventually made its way to your wife?"

"Yes."

"You have heard the testimony of Beverly Morgan concerning an exchange between you and your wife. Was her description of that exchange accurate?"

"Yes."

"And you didn't take your wife's threat seriously at the time?"

"No."

"Why not?"

"She was a sick woman. I didn't think she was capable of it."

"Mr. Rothberg, did you inject your wife with an overdose of insulin?"

"No, sir. I hated to even watch her do it to herself or watch the nurse do it. I usually left the room."

"No further questions, your honor."

McKensie rose slowly but stood by his desk. "Mr. Rothberg, didn't you see the insulin in your closet?"

"Yes, that morning, but I forgot about it. I got involved in some problems in the hotel and forgot to ask the nurse about it."

"Even though your wife threatened to implicate you in her death?"

"I just didn't think about it. It seemed . . ." He turned to the jury. "It seemed so incredible."

McKensie simply stared at him a moment and then shook his head. Most people thought it was in disbelief, but Kevin felt it was from frustration. "No further questions, your honor," McKensie said and sat down.

Kevin continued his game plan. He called Tracey to

the stand and went through her testimony, just the way they had gone through it in his office. She described Stanley Rothberg coming to her after the fight with his wife, and she related the same details, only adding how disturbed Stanley had been. She looked very sincere when she expressed her own remorse about the course events had taken. Kevin even found himself believing her when she talked about liking Maxine Rothberg.

McKensie didn't even bother cross-examining.

During his summation, Kevin developed the theme John Milton had suggested. Yes, Stanley Rothberg was guilty of adultery, Stanley Rothberg did not have the best character, but he wasn't on trial for those things. He was on trial for murder, and he was clearly innocent of murder.

It was obvious to everyone that Beverly Morgan's revelations had taken the wind out of McKensie's sails when he got to his summation. Kevin was surprised at how poorly he did, how he stuttered, paused, looked confused. After he sat down, there seemed to be no question in anyone's mind what the outcome of this trial would be.

And the jury reacted accordingly, returning a verdict of not guilty in less than three hours.

By the time Kevin arrived at the office, a celebration was in full swing. His victory was sure to be the lead story on the local television news, yet he didn't feel as good about it as he expected he would. He had felt better winning Lois Wilson's acquittal. When he examined his own feelings and the reasons for them, he realized it was because he had won that case with his own sweat, prodding, investigating, poking around until he found ways to discredit the prosecution's case.

But this time it was different. He wasn't fooling himself. What won the case was Beverly Morgan's testimony corroborating Stanley's claim. Despite the congratulations and compliments he received, he didn't feel as proud of himself. It was like winning an important baseball game because of rain after the fifth inning. It hadn't been a complete effort.

"I was just lucky," he told Ted.

"Luck had nothing to do with it. You structured the defense brilliantly."

"Thanks." He made his way back to Mr. Milton's office and knocked on the door. He was invited in, but he couldn't find the man.

"Over here," he said. He was suddenly standing by the large windows. "And congratulations."

"Thank you, but I was hoping to find you during the recess. I wanted to ask you about Beverly Morgan."

"Of course."

As Kevin joined him at the window, Mr. Milton put his arm around his shoulders and turned him so they were both looking out over the city. Darkness came late in the afternoon now. It was a sea of lights.

"Dazzling, isn't it?"

"Yes."

"All that power, all that energy concentrated in such a small area. Millions of people at our feet, incredible wealth, incredible energy, decisions being made that affect the lives of countless others." He held out his free hand. "All the drama of humanity, every known conflict, every known emotion, birth, death, love, and hate. It takes my breath away to stand above it all."

"Yes," Kevin said. He suddenly did feel overwhelmed. Mr Milton had a soft and enchanting quality to his voice. Hearing him speak and looking out at the lights twinkling like stars was mesmerizing.

"But you're not just standing above it all, Kevin," he continued, speaking in undulating tones that to Kevin seemed to be coming from within his own mind. It was as if John Milton had entered his very soul, had housed himself in some empty chamber in his heart and now truly possessed him. "You are above it all, and now we know, it will all be yours."

There was a long silence between them. Kevin simply stared out at the city John Milton continued to embrace him and hold him so he would stay close.

"You should go home now, Kevin," he finally whispered. "Go home to your wife and have your own private celebration."

Kevin nodded. John Milton released him and moved like a shadow to his desk chair. Kevin stared out a moment longer and then turned, remembering why he had come in.

"Mr. Milton, that note you sent me . . . How did you know Beverly Morgan had changed her story?"

John Milton smiled. In the subdued light of the desk lamp, he looked like he wore a mask. "Now, Kevin, you don't want me to give away all my secrets, do you? Then you young upstarts would all start thinking you could take my place."

"Yes, but . . ."

"I spoke to her," he said quickly. "I pointed some things out, and she relented."

"What did you say to change her mind?"

"In the end, Kevin, people choose to do what's best for themselves. Ideals, principles, whatever you call it,

228

in the final analysis, they don't matter. There is only one lesson to learn: everyone has his or her price. Idealists think that's a cynical lesson to learn. Practical-minded folk like you and me and the other associates know it's the key to power and success. Enjoy your victory." He turned away to look down at some papers on his desk. "In a day or two, I will have another case for you."

Kevin stared down at him a moment and debated whether or not to pursue the conversation. It was obvious John Milton wanted to end it. "Okay," he said. "Good night."

"Good night. Congratulations. You're a true John Milton associate now," he added.

Kevin stood by the door. Why didn't those words make him feel wonderful? he wondered. He walked out. As he started down the corridor, he thought about those city lights and standing by the window with John Milton beside him. His words returned. Strange, he thought, but they sounded so familiar. Where had he . . .

And then he remembered. Those were Ted's exact words when he had described a similar experience at the windows in John Milton's penthouse. In his heart he knew it wasn't just a coincidence.

Who was John Milton? Who were the associates? What was he becoming?

12

A cold, bleak rain had begun to fall over the city. Even though he was quite warm in the rear of the limo, Kevin shivered when they stopped at a traffic light, and he gazed out at people rushing to and fro, most caught without their umbrellas. Despite his having every reason to feel cheerful, the drops he saw streaking down storefront windows and over the windows of other cars looked like tears. He sat back and closed his eyes the rest of the way to the apartment house.

"Mr. Taylor," Philip cried, opening the lobby door for him as soon as he had stepped out of the limo. "Congratulations! I just heard the news bulletin."

"Thank you, Philip." He shook the icy drops from his hair.

"I bet it feels good to win such an important case.

Everybody's goin' to know your name, Mr. Taylor. You must be very proud."

"It hasn't all quite settled in yet," Kevin said. "I'm still in a bit of a daze myself." He started for the elevator.

"Nevertheless, it looks like Mr. Milton's got himself a reason for another party, eh?"

"I wouldn't be surprised. Thanks, Philip." He stepped into the elevator and pressed 15. As the elevator began its climb, Kevin settled back, still feeling a strange mixture of emotions, elation with an undercurrent of anxiety. Something wasn't right; something just wasn't right. He found himself twisting his gold pinky ring back and forth.

He stepped out when the doors opened but stopped immediately because he thought he heard someone whisper his name. Turning quickly to his left, he was shocked to find Helen Scholefield in a nightgown, her back against the wall, her eyes wide, maddening.

"Helen!"

"I saw you and Charon drive up," she whispered. She glanced back at her apartment. "I don't have long. She's sure to find me gone in a moment."

"What's wrong?"

"The same thing that happened to Gloria Jaffee will happen to Miriam. I refused to become part of it this time and tried to warn you with my painting, but if he's made her pregnant, then it's too late. He'll feed on her goodness, suck the life from her like a vampire sucks blood. You've got to find a way to kill him. Kill him," she demanded, her teeth clenched, her hands balled into fists. "Otherwise you'll be left with the same two choices Richard Jaffee had. Thank God he had too much conscience to do anything else . . . only

Richard had a conscience." Her lips began to tremble. "They're all his. Paul's become the worst. He's Beelzebub," she added, leaning into him, the madness in her eyes making his heart pound.

"Helen, let me help you back . . ."

"No!" She backed away. "It's too late for you, isn't it? You've won one of his cases. You're his, too, now . . . his. Damn you. Damn you all!"

"Mrs. Scholefield!" Mrs. Longchamp cried from the apartment doorway. "Oh my!" She rushed into the hallway. "Now you come back inside, please."

"Get away from me." Helen lifted her arms over her head, threatening to pound the nurse.

"Now just calm down, Mrs. Scholefield. Everything will be all right."

"Should I get some help?" Kevin asked. "Call her doctor?"

"No, no. It's going to be fine. Just fine," Mrs. Longchamp said, holding her smile. "Won't it, Mrs. Scholefield? You know it will," she added in a soothing voice.

Helen's arms began to shake. She lowered them slowly and began to cry.

"Here, here, now. It's going to be all right," Mrs. Longchamp said. "I'll take you back and you'll rest." She embraced Helen Scholefield around the waist firmly and turned her. Then she looked back at Kevin. "It's okay," she mouthed and nodded, moving Helen down the corridor toward the apartment door. Kevin watched until they reentered and the door closed. He wiped his face with his handkerchief before going to his own apartment.

The instant he closed the door, Miriam came running to him. She threw her arms around his neck and kissed him.

"Oh, Kev, I'm so excited. It was just on the early evening news. And I saw them talking to you as you were coming out of the courtroom! Your parents called just a minute ago. They saw it, too! And my parents. We'll go out; we'll celebrate. I've already made us a reservation at Renzo's. You'll love it. Norma and Jean said that's where they and their husbands always go to celebrate by themselves."

He just stood there, staring at her.

"What's wrong? You look . . . pale."

"A terrible thing just happened in the hallway. Helen Scholefield was out there in her nightgown. She had run away from her nurse."

"Oh no. What happened?"

"She said some wild things, but . . ."

"What kind of things?"

"About us, about John Milton and Associates."

"Oh, Kevin, don't let it get you down. Not now. Not when we have so much to be happy about," she pleaded. "You know she's been very ill, mentally sick."

"I don't know, I . . . how did you get that black and blue mark on your neck?"

"It's not a black and blue mark, Kevin." She turned and looked in the hallway mirror. "I guess I'll have to add some more body powder."

"What do you mean, it's not a black and blue mark?"

"It's a hickey, Kev." She blushed. "You vampire. Don't worry about it; it's nothing. Come on, shower and change. I'm ravishingly hungry."

He didn't move.

"Kevin? Are you just going to stand here in the hallway all night?"

"We've got to talk, Miriam. I don't know what's going on, what's happening, but I swear I don't remember doing that to you."

"Nothing's going on, silly. You've been distracted by the pressure of this case and worried. It's understandable. The girls told me something like this would happen to you in the beginning. You'd go around in a daze, forgetting this, forgetting that. They've been through it with Ted and Dave, too. It'll pass once you gain confidence in yourself and grow as an attorney. And what a start, huh? My big New York lawyer," she added and hugged him. "Now, come on. Let's get the show on the road." She started away. "I'll fix my makeup."

He watched her go and then followed slowly. He paused at the living room, thinking once again about the scene with Helen Scholefield in the hallway. Then he went into the living room to look at her painting.

But it wasn't hanging there, nor was it on the floor.

"Miriam." She didn't reply. He hurried to the bedroom to find her by her vanity table. "Miriam, what happened to Helen's painting?"

"Happened?" She turned from the mirror. "I just couldn't stand looking at it anymore, Kevin. It was the only depressing note in this apartment. The girls agreed we had been very kind to have kept it up this long."

"So where is it? In a closet?"

"No, it's gone," she said, turning to look at herself again.

"Gone? What do you mean? Gone where? You threw it out?"

"No. I wouldn't do that. It's still a work of art, and, believe it or not, there are people who like that sort of thing. Norma knew a gallery in the Village that would take it on. We thought we'd put it there, and if it got sold we'd surprise Helen with the good news. We thought it might cheer her up."

"What gallery?"

"I don't know the name of it, Kevin. Norma knows it," she said, annoyance slipping into her voice. "What are you so concerned about? Both my mother and your mother thought it was a horrible thing to have on our living-room wall."

"When did she take it?" he asked insistently.

Miriam turned back again. "Just shows how observant you've been these last few days. Two days ago, Kevin. The painting's been gone for two days."

"It has?"

She pressed her lips together and shook her head. "Are you going to shower and get dressed already?"

"What? Oh, yeah . . . yeah." He started to undress.

"It's so exciting, isn't it? You'll be in all the newspapers and on television stations throughout the country. I bet Mr. Rothberg's grateful, huh?"

"Rothberg?"

"Rothberg, Kevin. The man you defended?" She laughed. "Talk about your absentminded professors . . ."

"No, Miriam. You don't understand," he said, approaching her. "I won because a witness made a complete reversal of her original story, and I don't know why she did. I didn't know until it happened right there in court. Mr. Milton sent me a note to ask the right questions. He knew she would change. He knew!"

"So?" She smiled. "That's why he's Mr. Milton."

"What?"

"That's why he's the boss and you, Ted, and Paul are only associates."

He simply stared at her. She sounded like a little girl.

"Don't worry," she said, turning back to the mirror. "Someday you will be just like him. Won't that be wonderful?" She paused, her eyes growing smaller as if she were gazing into a crystal ball instead of a mirror. "Your own firm . . . Kevin Taylor and Associates. You'll send an associate around to find new, promising talent just the way Mr. Milton sent Paul to find you, because by then you'll know who to look for."

"Who to look for? Who put such an idea into your head?"

"No one, silly. Well, Jean and Norma said something like that at lunch the other day. They said that's what Mr. Milton wants to see happen." She threw her head back and rattled it off: "Dave Kotein and Associates, Ted McCarthy and Associates, Paul Scholefield and Associates, and Kevin Taylor and Associates. The four of you will cover the city. Mr. Milton will start with new associates, of course, and before you know it, there won't be a defendant in town who will want to go to any other firm but one of yours."

She laughed again and then stood up and turned to him. "Kevin, will you take that shower already?"

He thought for a moment and then stepped closer to

her. "Listen to me, Miriam. Something strange is going on. I don't know what just yet, but maybe Helen Scholefield isn't as off the wall as we think."

"What?" She retreated from him quickly. "Kevin Wingate Taylor, will you stop this and take your shower. I told you, I'm starving. I'll wait for you in the living room. I'll play the piano, but I hope you'll be out and ready before I do an entire concerto." She left him standing naked at her vanity table.

He turned and looked at himself in the mirror. The reflected image made him recall his strange erotic dreams. Were they dreams? They weren't dreams to Miriam. It was all very real to her. And those black and blue marks on her legs were real, too.

What about all those times she claimed they had made love and he couldn't remember doing it? No one could be that absentminded. Either she was going mad or he was.

". . . but if he's made her pregnant," Helen Scholefield had said, "then it's too late." He? Whom did she mean?

He turned away from the mirror. Could any of this be possible?

"We don't lose," Paul Scholefield had said. The three of them wore that same look of arrogance.

"You won one of his cases. You're his, too, now," Helen Scholefield had told him. "Damn you. Damn you all!"

He recalled how strange he had felt when Mr. Milton had said, "You're a true John Milton associate now."

He turned back to the mirror and looked at himself.

What was Helen talking about? Was he any different?

237

His reflected image did not respond, but there was something ominous in merely thinking the questions.

He made up his mind. Tomorrow he would go to see Beverly Morgan, and he would know before he left her how Mr. Milton had gotten her to change her story.

He called his parents and Miriam's parents before he and Miriam left to celebrate. During both phone conversations, he did nothing to let either set of parents suspect he was troubled. The only negative note was sounded by his mother, who said, "Now that you've finished this big case, Kevin, see if you can devote more time to Miriam. She sounds high-strung to me."

"What do you mean, Mom?"

"No one can be that up all the time. It's just a mother's instinct, Kevin. She's at such a feverish pitch. Maybe she's trying too hard to please you. Arlene feels the same way about it, Kevin, only she didn't want to say anything and appear to be an interfering mother-in-law."

"But she told me she thought Miriam was very happy."

"I know. I'm not saying she's not happy. Just . . . pay more attention to her, will you?"

"Okay, Mom."

"And congratulations, son. I know this is something you've always wanted."

"Yeah. Thanks."

He knew what she was saying was right. Miriam was so different and she had changed so quickly, he should have been more alarmed. He had ignored what was happening because he wanted all this so much—the wealth, the luxury, the prestige. Who wouldn't? He had brought her here; he had exposed her to all of it. To a large extent, what was happening, what already had happened, was his own fault.

He spun around as if someone had tapped him on the shoulder. "Uh-huh." His gaze went to the patio. Again he wondered why Richard Jaffee had taken his own life. What did Helen mean by "Only Richard had conscience"?

"I'm waiting, honey," Miriam called.

"Coming."

They left the apartment and went downstairs to get into the waiting cab and went to Renzo's, a five-star northern Italian restaurant, and he tried putting his worries aside.

But he spent his time noting how different Miriam was at this celebration from the celebration at the Bramble Inn in Blithedale after the Lois Wilson case. Gone was her concern about whether or not the client had really been guilty. Of course, she knew little or nothing about this case, so she had no questions or comments about the court proceedings.

He had to admit she looked good in her new bright red, snugly fitted pants and sweater outfit. The sweater had a ribbon of pearls criss-crossed over the bosom. She was still wearing a lot more makeup than she used to, and Kevin realized that without the rouge and the lipstick, she did appear pale.

He didn't think she would be as fond of a restaurant like Renzo's as she was, nor want to choose it for this occasion. It was a gaudy, brightly lit place with mirrored walls. Despite the poor weather, it was quite crowded, and tables were placed practically on top of each other.

Miriam was far more outgoing than she had been at

the Bramble Inn or, for that matter, than she had been while they lived in Blithedale. How could he have missed such a dramatic change in her? He chastised himself for being too occupied with his work. He was surprised at how many people she knew and how many knew her, from the maître d' to the waiters. Some other patrons nodded and smiled as well. She and the girls, she told him, had been there for lunch and dinner when he was tied up with work.

However, he found her very distracted by all this, dividing her attention between him and looking to see who had come in, who was sitting with whom, what other people were eating. How different this was from the intimate, candlelit meal they had enjoyed at the Bramble Inn, he thought. Yet she didn't mind or appear to notice.

Even their lovemaking afterward had a different character to it. She was impatient, demanding, and assertive. She turned and twisted beneath him and then took a commanding role, moving his hands to where she wanted herself touched more aggressively. He almost lost all interest, feeling more like a male prostitute, feeling like someone being used to bring pleasure. There wasn't the usual sense of consideration, the mutuality, the attempt at oneness.

And afterward she still appeared dissatisfied, frustrated.

"What's wrong with you?" he demanded.

"I'm tired. Too much wine, I guess," she said and turned her back to him. He lay there thinking, afraid to close his eyes, afraid that if he did, something . . . someone . . . would come. Finally he did fall asleep, but he awoke at about four in the morning and realized she was not beside him.

He listened for a moment and heard sounds coming from the front of the apartment. He got up quickly and put on his robe. The lights were on in the living room and in the entryway. Was this another erotic episode? Was he really up or dreaming? He moved forward slowly, his heart pounding with anticipation, until he saw Miriam standing in the doorway, holding the door open and looking out. There were other voices.

"Miriam. What's happening?"

"It's Helen," she said, turning back.

"What is it?"

He moved quickly to her side and gazed out. Norma and Jean were in their robes, too.

"What happened?"

"She went wild," Norma said. "Stabbed Mrs. Longchamp in the arm with a pair of scissors."

"What?"

At that moment the door to the Scholefields' apartment was opened and two ambulance attendants from Bellevue wheeled Helen out on a stretcher. She was belted down tightly. Paul, Dave, and Ted followed closely behind. Helen was turning her head rapidly from side to side as if trying to deny the reality of what was happening to her. Kevin pushed his way past Miriam and approached Paul.

"It was very bad," he said. "She just got up out of bed and attacked the nurse. Fortunately, it wasn't a bad wound, but I shouldn't have kept her in the apartment. They gave her a sedative, but it hasn't taken hold yet."

The elevator doors opened, and the attendants pushed the stretcher into the elevator. Paul turned to Dave and Ted.

"You don't have to come. It's late. I'll handle it."

"You're sure you're all right?" Ted asked.

"No problem. Everybody just get back to sleep. I'll talk to you all in the morning."

He stepped in beside the stretcher. The attendants turned it a bit to make room for him, and Kevin saw Helen Scholefield's face. Her eyes widened when she confronted him. Then she suddenly began to scream. It was a sharp, piercingly shrill shriek that made him wince. Even after the elevator doors closed and the elevator began its descent, he still heard her wail until it died out in the floors below.

"Knew this was coming," Dave said, turning away.

"Too bad," Ted said, shaking his head. "Jean?"

"Coming."

The three women embraced each other at Kevin and Miriam's doorway, and then Norma and Jean joined Dave and Ted to return to their apartments. Kevin watched them go.

"Kevin?"

He looked at Miriam and then looked at the Scholefields' doorway. Where was the nurse? he wondered. If she had been stabbed in the shoulder, why wasn't anyone concerned about her? He started for the doorway.

"Kevin, what are you doing? Where are you going? Kevin?"

He knocked on the door and listened. There was nothing, no sound, no voice. He pushed the buzzer.

"Kevin?" Miriam was out in the hallway. He still heard nothing.

He turned back to her. "They're lying," he said.

"What?"

He walked past her into the apartment.

"Kevin?" She followed him down the corridor to the bedroom. He sat on the bed staring down at his hands. He tugged at the gold pinky ring, but his finger was so swollen, he saw he would have to cut the ring off.

"Kevin, what are you saying? You saw how she was."

"They're all lying. They know she told me something. The nurse told them."

Miriam just shook her head. "You're acting very weird, Kevin. All of this is frightening me."

"It should." He stood up and took off his robe. "I don't expect you to understand what I'm saying right now, Miriam. I have some ideas which I'll pursue tomorrow. For now, there's nothing to do but go to sleep."

"That's a very good idea," she said and went out to turn off all the lights.

In the morning Kevin called the office and told Diane he wasn't coming in.

"Need a day's rest," he said.

"Understandable. Mr. Milton isn't coming in today, either. Isn't it terrible about Mr. Scholefield's wife?"

"Oh, you know about that already?"

"Yes. Mr. McCarthy called first thing. Maybe this is for the best, though. Maybe they'll be able to help her."

"Oh, I'm sure they will," he said. He didn't think she picked up his sarcastic note.

He put on his overcoat, but Miriam didn't ask him where he was going and he didn't volunteer information. She didn't seem all that interested in knowing, anyway. Norma and Jean called just as he was about

243

to leave, and the three of them began making plans to cheer themselves up.

"After all," he heard Miriam say, "it was such a downer last night."

"I see you're all overwrought with sympathy," Kevin remarked as soon as she cradled the receiver.

"Well, there's nothing we can do about it, Kev. Bellevue isn't the kind of place you go to pay a visiting call, and I don't think sending her flowers or candy would make much sense."

"No sense at all." He saw another one of those black and blue marks, this one on the back of her left calf muscle. "You've got another mark on you." He pointed.

"What?" She looked down. "Oh, yes," she said and followed it with a short laugh.

"Aren't you concerned? I'm telling you, it could be a nutritional problem or something."

She stared at him a moment and then smiled. "Kevin, don't be such a worrywart. It's nothing. I've had it happen before, especially before a period."

"Is your period due?" he asked quickly.

"Past due." Her eyes twinkled mischievously, but he didn't smile back.

"I'll call you later," he said and hurried out. He took the elevator down to the parking garage, got into his car, and drove off, heading upstate to speak to Beverly Morgan.

It was a crisp, cold winter day with a dark blue sky and clouds so still against it, they looked frozen in place. During the trip upstate, Kevin reviewed the past few months and thought about the things that had bothered him, things he had to admit he had chosen to ignore, now that he was honest with himself.

How did John Milton and Associates come to know so much about him and Miriam before he arrived? How did John Milton know so much about the Lois Wilson case? And what about everything being so perfect, such as the beautiful rent-free apartment that just happened to have a spinet and some of the other things Miriam always wanted? Was there something supernatural to the coincidences and the good fortune, or was he just being paranoid now? Was Miriam right? Was he reacting to the babblings of a mentally ill and depressed person? Maybe he was overworking.

Surely there had to be a logical explanation for Beverly Morgan's reversal. Perhaps she just didn't trust him because he was so young. If that were the case, she probably wouldn't talk to him now, either, he thought.

Kevin pulled up in front of the small house in Middletown. The windows were dark, shades drawn. A thin ten-year-old black boy eyed him suspiciously from the sanctuary of his own front porch as Kevin got out of his car and walked to the front door of Beverly Morgan's sister's house. He knocked and waited. His rapping echoed and died within and brought no response. He knocked again and then peered in a window.

"They ain't home," the little boy said. "They went off in the ambulance."

"Ambulance?" Kevin moved quickly to the side of the porch. The little boy retreated a few steps, frightened by his abrupt movement. "What happened to Mrs. Morgan?"

"She got drunk and fell down the steps," he said and pushed a metal toy firetruck along the chipped porch railing.

"Oh, I see. So they took her to the hospital, huh?"

"Yep. And my mother went, too. She drove Cheryl."

"Oh. Which hospital did they go to?"

The little boy shrugged.

"Probably only one hospital here anyway," Kevin mused aloud. He hurried back down the sidewalk to his car and drove off. At the first intersection, he got directions to the Horton Memorial Hospital and made his way there as quickly as he could.

The kindly faced elderly woman in pink behind the reception desk had no information concerning any Beverly Morgan being admitted. "She might still be in the emergency room," she offered as the only possible explanation. She gave him directions, and he hurried down the long, wide hallway.

He was surprised at the activity. Small city or no small city, emergency rooms were all the same, he thought. Nurses moved frantically from one examination room to another. An overwhelmed intern stood staring at his clipboard while another nurse recited the symptoms of a patient in the room behind her. No one seemed to notice Kevin. He spotted two black women standing outside an examination room door on the other side of the emergency suite talking softly and made his way to their side.

"Excuse me."

They turned curiously.

"Is Beverly Morgan in there?"

"She sure is. Who are you?"

"I'm Kevin Taylor, an attorney. I defended Stanley Rothberg."

"Oh, well, what do you want with my sister now? She told everything in court, didn't she?"

"Is she all right?" he asked, smiling.

"She's goin' to live," her sister said, smirking. "But things are sure goin' to change in my house if she wants to live there."

"I bet." He nodded and looked at the other woman, who stared at him as if he were some total nut. "Do you think I could speak with her for a few minutes?"

"Well, seein' as we're goin' to be waitin' here forever to get her into a room, I guess so. She ain't fully sobered up yet, though," Beverly's sister said. Kevin didn't hesitate, however. He walked into the examination room.

Beverly Morgan was on a gurney, the thin white blanket brought up to her neck. Her head was wrapped in a gauze bandage; there was a blood stain over the right side of her forehead. She stared up at the ceiling. Her sister and their neighbor came in behind him and stood in the doorway. He approached Beverly slowly.

"Beverly?" Kevin said. "How are you doing?" She blinked, but she didn't turn his way. "It's Kevin Taylor. I'd like to talk to you, if I can, even though the trial is over. Beverly?"

She turned her head slightly.

"She's too drunk to hear ya, mister. She don't even know where the hell she is. Went head over heels down the stairs. I didn't find her right away. Lucky she's livin'."

"Beverly," he said, ignoring her sister. "You know I'm here. You know it's me. You have to talk to me, Beverly. You know it's important."

She turned her head some more until she was facing him. "He send you?" she asked in a hoarse whisper.

"Who? Mr. Milton?"

"He send you?" she asked again. "Why? What's he want now?"

"He didn't send me, Beverly. I came on my own. Why did you change your story, Beverly? Did you tell the truth in court? Or were you telling me the truth when I came to see you in your sister's house?"

She stared at him, and he thought it was going to be useless. "He didn't send you?" she asked suddenly.

"No. I came on my own," he repeated. "I didn't know you were going to change your story until I asked you those questions in court, and I didn't believe you, Beverly. Even though you helped me win my case, I didn't believe you. You lied, didn't you?"

Tears began to flow from Beverly's bloodshot eyes.

"Hey, mister, what are you doin' to my sister?"

"Nothing," he said, practically snapping at them. He turned to them. "I've just got to get some answers from her. It's very, very important. Beverly, you lied, didn't you? Didn't you?" he pursued.

"Mister, you'd better go," her sister demanded.

Beverly nodded.

"I knew it. But why? Why did you lie? How did he get you to lie?"

"He knows," she whispered.

"Knows what?"

"Mister, you better leave her be now."

"Knows what?" he insisted.

Her lips began to move. Kevin lowered his head. She whispered her confession into his ear as if he were a priest. Then she turned away.

"But how did he know those things?" Kevin wondered aloud. She didn't attempt any answer, but he didn't need the answer. It was already in his heart.

* * *

It was a strange ride back to the city. He was in such deep thought most of the way, he couldn't recall the drive. Suddenly, he found himself approaching the George Washington Bridge almost as if he had been transported to it. He shuddered. Perhaps he had. Where was reality in relation to illusion? What was magic and what was not? Was Mr. Milton just a shrewd, conniving, and ruthless man or . . . was he more?

How could John Milton have known the sins Beverly Morgan had locked in her heart: that she had stolen from Maxine Shapiro's mother while she was taking care of the old lady after her stroke, and that she had been doing the same thing to Maxine—pilfering jewelry, loose cash, robbing from the dead; she had characterized it herself, for they were in death's grasp. Once he knew those things, how easy it was for him to blackmail her, telling her she would become a prime suspect now, not accidentally killing Maxine through negligence brought on by her alcoholism, but deliberately, planned. Maxine had found out what she was doing and what she had done, as had, God forgive her, Maxine's mother.

Too much digitalis, undetectable unless the pathologist had reason to look for it. She had pushed the old lady on to glory and kept herself from being exposed.

Kevin had heard it all, but, unlike a confessor, he gave her no hope of redemption, for at the moment he wondered if he had any hope for redemption himself.

But he had no time to think about himself now. Helen Scholefield's warning was for Miriam, not for him. Helen had said the same thing that had happened to Richard Jaffee's wife would happen to

Miriam. How much of what he felt and knew had Richard Jaffee known?

Now that his curiosity about the firm and the other associates had peaked, he decided to go to the offices and do some research himself. He had an idea about where to look, and he knew he had to have something more concrete to go on, something more that he could tell Miriam and anyone else, for that matter.

Diane was surprised to see him. "Oh, everyone's left for the day, Mr. Taylor," she said. "Matter of fact, Mr. McCarthy just walked out." Kevin knew that. He had seen Ted emerging from the office building and had remained back so Ted wouldn't spot him.

"That's all right. I just wanted to clean up some loose ends and look up something."

She smiled and then shook her head sadly. "Did you hear the latest about Mrs. Scholefield?"

"No. I was out of town most of the day. What's happening?"

"She's gone into a comatose state. Won't respond to anything. They might use electric shock treatment eventually," she whispered.

"Uh-huh. That is too bad. Mr. Scholefield still over at the hospital?"

"Yes. Will you need anything, Mr. Taylor? Wendy left early today."

"No, I'm fine," he said and went back to his office, where he found a new file on his desk and a note on top that said, "Kevin, a new case for you. We'll discuss it today. J.M." Of course, Mr. Milton hadn't intended for him to discuss it until tomorrow. He opened the cover and perused the first page.

Elizabeth Porter, a forty-eight-year-old woman, the owner and operator of a rooming house specifically for elderly people, and Barry Martin, her forty-five-year-old handyman lover, had been arrested and charged with the murder of four of the elderly people, killing them for their social security checks. All four were found buried behind the rooming house. He was to represent and defend the handyman, who was now apparently willing to turn state's evidence against his former lover to save his own neck.

The material in the folder delineated each murder, who the victims were, how long it had been going on, the landlady's past, as well as the handyman's past. Once again, Kevin saw thorough, detailed reports worked up and ready at instant notice. It fanned the fires of his suspicions, and he went to the computerized law library. He flicked on the library light. The neon lights blinked and then came on to illuminate the long, narrow room with its walls of bookshelves. The computer station was directly on his right. He pulled the chair up before the keyboard and turned on the machine. The screen blinked and, with a beep, lit up before him.

The secretaries kept a template beside the keyboard for quick, easy reference. Studying it for a moment, Kevin was able to tap the right keys and bring up the menu of files in the computer's hard disk. He wanted to run through the past cases, the firm's history, so to speak. He saw that cases were organized by the name of the associate who handled them. Since Paul was the earliest to join the firm, he called up his first.

He flipped through each quickly, noting the clients and the outcomes. Then he moved on to Ted's cases and finally to Dave's. On and on he went, reading and confirming a premise that he knew in his heart was true. Every client that John Milton and Associates had defended was either guilty and argued down to a lower plea or a reduced sentence, or apparently guilty and exonerated through legal maneuvering. No one could say that John Milton and Associates had lost or done poorly with any of their cases.

No wonder the three of them looked so arrogant when they said, "We don't lose," he thought. They knew. They don't.

Kevin saw that his own name was already listed, so he called up his file and was shocked to discover a description of the Lois Wilson case. But why was it in these files? He hadn't been working here at the time. Of course, the Rothberg case was there, and now, already entered, was the rooming-house case.

But what brought the blood to his face was the discovery that the outcome was already written in. Was that just confidence or what? He could screw something up, couldn't he? Or the prosecution could introduce something they knew nothing about, couldn't they? It would be a while before the case came to trial. How could this be written in?

He sat back and thought for a moment. Then he leaned in and brought up the main menu of files again. One in particular caught his eye. All it said was "Futures."

He called it up and sat waiting tensely. He read slowly, noting the dates. His heart was pounding before he got down the first page. He couldn't believe his eyes.

John Milton and Associates was listing more than two years of future legal work based on crimes yet to be committed!

13

"I'm leaving now, Mr. Taylor," Diane said. She was suddenly standing in the library doorway. He hadn't heard her come down the corridor, because he was entranced with what he saw on the computer screen. Even though she spoke softly, he spun around so abruptly, he felt as if he had leaped out of his skin. The beautiful secretary smiled innocently at him, seemingly unaware of what he was doing or what he was looking at. Perhaps she didn't know. Perhaps none of them truly knows, he thought.

"Oh, yes, Diane. I'll be going myself in a moment or two."

"No need for you to rush, Mr. Taylor. The door's set to lock when you leave."

"Thank you. By the way, where has Mr. Milton been all day?"

"He had various appointments throughout the city,

253

but he's been fully informed about everything, including Mr. Scholefield's wife. He'll definitely be in tomorrow. See you in the morning then," she added.

"Yes. Good night." He waited for her to turn away before looking at the screen again. No one would believe this unless he saw it for himself, he decided, so he tried to print out the "Futures" file, but when he went through the function keys, the screen responded with "File not formatted for printer." He started to go through the process of doing just that when, suddenly, the screen went blank. He drew the files list up again and tried to retrieve "Futures," but this time the screen responded with a demand for the password.

How could that be? he wondered. Why was he able to bring it up once and not again without knowing the password? It was as if the computer were tormenting him, as if it, too, were a part of this . . . evil.

He lifted his fingers off the keys, fearful that somehow it could do something to him, but the computer screen remained bright, innocuous-looking. He shook his head. Madness, he thought. His paranoia was rapidly expanding. He flicked the computer off quickly, retreated from the library, and went into his office to call home.

After four rings, Miriam's answering machine came on, and in a sweet yet unfamiliar voice, she asked the caller to leave a name, number, and message. Then, after a short laugh, she said, "Thank you," and the beep was sounded. He held the receiver in his hand, listening to the soft whir of the turning tape on her machine. Why hadn't he heard it in her voice before —this thin, distant tone, the tone of someone quite distracted, someone only vaguely paying attention? Had he been under some spell, a spell that had cracked as soon as he felt guilty about the things he had been doing?

A cold sweat broke out over his forehead and down the back of his neck. He cradled the receiver slowly without leaving any message. Where was she? Was she upstairs, in the penthouse again? Maybe with him? What kind of hold did he have on the women, and why didn't the other associates see it, or if they did, why didn't they care? The three of them were so competent and so bright, surely they were just as aware of things as he was now. He couldn't trust them. He couldn't trust any of them; he especially couldn't trust Paul, for Paul had brought him here, and Paul had permitted his wife to be incarcerated in Bellevue.

Yet what was he to do with what he had learned? He thought for a few moments, looked at the clock, and then went through his phone directory to find the number of the district attorney's office. As soon as the receptionist answered, he asked to speak with Bob McKensie. He was switched to McKensie's secretary.

"He's just leaving," she told him. "I can have him call you tomorrow first thing in the morning."

"No," he snapped, almost shouting into the receiver. "I must speak with him now. It's an emergency. Please . . ."

"Just a moment." From what he heard, he surmised she had put her palm over the mouthpiece and that Bob McKensie was standing right by her desk. "All right," she said. "Mr. McKensie will be right on the line." A moment later he was.

"Kevin, what's up?"

"I know you're on the way out for the day, but believe me, Bob, I wouldn't do this if it weren't critical."

"Well, I was going home. What is this about?"

"It's about every case you've tried against a suspect represented by a John Milton associate. Not only you, but every member of the district attorney's office," Kevin replied, his voice a deep whisper. There was a long pause. "I promise you, you won't regret seeing me."

"How soon can you get here? I do have to be home."

"Give me twenty minutes."

After another pause, McKensie said, "All right, Kevin. Everyone else could be gone by then, so just come in. My office is the third door on the left."

"Right. Thanks."

He cradled the receiver and hurried out, flicking off lights as he went. Just before he closed the front door behind him, he turned back and looked at the dark corridor. Perhaps it was only his overworked imagination, but it seemed to him that there was a glow coming from the law library, a glow that might be coming from a computer screen. But he was positive he had turned it off, so he attributed it to his stimulated imagination and didn't hesitate a moment more.

When he told McKensie twenty minutes, he hadn't considered the end-of-the-day traffic. It was closer to forty minutes before he finally pulled into the garage servicing the prosecutor's office. He parked and hurried to the lobby and elevator. He was so intent on getting to McKensie as quickly as possible, he hadn't thought much about how he was going to present what he had discovered and what he believed. Now that he was at the door of the prosecutor's office, the full impact of what he was about to do struck him, and his hand froze on the doorknob.

He'll think me mad, Kevin thought. *He won't*

believe a word. But I've got to tell someone, someone who would care and would want to investigate further. Who better than the man John Milton and Associates had defeated and embarrassed a number of times? He opened the door and entered. All the lights were still on in the lobby, but there was no receptionist at the front desk. Kevin made his way quickly to the third door on the left and opened it.

McKensie was standing by a window, gazing out at the darkened city, his hands behind his back. The tall, lanky prosecutor turned quickly when the door was opened and raised his eyebrows. Kevin thought McKensie's face looked longer, glummer, his eyes deeper and sadder than usual.

"Sorry. I got caught up in some traffic."

"Knew that would happen." He looked at his watch. "All right, let's make this quick, please. I phoned my wife, but I forgot we were having company tonight."

"I'm sorry, Bob. I wouldn't do this if . . ."

"Sit down, Kevin. Let's hear it. What's gotten you so worked up?" He moved to his own seat. Kevin sat down and leaned back a moment to catch his breath.

"I don't know where to start. I hadn't thought about how I would present this to you until now."

"Just cut right to the heart of it, Kevin. We can discuss details later."

Kevin nodded, swallowed, and then leaned forward.

"All I ask is that you give me a chance," he said, holding his left hand up like a traffic cop, "and don't dismiss what I have to say out of hand, all right?"

"You've got my full attention," McKensie said dryly, gazing at his watch again.

"Bob, I have come to the conclusion that John Milton is an evil man with supernatural powers. Probably he's not a man, or, what I mean is, he's more than a man. He's most probably Satan himself."

McKensie simply stared, the only reaction in his face coming with the raising of his eyebrows again. The absence of disdain or laughter encouraged Kevin.

"I visited Beverly Morgan today. You see, I was just as surprised as you were by her testimony. When I interviewed her before trial, she rejected Rothberg's story, even ridiculed it. She evinced a deep dislike for the man and wanted no part of anything that would help him."

"Yeah, so . . . she had pangs of conscience, maybe. You know as well as I do that there are often witnesses to crimes who refuse to testify. Most rationalize away their guilt," he said and shrugged. "She couldn't when it came right down to it."

"Mr. Milton sent me a note just before I began to question her in court. He knew she was going to change her mind."

"And you think that took supernatural powers?"

"No, not that. I told you. I visited Beverly Morgan today. She had had an accident . . . drinking. She fell down some stairs and was already in the emergency room in the hospital when I arrived at her home. I went to the hospital emergency room and asked her why she had changed her story. Perhaps because she thought she was near death or maybe because her conscience finally got to her, she confessed things to me, things she had done in the past. Bob," Kevin said, leaning over the desk, "she told me she had killed Maxine Shapiro's invalid mother after the old lady discovered she had been robbing her. She gave her an overdose of digitalis. No one knew; no one suspected. She had been robbing from Maxine as well, a little jewelry here, some money here and there."

"So she killed her, too?"

"No, Maxine didn't know what she was doing, or, if she did, she didn't care. Stanley Rothberg killed his wife. I'm convinced of that, and I'm convinced Mr. Milton knew he had. In fact, I know that he knew he would."

"Huh? What are you saying?" McKensie sat back. "John Milton was in on this?"

"In a way, I suppose he is. He knows the potential for evil in our hearts," Kevin said, thinking a moment. Then he looked up quickly. "I thought it was just a clerical error when I was first given the Rothberg file, but John Milton had been working up information before Maxine Rothberg had been murdered. He knew she would be killed and Stanley would be charged."

"Or maybe you were right when you thought it was just a clerical error, Kevin," McKensie said softly.

"No, I'll tell you why I'm sure it wasn't. He not only knows what evil men will do; he knows what evil we have done and hidden in our hearts. He went to Beverly Morgan and blackmailed her. He knew what she had done, and she knew she was confronting some terrible evil force. So she submitted and did what he wanted."

"And she told you this in the hospital today?"

"Yes."

"Kevin, you said yourself she got drunk and had an accident. I was almost ready to discredit her testimony by showing she was an incompetent alcoholic, but I knew you would use that to suggest she could have killed Maxine Shapiro accidentally, so I didn't bother. But what kind of a witness would she make against the likes of John Milton?"

"Bob, John Milton and Associates have won or done well with every criminal case they've been involved in," Kevin replied. "If you examine the court records carefully, you'll see that. And note the kinds of clients . . . many are guilty beyond doubt, but they get their sentences reduced or . . ."

"Any defense lawyer would try to do that, Kevin. You know that."

"Or they find ways to get evidence thrown out."

"Just good defense lawyers, Kevin. That's their job. We understand that. Why do you think I'm on the tails of the police all the time? They're so fed up and eager, they make mistakes, and they hate me and the other AD's for pointing out what they can and can't do."

"I know all that. I know all that," Kevin said impatiently. "But there's more to it here, Bob. They —especially he—enjoy getting guilty people off. He's the true defender of evil, the devil's advocate, if not the devil himself."

McKensie nodded and sat forward. "What else do you have to support such a wild story, Kevin?"

"I just came from the office. I went in and used the computer to review all the firm's cases. As I said, they haven't lost one. They had me in there, too, but not only credited with the Rothberg case. They had my first real criminal case, the one I tried on Long Island."

"Defending an elementary schoolteacher accused of sexually abusing children." Kevin looked at him sharply. "I had my people do some research on you,

Kevin. I had to know what kind of an attorney I was up against."

"It was eerie seeing it there in John Milton's firm's file. It was almost as if he thought I was working for him when I was defending Lois Wilson. Then I thought to myself, maybe I was."

"I don't understand."

"I think in my heart I knew she was guilty of fondling one girl, but I deliberately ignored my instincts to attack the prosecution's case where I knew it was weak."

"That's what you were paid to do," McKensie said dryly.

"Yeah, but I didn't realize at the time that I was auditioning for a position at John Milton and Associates, a firm that seeks attorneys who will go that extra mile to get a defendant exonerated, even a guilty one. Anyway, what shocked and frightened me the most in the computer was a file entitled 'Futures.' It listed crimes that would be committed over the next two years and clients we would have."

"Predictions?"

"Not just predictions, positive predictions— robberies, rapes, murders, extortions, embezzlement—I saw the whole gambit. It read like a description of the graduating class of Hell University."

"Actual names of people and what they would be charged with?"

"Yes."

"Did you run off a copy of this?"

"I tried, but I couldn't get the computer to do it, and then I lost the file and was unable to bring it up on the screen again, but if you go over there . . ."

"Easy, Kevin. I can't see myself marching into John Milton's office with a subpoena to look at a computer file listing crimes yet to be committed. Anyway, if he's got the power you think he does, he would have it deleted before I arrived anyway, wouldn't he?"

Kevin nodded, his frustration building. "Paul Scholefield's wife's in Bellevue," he said quickly. "She told me things last night, told me that John Milton was evil and had a spell over everyone, even our wives. She said he was responsible for Richard Jaffee's death."

"She said he pushed Richard Jaffee off his patio?"

"Not literally, but Jaffee felt responsible for what had happened to his wife and felt guilty about the things he had been doing as a John Milton attorney. The way Helen put it, Richard was the only one with a conscience."

"Helen Scholefield told you these things?"

"Yes."

McKensie nodded and sat forward again, resting his long right hand over his left. "Milt Krammer told me about her today. News travels quickly in the legal community. Nervous breakdown, right?"

"It's just a coverup."

"So you're saying they're all in on it—Dave Kotein, Ted McCarthy, and Paul Scholefield?"

Kevin nodded. "I really think so now."

"And their wives?"

"I'm not sure about the wives."

"But definitely not Paul's?"

"You see, she had done this painting, an abstract work, but terrifying . . ."

He stopped. McKensie was shaking his head slightly, and Kevin realized he was losing it.

"Let's be calm for a moment, Kevin, and review what you've been telling me so far. Okay?"

"Bob, you have to listen to me."

"I'm listening, and I haven't laughed at you or called for the men in white coats, have I?"

"No."

"Okay. You're worked up. Beverly Morgan apparently lied to cover her own ass. John Milton knew about her crimes. Whether or not he knew through supernatural powers remains to be seen. He might have done some investigating himself. He has good private dicks out there. I should know.

"You've looked at his firm's history, and you've discovered it's a very successful firm. But none of the cases they won were won using any supernatural power. They took advantage of police procedural errors whenever they could, negotiated settlements whenever they could, and won cases outright when circumstantial evidence came under question.

"Stop me when you think I've said something wrong."

"No, I know how that all looks, but . . ."

"But you saw this other computer file that you can't reproduce or call up again. It lists possible crimes."

"Not possible, definite."

"You say they're definite because you believe John Milton started to research the Rothberg case before Maxine Rothberg was murdered, but you also admit you first thought it was a clerical error. You want to refer to the testimony of a woman who is now in Bellevue and diagnosed with a nervous breakdown or the testimony of a known alcoholic who may or may not be a murderer and a thief herself.

"Kevin," McKensie said, leaning forward. "Why

don't you just quit the firm? Go back to practicing on
the Island?"

"How many cases have you tried against clients
represented by John Milton?" Kevin asked as calmly
as he could.

"Personally? Five, including yours."

"And you lost every one of them, right?"

"I can't question why I lost them. The reasons were
all logical. Nothing supernatural at work. Look, I've
known John Milton for a while. You saw me at one of
his parties. Other AD's have been to his parties, too.
The boss has been there. No one's ever felt he was in
the presence of the devil or the devil's advocate,
believe me, although some of those parties were a bit
risqué."

Kevin nodded, a terrific sense of defeat coming over
him. Suddenly he felt very tired, very old. "I'm sorry,
Bob. I wish there was some way I could make you
understand."

"If you really believe you and your wife are in the
presence of some evil, Kevin, you should get out."

"I intend to, but I wanted to do more. I wanted to
stop it because I had contributed to it."

McKensie smiled for the first time. "I wish all
defense lawyers would have pangs of conscience like
that. It would make our job a little easier." They
stared at each other for a moment. "I shouldn't do
this," McKensie added. "But I can see you're serious
about everything you've told me. I know someone
who might be able to help you, clear things up for you,
explain some of what you think you've seen or experienced."

"Really? Who?"

"A friend of mine, more of a friend of my father's, I

should say. He's a retired priest, Father Vincent, who in his retirement has been researching and writing about the occult, the devil in particular, I believe. He's not one of these kooks, either. He does what most authorities recognize as scholarly work because he was a psychiatrist, too. He still takes on a patient here and there, even though he's nearly eighty."

"You think I need a psychiatrist, is that it?" Kevin asked. He nodded. "I suppose I can't blame you."

"I'm not saying you're crazy, Kevin. But Father Vincent could very well be of some help to you. Maybe he'll tell you how to go about confirming or disproving your theories and thereby settle your own mind," McKensie said. "Is that so bad?"

"No, I suppose not."

"Now you're being sensible," McKensie said and looked down at his watch again. "I really better get my ass in gear."

"Right. Thanks for listening." Kevin extended his hand.

McKensie stood up, and they shook. "Kevin, don't misunderstand me. I'd love to knock off John Milton and Associates. They're too good at what they do, and, I agree, a number of their clients have gotten away with criminal activities, but that's the system, and right now it's the best system in town. You probably discovered you don't have the stomach for this sort of thing. It happens," McKensie said, shrugging. "Maybe you ought to think about coming over to our side. Pay's not as good, but you can sleep better at night."

"Maybe," Kevin said. He started to leave McKensie's office.

"Wait. I'll walk out with you."

McKensie put on his overcoat and grabbed his briefcase. He flicked off his office lights, and once again, Kevin was the last to leave an office, lights turned off behind him, doors locked.

"Where is this Father Vincent?" Kevin asked when they got into the elevator.

"He lives in the Village," McKensie said, smiling. "Apartment 5, One Christopher Street. His first name's Reuben. Mention my name if you call him."

"I might just do that," Kevin said, even though his enthusiasm for doing anything was low.

But the moment he returned to his apartment and opened the front door, that all changed.

Miriam was there in the entryway waiting for him.

"I heard you put the key in the door lock," she explained, "and came running."

She was beaming, her face flushed, her eyes brilliant.

"Why?"

"I didn't want you to know until I was sure, but I confirmed it today. I'm pregnant," she said, and threw her arms around him before he had a chance to respond.

"What are you saying?" Miriam got up before he could continue. After getting hold of himself, Kevin had taken her into the living room to talk, but he had barely begun before she clenched her hands into fists and pressed her knuckles against her temples. "An abortion!"

"I don't think the baby's mine," Kevin said as calmly as he could. "And if Helen's right, which I think she is, it will kill you."

"Helen? Helen Scholefield? My God, you're mad.

You've gone mad. You've let Helen Scholefield drive you crazy, haven't you?" she said. "What did she tell you last night? How can the baby not be yours? Who do you think I've been sleeping with? Did Helen tell you I was with another man? And you believed her, a crazy woman? Someone who's now in a straitjacket babbling in Bellevue!" Her face turned blue with anger.

"Just sit down again and listen to what I have to say. Will you do that?"

"No, not if it has anything to do with getting an abortion. We wanted this baby; we wanted to start our family. I have the nursery all planned out." She shook her head vehemently. "I won't listen. No. I won't," she repeated and suddenly bolted from the living room. He sat there a moment and then got up and followed her to the bedroom. She was sprawled across the bed, facedown, sobbing.

"Miriam." He sat down beside her and stroked her hair softly. "It's not your fault. I didn't mean you deliberately slept with someone else. You weren't really unfaithful. That's not what this is about. He had you under a spell and made love to you as me. I saw it . . . twice, but I was unable to do anything about it each time."

She turned around slowly and studied his face. "Who had me under a spell and made love to me while you watched?"

"Mr. Milton."

"Mr. Milton?" He nodded. "Mr. Milton?" Her smile of disbelief expanded into a laugh. "Mr. Milton?" she said again as she sat up. "Do you know how old Mr. Milton is? I found out his true age today. He's seventy-four. That's right, seventy-four. I know he looks great for his age, but if you want to imagine me being unfaithful with someone, why not pick one of the associates?"

"Who told you his true age?"

"Dr. Stern."

"Who's Dr. Stern?"

"The doctor the firm uses," she said, wiping tears of both laughter and sorrow from her cheeks. "Norma and Jean took me to see him, first because I wanted to check out those black and blue marks that worry you so, and second to take a pregnancy test. You'll be happy to know that he agreed with your diagnosis and put me on some vitamin therapy. Why I should be so deficient in vitamins might be related to my pregnancy. I have to eat for two people now," she added, smiling.

"Oh, Miriam . . ."

"He was a very nice man, and we talked about the firm and you and Mr. Milton. That's when I found out his true age."

"Is he the same doctor Gloria Jaffee used?" Kevin nodded as if she had already replied in the positive.

"Of course. And I know what you're going to say next," she added quickly. "But her death wasn't his fault. The girls and I talked about it, and he even brought it up. It still bothers him. It was her heart. Just a freak thing, quite unexpected."

"It was a freak thing all right, but not unexpected. I'm not sure exactly why it happened yet, but the baby killed her, and her husband knew it and knew why."

"How come nobody else thinks such terrible things, not Norma or Jean or their husbands? They work with John Milton and have worked with him much longer than you have. How come they don't come home and tell their wives how evil he is? Or is it that they just don't know as much as you do, Kevin?" she asked disdainfully.

"They know," he said, nodding. A thought came to him. "Do Norma and Jean ever talk about their husbands?"

"Of course."

"I mean, their pasts, their family life?"

"Some. So?"

"Anything unusual about either Ted or Dave that I don't know?"

She shrugged. "You knew Ted was adopted, didn't you?"

"No, I didn't. He never said anything to me to suggest it. The way he talked about his father's firm, I just assumed he was his natural father and his mother was his natural mother." He looked at her. "Dave doesn't talk much about his parents, now that I think of it. If he does, it's always about his father." He nodded. "Dave's mother died when he was born, didn't she?"

"So you knew."

"And I'd bet Paul's . . ." He widened his eyes with the realization. "Don't you see?" He stood up. The impact of the realization was shooting through him with electric speed.

"See what, Kevin? You've really got me frightened."

"They mean it when they say this firm's a family. It is. He's their father, really their father!"

"What?" She grimaced.

"I should have known . . . the way they talk about

him. 'He's like a father to me,' Paul once said. I think they've all said it one time or another."

"Really, Kevin. They were just speaking figuratively."

"No, no, it's all making sense now. Someday Gloria Jaffee's son will be in this firm, too. And so . . ." He looked down at her. "So would your child, if you had it."

"The Jaffee child . . . twenty-five or twenty-six years from now? Will join Mr. Milton's firm? Why, let me see," she said, closing her eyes and calculating. "Mr. Milton will be a ripe old one hundred and nine or ten by then."

"He'll be a lot older than that, Miriam. He's at least as old as creation."

"Oh, Kevin, really," she said, shaking her head. "Where are you getting these wild ideas? Helen Scholefield?"

"No."

"Then where?"

"First, from my own good instincts, whatever's left of them." He paused for a moment and then, after a deep breath, said, "Miriam, you were right about Lois Wilson."

"What do you mean?"

"In my heart I knew she was guilty of fondling Barbara Stanley. Barbara Stanley was embarrassed and frightened because initially she permitted Lois to do it, so she got the other girls involved, got them to agree to lie so she could go forward with allies. I saw the lie and used it against the prosecution. It was a despicable thing to do, but I wanted to win. That's all I cared about, winning."

"You did only what you were trained and paid to do," Miriam recited.

"What? Since when do you believe that? What happened to your revulsion at the idea of my defending her in the first place?"

"Norma, Jean, and I discussed that. It was good for me to have other lawyers' wives with whom to share my feelings and thoughts. They helped me a lot, Kevin. I'm glad we've come here and been around more intelligent and sophisticated people."

"No! They're not more intelligent and sophisticated; they're more evil, that's all."

"Really, Kevin, I don't understand why you're saying these things and why you suggested such a terrible thing—aborting our first child."

"I'm going to tell you everything, and after I do, you'll agree with me about the abortion. First, though, I want to see someone, learn some more, learn what to do, learn how to confirm all this so other people, you especially, will believe me."

He got up and went to the phone and tapped out the numbers for information. When the operator came on, he asked for Reuben Vincent's number. Miriam watched him with interest as he wrote it down quickly and then tapped it out.

"Who's that?" she asked. He indicated she should wait.

"Father Vincent? Good evening. My name's Taylor, Kevin Taylor. Bob McKensie gave me your name. Is this a good time to talk? Fine. I'm very interested in the work you're doing, and I think I need your help. Would it be possible for me to see you now? Yes, tonight. I could be there in a half-hour or so. Yes.

Thank you very much. See you soon." He cradled the phone and turned to Miriam.

"Who was that?"

"A man who might be able to help."

"Help do what?"

"Beat the devil," he said and left her sitting on the bed, a look of amazement on her face.

14

There were times before in his life when Kevin felt as if he were moving in a dream. Caught up in an intense moment or doing something he had dreamed about doing so often, he saw himself as outside the actual events, an observer of himself, almost the way he had been an observer of what he thought was himself in those erotic scenes played out with Miriam. He felt the same way now.

Stopping at a traffic light on Seventh Avenue, he saw someone standing on the corner, looking his way. The man, his overcoat collar up, his hands in his pockets, his face partly in shadows, partly in dim light, reminded him of himself, and for a moment he saw himself as that man might be seeing him—crunched up intently over the steering wheel, his hair disheveled, a wild-eyed, frantic look on his face.

The light changed, and the driver in the car behind

him hit his horn angrily. Kevin pressed his foot down hard on the accelerator, but as his car tore on through the night, he gazed up once in his rearview mirror to see the shadowy figure crossing the street quickly, looking like someone in flight. He drove on with that image of himself lingering on the surface of his eyes just the way light lingers for a split second after it has been turned off.

Kevin knew this section of the Village well. He had gone there often to have lunch at a nearby delicatessen. He went directly to the parking lot next to Father Vincent's building, and, just a little over a half an hour since he had called him, he rang the man's apartment and entered as the door was buzzed open.

Father Vincent opened his apartment door for Kevin as soon as he emerged from the elevator. "Right this way," he called in a deep, resonant voice. Kevin hurried toward him.

A short, stout, bald-headed man in a crisp white shirt and black slacks stepped back so he could enter.

Father Vincent had two lean puffs of starch-white hair over his ears. They combined at the rear of his head to emphasize the oval shape of his shiny crown, spotted with brown age spots. His eyebrows were gray and bushy, but his eyes were a soft, youthful blue, revealing the spirit and intellectual energy of the man. His cheeks were inflated just under his eyes. In fact, there was a bloated look to his entire face, all his features somewhat large. His chin dipped and curved smoothly, rounding off his elliptical visage.

He was barely over five feet tall, and Kevin thought there was something dwarfish about his hands. He extended his left one quickly, seizing Kevin's right hand and pumping his palm with unexpectedly strong stubby fingers.

When he smiled, the softness in his cheeks folded to form two dimples just above the corners of his mouth. Kevin decided he was a cuddly, cute man, lovable, a beardless, albeit a bit diminutive, version of Kris Kringle.

"Cold as hell out there, I bet," Father Vincent said, rubbing his hands together sympathetically.

"Yes. The wind is especially biting tonight," Kevin said, and for an instant he replayed the image of the shadowy man on the corner, his collar up against the frosty air.

"Go right into the living room. Make yourself comfortable," Father Vincent said, closing the door. "How about a hot drink or a stiff one?"

"I think . . . a stiff one."

"Brandy?"

"Fine. Thank you."

Kevin followed him into the cozy little living room, its furniture consisting of an egg-white large cushioned sectional, two glass and wood end tables, and a matching table at the center of the sectional. There was a dark pine rocker in the far left corner with a pole lamp beside it. On the right and to the immediate left were shelves and shelves of books. The far wall consisted of a fake marble fireplace. There was a false log with a glowing red light in it. The light blue nylon carpet looked old but not yet worn.

Father Vincent went to a small liquor cabinet on the immediate left and poured two snifters of cognac.

"Thank you," Kevin said, taking his.

"Have a seat. Please." Father Vincent gestured

toward the sectional, and Kevin sat down, unbuttoning his top two overcoat buttons.

"I'll give you a chance to warm up before taking your overcoat, if you like."

"Yes, thank you," Kevin said. "This will help," he added, indicating the brandy. The drink did feel wonderful as it burned its way gently down his throat and into his stomach. He closed his eyes and relaxed.

"You look like a very troubled young man," Father Vincent said. He sat across from Kevin and studied him as he sipped his own brandy.

"Father, that's an understatement."

"Unfortunately for me, it often is." He smiled. "People come to priests or psychiatrists only as a last resort, usually. So," he said, relaxing himself, "you're a friend of Bob McKensie's, huh?"

"Not exactly a friend. I'm a defense attorney. I opposed him in a case recently."

"Oh?"

"Father Vincent," Kevin said, thinking it was best to get right down to it, "Bob explained that you have done considerable research in what we call the occult."

"It's been one of my passions, yes."

"And he told me you are a practicing psychiatrist as well as a priest."

"To be honest, I wasn't all that active as a psychiatrist. I dabble in it now and then on a part-time basis. And I'm sure he told you I have retired from my clerical duties."

"Yes. Well, to be honest, I think Bob wanted me to see you as both a priest and a psychiatrist."

"I see. Well, why don't you begin at the beginning? What seems to be the problem?"

"Father Vincent," Kevin said, fixing his eyes on the little man, "I have good reason to believe I work for the devil or the devil's advocate. Whatever we call him, he's someone or something with supernatural powers, and he uses these powers to assist the forces of evil at work in our world." He paused and took a deep breath. "Bob McKensie has told me about your work with the occult, and he assured me you wouldn't laugh when I told you all that. Was he right?" Kevin paused and waited for the elderly man's reaction.

Reuben Vincent remained stoical, thoughtful for a moment, and then nodded. "You mean all this literally, I assume?"

"Oh yes."

"No, I won't laugh, nor will I embrace your statement as would so many, what shall I call them, religious fanatics, without satisfying my own criteria. I do believe in the devil's literal existence, although I am not certain that he has manifested himself in a human form continually since the loss of Paradise. I think he has chosen his moments, much as God has chosen His."

Father Vincent pressed his hands together piously and rocked slightly in his seat, his eyes fixed on Kevin. He was such a diminutive man, it was difficult for Kevin to imagine that he could offer anything to combat the powers of John Milton.

"However," he continued, leaning forward, his eyes small, scrutinizing, "there is no question that the devil is always with us. Some of his essence exists in all of us, just as some of God's essence exists in all of us. Some believe that is all the result of Adam and Eve's blunder. I don't know whether I subscribe to that theory so much as I feel we have the potential to be either good or bad.

"So to answer your question fully, I believe in the devil and I believe he lives in us waiting for his opportunity. Sometimes, to tempt us, he takes a human form and wins our confidence and trust in some way."

Father Vincent sat back, smiling. "What makes you think you are working for the devil himself?"

Kevin began with the Lois Wilson case, his decision to take it, and Paul Scholefield's attendance at the trial. He traced the history of events, Miriam's change in character, Helen Scholefield's cryptic warnings, the Rothberg trial, and brought his story up to his discoveries at the computer in the office.

Throughout it all, Father Vincent listened attentively, nodding occasionally, occasionally closing his eyes as if he had just heard something with which he was well familiar. When Kevin was finished, the old man did not say anything for a few moments. Instead, he got up and went to a window to look out at the street below. He stood there thinking. Kevin waited patiently. Finally, Father Vincent turned to him and nodded.

"What you say makes a lot of sense to me. Stories, anecdotes, histories, and philosophies I have read convinced me quite a while ago that the devil has a sense of loyalty to his followers. Perhaps you remember a great literary work about good and evil, *Paradise Lost,* by the English poet John Milton?"

"John Milton! John Milton!" Kevin sat up. A sharp, deep smile cracked across his face. Then he sat back and laughed.

"What's the joke?"

"It's his joke, his in joke, his own sick sense of humor. Father Vincent, John Milton is the name of the man I work for."

"Really?" Father Vincent's eyes brightened. "This is getting interesting. Obviously, you didn't recall the poetic narrative before this."

"It must have been one of those things I fudged at college, bought those summarized versions to read instead of reading the work itself."

"It's not an easy thing to read . . . Latinate syntax, loads of classical references, metaphors born out of metaphors," he said, making S's in the air with his right hand like an orchestra conductor. "Anyway, according to the poet John Milton, after the devil, Lucifer, is thrown out of Heaven for leading a rebellion against God, he finds himself and his followers in hell, and he feels sorry for his followers. Milton described him as a classic leader, don't you see? He had vision, charisma, saw himself as destined to lead and care for his followers."

"John Milton cares for his associates, provides well for them: homes, money, medical care . . ."

"Yes, yes. What you are telling me is very, very interesting. He knows the evil that lurks in the hearts of people, predicts, perhaps even encourages it, and then, like a true leader, stands by his troops, supports and defends."

"No matter how heinous the crime or how guilty they might be," Kevin added, as if he and Father Vincent were solving a great mystery together.

The short, grandfatherly man pressed out his lips and clasped his hands behind his back. "Intriguing. Manifesting himself as a lawyer. Of course. All the opportunities . . ." He shook his head, his face brightening with excitement. "I have some observations I'm going to want you to make. In time . . ."

"Oh no, Father. You don't understand. I've come here tonight because I'm desperate. There is one thing I haven't yet told you. It involves my wife. I believe she is in great danger and must have an abortion, only I don't know how to get her to believe what we are saying."

"An abortion!"

Kevin related what he knew about Gloria Jaffee's death and Richard Jaffee's suicide, and then he began to describe what he had first thought were the strange erotic dreams. He reiterated Helen Scholefield's warning concerning Miriam and finished with Miriam's announcement about her own pregnancy.

"As soon as she told me, I knew I had to see you immediately."

"Children of the devil," Father Vincent said, quickly sitting himself down again as if the weight of this information was too heavy. "Completely his own, of his essence. Children without conscience who could imagine things more evil than ordinary people . . . Hitlers, Stalins, Jack the Rippers, who knows what?"

"Intelligent children," Kevin said, feeling the need to contribute to the scenario Father Vincent envisioned. "Clever, conniving people who work within the system to carry out the devil's orders."

"Yes." Father Vincent's eyes lit up with the realizations. "Not only lawyers, but politicians, doctors, teachers, just as you suggest: everyone working within the system to corrupt the soul of mankind and defeat God Himself."

Kevin took a deep breath and sat back. Could it really be that he had discovered the greatest conspiracy of all time? Who was he to have been chosen to bring down the devil himself and be the defender of God? And yet there was Miriam to think about. He would fight devils and demons to protect her, he thought, especially since he had brought her to this . . . this hell on earth, just as Richard Jaffee had brought his wife. Only he wasn't going to choose suicide. Helen Scholefield had told him Jaffee had two choices. Well, there were three: join Milton, commit suicide, or destroy him. Miriam's immediate danger made this paramount.

"The analogy you made between the weaknesses in the physical body and the weaknesses in the soul might be closer than you think," Kevin said. He described Miriam's tendency to develop black and blue marks. "I've been telling her it could be a nutritional deficiency."

"Evil draws from good, feeds on it. It will be the reason why the evil child will take its mother's life in the end."

"That's what I thought," Kevin said, excited because Father Vincent had reached the same conclusion so quickly. "What can I do?" he asked in a voice that was no more than a shade above a whisper.

"I don't doubt any of the things you have told me, things you have seen and heard, things you have felt, and if what you tell me is true, there is only one course of action," Father Vincent said, nodding after his words as if to convince himself first. "Only one course—we must destroy the devil in the body he has chosen.

"First," the elderly priest continued, "you must carry out two additional tests to satisfy yourself that you are indeed in the presence of Lucifer." He rose from his seat and went to his bookshelves to pull out an old Bible, its brown leather cover quite faded. The words "Holy Bible," however, were still remarkably bright, almost as if they had been retouched. He brought the Bible to Kevin, who took it slowly and waited for some explanation.

"The devil can't touch the Holy Book. It burns his fingers. God's words sear his polluted soul. He will howl hideously."

"But knowing that, he will never touch it."

"Yes. I want you to give this to John Milton, but . . ." He looked around the room a moment and then went to a cabinet and took out a plain brown paper bag. "Here. Put the Bible in this bag. Offer it to him as a gift. If he is truly the devil, when he takes it out and sees what he has touched, he will drop it as if he has grasped the center of a flame and howl in pain."

"I see." Kevin slipped the Bible into the paper bag carefully. He handled it as gingerly as he would handle an explosive. "And if he does what you have just described?"

Father Vincent stared down at him a moment and then turned and went to the bookshelves again. He reached into a corner of a shelf and came out with what looked to be a gold cross with a silver replica of Christ crucified upon it. The cross was nearly eight inches long. Father Vincent held it at the bottom in a tightly closed fist.

"Take this out and put it as close to his face as you

can. For him, if he is truly the devil, it will be like looking directly into the sun. It will blind him momentarily, and in that moment he will be a helpless old man."

"And then?" Kevin asked.

"And then . . ." Father Vincent opened his fist. The bottom of the cross was a sharp dagger. "Drive this into his corrupted heart. Don't hesitate, or you and your wife will be lost forever." He leaned closer. "Eternal forever," he added.

Kevin barely breathed. His heart was pounding, but he reached up slowly and took the cross from Father Vincent. The small face on the statue of Christ looked different from any he had ever seen. The expression was one more of anger than forgiveness, a face intended to depict a soldier of God. The cross was heavy, the end very sharp.

"Once you have driven this into his heart, he will fall."

"But what about my wife and that . . . child?"

"When the devil is killed in one of his human forms, his progeny will die with him. She will abort naturally. And so," Father Vincent concluded, pulling himself into an erect position, "you will have saved your wife.

"But do nothing," Father Vincent warned, "if he does not meet the two tests I have described. Come back and we'll talk some more. Is that understood?"

"Yes," Kevin said. "Thank you." He stood up, pressing the Bible in the brown bag under his arm and clutching the gold cross dagger. He inserted it between his belt and his pants.

Father Vincent nodded. "Good. Go, and may God

be with you, my son." He placed his hand on Kevin's shoulder and mumbled some prayer under his breath.

"Thank you, Father," Kevin whispered.

The apartment house was quieter than usual. Even the security guard, a man named Lawson who replaced Philip for the night shift, was nowhere to be seen when Kevin drove up and looked through the glass doors. He turned into the driveway and pressed his clicker. The gate lifted, and he drove into the garage. It was deadly still. The sound made by closing his car door echoed through the dimly lit garage and then died. He heard the soft hum of motors.

Kevin saw that all the associates' cars were there. Way down in the far right corner was the firm's limo. For the first time, he noticed a doorway that he now understood must be the way to Charon's apartment. Charon . . . it came to him because now he was thinking about definitions. Wasn't Charon the mythological boatman who took dead souls on the ferry ride down to Hades? His name was surely another one of John Milton's jokes, but their Charon did ferry them deeper and deeper into hell, didn't he? *The joke's been on us,* he thought.

Kevin went to the elevator. First, he would go to Miriam and tell her all he had learned, make her understand the danger, force her to see. If need be, he would call Father Vincent and have her speak to him, too, he thought, but when he arrived at their apartment, she was already gone. She had left him a note on the kitchen table.

"Forgot, tonight the girls and I had tickets to the ballet. Don't wait up. We'll probably stop for something after. There's a gourmet lasagna in the fridge.

Just follow directions and microwave as directed. Love, Miriam."

Is she mad? he thought. *After all I said to her, after the way I ran out of here, to just go on with her schedule, not wait for me!*

She's lost, he thought. Talking to her would have done no good. It was all in his hands now. Kevin's gaze fell on the small table by the phone in the kitchen. There lay a godsend, the gold key. He could go up and face John Milton and put an end to it all. He grabbed it, and with the Bible in the paper bag under his arm and the gold cross dagger in his belt, Kevin rushed out to the elevator.

He inserted the key and pressed "P" for penthouse. The doors closed, and he began to ascend, imagining that he was truly rising up out of the confines of hell. He had his soul to save and his wife's life.

The doors opened slowly, more slowly than they opened on any other floor, he thought. The great room was dimly lit, the lights in the ceiling turned down, most of the lamps off. Candles burned in the candelabra on the piano. Their tiny flames threw enormous, distorted shadows on the far wall. A very slight breeze in the room made the small flames flicker, making it seem as if the silhouettes trembled.

The stereo was on very low, the tape deck playing a piano piece that was at first only vaguely familiar. But after a few seconds of listening, Kevin realized it was the concerto Miriam had been playing the night of the party. In his mind he could almost see her sitting there, playing it now.

Kevin stepped out of the elevator and paused to listen for other sounds. At first there were none. Then, as if he materialized right before Kevin's eyes, John

Milton was suddenly sitting at the right corner of the sectional couch, sipping wine. He was in his burgundy velvet smoking jacket.

"Why, Kevin. What a pleasant surprise. Come in, come in. I was just sitting here, relaxing. And, as a matter of fact, I was thinking about you."

"Were you?"

"Yes. I know you took the day off. Are you feeling better, rested?"

"Somewhat."

"Good. Once again, congratulations on a wonderful defense."

"I didn't have to do that much," he said, stepping farther forward. "It was handed to me when you had that note delivered."

"Ah yes, the note. Still wondering about that, are you?"

"No."

"No? Good. As my grandfather used to say, 'Never look a gift horse in the mouth.' "

"My God."

"What?"

"It was my grandfather who said that."

"Was it?" John Milton's smile widened. "Everybody's grandfather probably said things like that. When you're a grandfather, you'll say the same sort of things, too." John Milton put his glass of wine on the table. "Come on in. You're standing there like some sort of messenger boy. Would you like a glass of wine?" He held the glass in the light so that the red liquid looked more dazzling.

"No, thank you."

"No?" He sat back and studied Kevin for a moment. "What's that you're carrying under your arm?"

"A gift for you."

"Oh? That's kind of you. What's the occasion?"

"Let's call it gratitude, appreciation for all you've done for me and for Miriam."

"I've already gotten my gift in seeing you do so well in court."

"Nevertheless, I wanted to give you some small token of our . . . affection."

Kevin moved forward until he was standing before him. Slowly, he brought the brown bag out from under his arm and handed it to John Milton.

"Feels like a book."

Kevin reached in under his jacket and grasped the gold cross.

"Oh, it is. One of the best."

"Really? Well, thank you." He put his fingers in the bag and pulled out the Bible. It wasn't until it was completely out of the bag that the words "Holy Bible" were visible. The moment they were, John Milton's eyes bulged. He screamed just as Father Vincent had predicted, howled as if he had tried to seize the center of a fire, a hot, burning coal. The Bible fell to the floor.

Kevin pulled out the cross and extended his arm, shoving the face and body of an angry-looking crucified Christ in John Milton's face. He screamed again and brought his hands to his eyes, covering them as quickly as he could with his palms, and fell back against the sectional. Kevin clutched the cross as he would a dagger, and without a moment's hesitation he drove the sharpened end into John Milton's heart. It cut through the garment and his flesh with the speed and precision of a heated knife cutting through soft ice cream, the cross cooling down as it entered. Blood spurted out and over Kevin's fingers, but he didn't retreat until he had driven the cross as deeply as he could.

John Milton never lowered his hands. He keeled over and died on the luxurious couch, with his palms still pressed firmly against his eyes to block out the light. Kevin stepped back. The replica of Christ on the cross was planted firmly in John Milton's chest, only now Kevin thought the small face looked satisfied, fulfilled.

Kevin stood there, staring down at the body until his own body stopped shaking. It was over, he thought. He had saved his soul and his wife's life. He went directly to the telephone to call Father Vincent. It rang and rang and rang. Finally, he heard the old man's voice.

"I'm here," Kevin said. "In his apartment, and it all went as you described."

"Pardon?"

"I've done it, Father. He couldn't touch the Bible, and he howled when it was in his hands, and then I showed him the crucified Christ and he was blinded, so I drove the dagger into his heart just as you directed."

There was only silence on the other end.

"It was what I was supposed to do, wasn't it?"

"Oh yes, my boy." Father Vincent burst into a hollow laugh. "It was what you were supposed to do. Don't do anything else. Just stay put. I'll call the police."

"The police?"

"Just stay put," he repeated and hung up. Kevin held the receiver in his hand a moment and listened to the hum. Then he cradled the receiver.

He looked toward the couch and John Milton's

body. There was something different about it. Slowly, he walked back to the sectional and stared down at the body. His heart began to pound, and a cold, chilling wave traveled up his legs, making him feel as if he had just stepped into an icy pond.

John Milton was still dead. The dagger was still firmly planted in his heart.

But his hands were off his face.

And he was smiling!

15

There's no one better to defend you," Miriam pleaded. "Why don't you listen to reason? You should be grateful that they're willing to do it, considering what you've done. I'm amazed they don't hate us."

Kevin said nothing. He sat in the prison visiting room and stared straight ahead, his mind still jumbled. Had he gone mad? Was this what it was like to go completely mad?

The police had come, followed by the associates, and then Miriam and the girls had arrived. He had said nothing to anyone, not even Miriam, who became hysterical and had to be comforted by Norma and Jean anyway. The associates thought he was just being a good defendant, refusing to speak until represented by an attorney, but he wasn't going to speak to any of them now, despite Miriam's pleas.

And as for the associates not hating them, of course they hated them. They were just being their old conniving selves. But he understood why Miriam would be blind to that. She was so vulnerable, he thought, and looked at her.

She was still pregnant. There hadn't been any immediate subsequent abortion, but surely it would happen. Everything else Father Vincent had predicted had happened. That thought brought him back to the moment. He studied her face more closely.

Miriam didn't look sick or in pain. She had been crying and her makeup was streaked with tears, but she didn't look physically uncomfortable. In fact, the paleness he had seen in her face recently was gone. She looked like a healthy pregnant woman, blooming because of her pregnancy. Maybe that meant the evil fetus within her was dying, losing its power to draw on her nutritional health. He was hopeful.

"How do you feel?" he asked her.

"I feel terrible. What do you mean? How can you ask me that now?"

"I don't mean about any of this. I mean, physically . . . your pregnancy . . . any more black and blue marks?"

"No. I'm all right," she said. "I've seen the doctor, and he says everything is fine." She shook her head. He continued to stare at her, studying her, searching her eyes, searching the expression in her face. She looked so different to him. He sensed that the intimacy that had once been between them was gone. They were no longer a part of each other. She had become a stranger. Her eyes no longer had that warmth he had once cherished. It was as if someone else was in her body, he thought, and then he thought, of course, there was . . . that child, draining her, drawing out her warmth, her love for him.

The doctor was one of them. Maybe he was keeping the baby alive.

"I want you to stop seeing their doctor, Miriam. Stop seeing him," he demanded.

"My God, Kevin, I didn't realize how crazy you had become. My God."

"I'm not crazy, Miriam. You'll see. I'm not crazy."

She sat back and stared at him, any sympathy or pity for him slipping away. He sensed her disgust and dismay.

"Kevin, why did you do it? Of all the people in the world to kill, how could you kill Mr. Milton?"

The guard standing by the door lifted his eyebrows, looked their way, and then pretended interest in something across the room.

"You didn't believe me when I first told you, you won't believe me now, but it will all come out at the trial."

"The trial?" She smirked. All these expressions and reactions, they were so unlike her. That thing was taking over, he thought, possessing her just as the one in Gloria Jaffee had surely possessed her. "What kind of a trial do you expect? You admit to having done it, and you won't permit Paul or Ted or Dave to represent you, even though they are the best defense lawyers in the city, probably in the country."

"I've made inquiries and sent for an attorney."

"Who?"

"Someone barely known as a criminal attorney. He's not a high-powered lawyer; he's not rich, and, most importantly, he's not any of them." *Yet,* he added to himself, *if I lose, he might just become one of them.*

"But Kevin, is this wise?"

"Most wise. I have a chance this way, a chance to demonstrate the truth."

"Paul says the first thing that must be done is you must be examined psychiatrically. The prosecution is going for first-degree murder. He said the psychiatrist the prosecutors appoint will most likely support their contention that you knew what you were doing. Paul said they'll block that avenue of defense, which, he feels, is your only defense."

"He would say that. He's even recommended some psychiatrist for us, no doubt."

"Oh yes. He offered some wonderful doctors," she said. "Ones the firm has used before."

He thought she winked. She was becoming one of them. It was almost useless to talk to her until it was all over.

"Doctors who will definitely claim I'm crazy. That's what they hope will happen: I'll be declared insane, and the truth will be buried, don't you see?" He leaned forward, getting as close as he could to her without the guards noticing. "But that won't happen, Miriam. We're not going to ask for any psychiatric tests. None." He slapped the table between them so hard, she jumped in her seat.

Miriam made a small, mouselike sound and pressed her right hand against her mouth. Her eyes were glassy, wet. She shook her head.

"Everyone's devastated—your parents, mine, the associates, Norma and Jean."

"What about Helen?" He smiled madly. "You don't

want to conveniently forget Helen Scholefield now, do you? Just because the others have."

"I won't forget her, and they haven't either. I'd blame her for all this, only she was very sick herself at the time and not responsible for the things she said and did." She opened her purse and took out a handkerchief to dab her cheeks. She followed that with a small mirror and started to wipe away the streaks. "Thank God, she's improved."

"Improved?" He sat back. "What's that supposed to mean? Is she dead?"

"Oh, Kevin, really. What a thing to say. Improved means getting better. The treatments have helped. She's out of her comatose state. She's eating well and conversing intelligently. Paul hopes to bring her home in a week or so if she continues to progress."

"Bring her home? She'll never come back to that apartment building."

"She asks to be brought home every day, Kevin. Norma and Jean have seen her. They say the change in her is dramatic, nothing short of miraculous.

"Don't you see?" she said quickly, pressing forward. "That's why you need to have a psychiatric exam and treatment and . . ."

"No!" He rose out of his seat and shook his head vehemently.

"Kevin."

"You'd better go, Miriam. I'm tired, and I have to prepare for my attorney's first visit. Let me know the minute something happens to you. It should happen soon."

"Something happens? What's supposed to happen?"

"You'll see," he said. "You'll see," he muttered hopefully and turned to go back to his cell.

How odd, Kevin thought. Why would Helen Scholefield be improving and want to come back knowing all she knew? Had they done something to her in Bellevue, something to erase all her memories and knowledge? Maybe they had given her a lobotomy. Yes, that was it, a lobotomy.

And why was Miriam still pregnant? Father Vincent had said once the devil in his human form was killed, all his human progeny would die. Why was it taking so long? Father Vincent didn't say the firm's doctor could block it. Could it be he didn't know? He had to talk to him. Why hadn't the priest come to see him? And why was he the one who called the police? Was it all part of the process?

There was so much to understand . . . so much. He had to go back and think, plan, reorganize. He had to work on his own defense. He had to show he had killed in self-defense. It would be the greatest brief of his career, he and the nobody lawyer proving to the state and to the people that he had saved mankind by killing the devil.

"We've got to subpoena the computer files in the office," he muttered, "and Beverly Morgan." And then McKensie would describe his meeting with him, he thought, and Father Vincent would be called . . . a man of the cloth, a man of authority, a psychiatrist in his own right who believes in the existence of the devil.

"I'm all right. I'm all right," he concluded. "It will be just fine."

"Sure," the guard walking behind him replied.

"Everything's going to be great now that you're in our hands."

Kevin ignored him, and moments after his cell door had been closed behind him, he was on his bunk bed scribbling madly over a long yellow legal pad.

His lawyer's name was William Samson. He was only twenty-seven and looked like a young Van Johnson—fresh, pure American apple pie. Samson couldn't believe his luck. It was a dramatic case, high profile, heavy publicity. He had really had only one criminal trial experience, defending a nineteen-year-old college man accused of robbing a liquor store at gunpoint near the campus. The thief wore a ski mask, and the police, acting on a tip, had found an identical-looking ski mask in his apartment, and there wasn't any other ski equipment. He wasn't a skier. He fit the physical description as well, and there was evidence that he had some serious gambling debts. Yet it wasn't an open-and-shut case because the police didn't locate any weapon and the defendant's girlfriend claimed he was with her at the time.

However, Samson knew she was lying, and he had little faith in her credibility on the witness stand. When he spelled out the punishment for perjury and explained that the prosecution was already working to disprove and/or discredit her testimony, she became very jittery. A day before the trial began, he advised his client to plea bargain and went to the district attorney's office to negotiate. He convinced the AD to drop the armed robbery charge, replacing it with a simple robbery charge. Since his client had no priors, he got the prosecution to recommend six months and five years probation.

Kevin didn't really know the details of this case. He didn't care. In his way of thinking, he was simply looking for someone capable of being a criminal attorney who was least likely to have been corrupted by the devil. At their first meeting, Kevin explained why he wanted to plead self-defense. Samson listened and took notes, but as Kevin went on and on, Samson's heart sank. This wasn't going to be much of a case after all. His client, he decided, was crazy, suffering from hysterical paranoia. Very gingerly, he recommended a psychiatric examination.

Kevin refused. "That's just what they want me to do—plead insanity so no one will listen to my evidence and my witnesses."

"Then I can't in good conscience defend you," William Samson declared. "No one will believe your motives or your story. I have no defense to offer under these circumstances, Mr. Taylor."

Kevin was disappointed with Samson's reaction, but he was also impressed. William Samson was a bright young attorney who would do his best for his clients, but he operated under a system of morality, too. This was the kind of attorney he could have been, he thought. It gave him hope and renewed his faith in himself and his actions.

"Then I'll defend myself," he said. "But come to the trial anyway. You may be surprised."

William Samson was surprised to learn that the prosecution's psychiatrist had concluded that Kevin Taylor was not insane, that he knew the difference between right and wrong at the time he committed the murder of John Milton, and that what he was probably doing was trying to disguise his real motives with this act and this ludicrous tale about Satan and his followers.

When Kevin read the psychiatric report, however, he thought it was his first real piece of luck. Now he would be able to prove his case. People would listen and give him an opportunity. If he had convinced a man as religious and as scholarly as Father Vincent, surely he could convince twelve ordinary citizens. He was buoyed by the belief that once they saw the evidence and heard the testimony of his witnesses, the jury would support his contention that he had killed John Milton in self-defense. He wouldn't have been able to call witnesses and cross-examine them himself if the prosecution's psychiatrist had contended he was insane.

But everything crumbled after that.

He subpoenaed John Milton and Associates' computer files, but the "Futures" file he wanted wasn't there. He insisted that he hadn't been given all of them and, accompanied by court-appointed police guards, went to the office himself and tried to bring up the files on the computer. He met with no success. The file was gone. It was no longer even listed on the menu.

"They've deleted it," he declared. "I should have known they would."

Of course, no one believed him, but he thought he could go on without it.

On the opening day of the trial, Todd Lungen, another assistant district attorney, not much older than Bob McKensie but considerably better-looking, outlined the prosecution's case. Lungen reminded Kevin of himself because he had a similar confident, almost arrogant air about him. He promised to show how this was a simple open-and-shut case involving a husband, a wife, and a victim the husband believed had been having an affair with his wife and had impregnated her. Lungen contended that after Kevin had committed the cold-blooded murder, he concocted a ridiculous story in the hope that he would be declared insane. Thus, his ludicrous claim that he had killed John Milton in self-defense. His refusal to have his own psychiatrist examine him was motivated by the realization that any competent doctor of mental health would know he was faking it.

Norma and Jean were called to the stand, and both testified that Miriam had told them about Kevin's jealousy of John Milton. They related how he had even demanded she get an abortion after she announced her pregnancy. He had accused her of making love with John Milton and declared the child was Milton's. They said Miriam was terribly upset and was actually afraid of Kevin at this point.

In cross-examination, Kevin tried to get both of them to talk about Gloria and Richard Jaffee, but they gave his assertions no support, and when he brought up Helen Scholefield and the things she had told him, they both said that Helen had never said anything like that to them. Lungen then reexamined Jean, who revealed that Helen was still at Bellevue for psychiatric treatment.

"So even if she had said any of these fantastic things, we could hardly consider them sensible," Lungen concluded. Then he turned to the jury and added, "And surely, Mr. Taylor, a bright young attorney who had just won a major case in these courts, would have realized that."

Paul, Dave, and Ted were then called up. Each testified to John Milton's good character and charitable acts. They talked about his love of the law and all that he had done for each of them and their wives. They stressed the familial nature of their firm and vehemently denied that John Milton was a womanizer or had ever made advances to their wives. Each commented about Kevin's seeming inability to grasp that nature and his distrust of John Milton's intentions.

Kevin announced that he would not bother to cross-examine any of the associates because they would lie, oath or no oath. They were John Milton's sons, sons of the devil, he added. The judge pounded his gavel to quiet down some snickering in the audience.

The prosecution then offered the physical evidence —the cross dagger. Even though Kevin wasn't contesting that he had stabbed John Milton with it, a forensics expert was brought in to testify to his fingerprints. Kevin was placed at the scene of the crime, and the police officers who had arrived at the scene testified that Kevin's hand was bloody and that he did not deny he had killed Mr. Milton, even though he refused to answer any questions.

Confident, Lungen rested the prosecution's case.

Kevin was going to take the stand himself and offer his story, but he decided it would be better to first build some supportive evidence. He intended to begin with Beverly Morgan. However, when it came time to begin his defense, Beverly Morgan was unable to appear. She was comatose in the hospital, suffering from acute alcoholic poisoning. The attending physician did not hold up much hope for her.

Since another assistant district attorney, Todd

Lungen, had argued the state's case, Kevin was able to call Bob McKensie to the stand. However, McKensie's recollections of their clandestine meeting were quite different from Kevin's. McKensie admitted to Kevin's concerns about John Milton's law firm and that Kevin had claimed the firm would go to any lengths to win a client's acquittal, no matter how guilty he or she might appear. Yes, he said, Kevin had come to see him to discredit the firm.

"But it was apparent to me," McKensie added, "that his motive was revenge. He believed his wife was having an affair with the man."

Kevin couldn't believe his ears. "You're lying! I never said anything like that!" he declared. Lungen objected to Kevin's outburst, and the judge sustained.

"Either you continue questioning the witness or he will step down."

"But your honor, he's lying."

"That's for the jury to decide. Any other questions for Mr. McKensie?"

"Yes. Did you recommend I see Father Reuben Vincent?"

"Yes I did," McKensie said.

"Good. Now tell the court why you made such a recommendation, please."

"Because I thought he could help you. He is a licensed psychiatrist. He could counsel you and help you to find other ways to deal with your jealousy."

"What?"

Stoically, McKensie stared back.

Kevin spun around and looked into the audience where Paul Scholefield, Ted McCarthy, and Dave Kotein sat. He thought they were smiling contentedly.

Norma, Jean, and Miriam sat beside them, Norma and Jean comforting her. Miriam looked as sad to him now as she had looked during Lois Wilson's trial. She ran the back of her hand over her cheeks to wipe away tears.

For a moment he thought he was back at the Lois Wilson trial. It was the moment before he was going to question the little girl. He could do it or not. Was he there? Had all this been a dream? Could he turn back time?

The judge brought him back to reality. "Mr. Taylor?"

He looked back at McKensie, who had the same smile on his face as the associates. Of course, Kevin thought. Of course.

"I should have known," he laughed. "I should have realized. What a fool. I was a perfect fool, a perfect victim, wasn't I? Wasn't I?" he demanded of McKensie. The lanky man crossed his legs and looked up at the judge for assistance.

"Mr. Taylor?" the judge said.

"Your honor," Kevin said, moving toward the witness stand and shaking his finger at McKensie, "Mr. McKensie was part of it . . . the cases he lost, the deals he made . . ."

Lungen rose to his feet. "Objection, your honor."

"Sustained. Mr. Taylor, I've warned you about these speeches. Save them for your final arguments or I'll find you in contempt."

Kevin stopped and looked at the faces of the jury members. Most looked amazed, confused. Some looked disgusted. He nodded, a sense of overwhelming defeat washing over him with the impact of an

ocean wave. But surely, Father Vincent, a priest . . .
He was his last hope.

He called him to the stand.

The small elderly man looked very distinguished in
his double-breasted suit and tie. He looked more like a
psychiatrist and less like a priest.

"Father Vincent, will you relate to the court the
substance of the conversation you and I had concerning John Milton."

"I'm afraid I have to decline that request on the
basis of doctor-patient privilege," he said.

"Oh no, Father. You can say anything. I waive all
that."

Father Vincent looked to the judge.

"It's his right to do so," the judge said. "Go on with
your testimony."

Father Vincent shook his head sympathetically.
"Very well." He turned toward the jury. "Mr. Taylor
was referred to me by Bob McKensie. I had one
session with him during which I detected great anger
and antagonism. He revealed his desire to do harm to
Mr. John Milton because he believed Mr. Milton had
impregnated his wife. He rationalized his desire by
declaring that Mr. Milton was an evil man, a devil in
disguise.

"I tried to point out this rationalization and lead
him to an understanding of what he was feeling in the
hope that he would be able to deal with his anger and
suspicions. We were to have more sessions together.

"But that night, Mr. Taylor phoned me and told me
he had killed John Milton. He was hysterical but, in
my opinion, quite aware of what he had done."

"I'm not interested in the psychiatric end to all

this," Kevin snapped. "I came to see you in your role as a priest, an expert on the occult and the devil. Wouldn't you consider yourself an expert on these matters? Haven't you done very scholarly research on them?"

"Scholarly research on the devil? Hardly."

"But . . . didn't you give me a Bible to give to Mr. Milton as a way of testing whether or not he was the devil?" Rather than reply, Father Vincent started to smile. Kevin practically lunged at him. "And didn't you provide me with a cross that was a dagger as well?"

Father Vincent looked at him and then turned slightly to the jury again. "Absolutely not. These statements are as fantastic to me as they must be to all of you."

Kevin reddened. He turned back to look at the associates. Their smiles were wider, deeper. Norma and Jean were turned to Miriam, who had her hands over her face. He looked at Bob McKensie, who now seemed to be laughing.

"Even priests! Even priests!" Kevin shouted, raising his hands toward the ceiling. "You're one of his sons, too, aren't you?" he demanded, turning back to Father Vincent. "Aren't you?" He spun around. "How many more of you are there here?"

"Mr. Taylor." The judge rapped his gavel. Kevin turned to him and pointed a finger of accusation.

"You're his, too. You're all his. Don't you see?" he screamed at the jury. "They're all his sons."

In the end the court marshals had to subdue Kevin so the prosecution could cross-examine Father Vincent. Lungen presented him with the Bible.

"This was the Bible found at John Milton's feet.

You've already said you didn't give it to Mr. Taylor to use for some voodoo test of the devil, is that not so?"

"Yes."

Lungen opened the Bible. "In fact, would you read to the jury what is written here?" He handed the Bible to Father Vincent.

"'To John. May this bring you comfort whenever you need some. Your friend, Cardinal Thomas.'"

"So much for that part of his ridiculous story," Lungen said, taking the Bible back and returning it to the exhibit table.

Kevin had no other witnesses, nothing else to offer in his own defense, but the prosecution recalled Paul Scholefield, Dave Kotein, and Ted McCarthy and had them each testify that they had seen the cross dagger in John Milton's apartment from the first time they had entered it. It was something he had picked up on one of his European holidays and, they all agreed, something he had cherished.

"Certainly, it wasn't something Father Vincent had given Kevin to use to kill the devil," Paul Scholefield said.

In his closing argument, Lungen contended that Kevin Taylor, a proven successful criminal trial lawyer, had committed a cold-blooded, premeditated murder and then devised this ridiculous story about the devil to get the jury to think him insane so he would get away with it.

"Trying to employ some of the very skillful yet conniving techniques he employed as a defense attorney for other clients. No," Lungen concluded, "there'll be no confusing of this jury." He pointed at Kevin. "Kevin Taylor, driven by an insane jealousy of a talented, debonair older man, plotted against that man and stands guilty of murder. This is one time a clever defense attorney will not manipulate the truth."

The jury agreed. He was found guilty of murder in the first degree, and he was sentenced to twenty-five years to life.

Epilogue

He moved like one in a daze. At first no one bothered with him; practically no one spoke to him. He thought maybe he had become invisible, or maybe he wasn't really here in a maximum-security prison in upstate New York.

Miriam came to visit on the third day, but mostly they just stared at each other. She seemed a thousand miles away anyway, and when she did speak, some words were lost, like a television set on the blink. What he remembered of their conversation was broken up into phrases: "Your parents and mine . . . I tried to play piano . . . Helen's back."

"Isn't it wonderful," she remarked at the end, "that John Milton had put aside a trust fund for our child? It was something he did for the Jaffee child, and there are trusts for Ted and Jean and Norma and Dave. Paul and Helen are talking about adopting."

Of course, she was still pregnant. There was no reason for her not to be. He understood that now. He understood that it was too late for her.

"I don't want my parents to have the baby," he finally said.

"Have the baby?" She smiled with confusion. "What baby, Kevin?"

"His," he said.

"Oh no, not that again." She shook her head. "I was hoping you would stop saying those things now that it's over."

"It's over. I repeat, I don't want my parents bringing up this baby."

"All right, they won't," she said, not cloaking her anger. "Why should they?"

"They shouldn't. Nor should yours."

"I'll bring up our child."

He shook his head. "I tried, Miriam. In the end I tried for you, to save you. There'll be a moment, one final moment near the end, when you'll realize all this and you'll think of me as I am now, and if you are still able to, you will shout my name. I'll hear you, but there will be nothing I can do."

"I can't take this, Kevin. It's hard enough for me to come here, but I can't take this talk. I won't come back until it stops, do you understand?"

"It doesn't matter anymore. It's too late," he repeated.

She jumped up. "I'm going. If you want me to come back, write and promise you won't talk like this when I do," she said and started away.

"Miriam!"

She turned back.

"Ask them where Helen's painting is and go

look at it if they haven't destroyed it. Look at it closely."

"It wasn't destroyed. It was sold. Bob McKensie bought it. He likes that sort of thing."

Kevin laughed. In fact, it was the mad sound of that laughter that drove her out.

He spent his time trying to understand. How did his demise fill any of their purposes? So he had discovered who John Milton really was and what the firm was really doing. What could he do with this information? Bring it to McKensie, and then when he got no satisfaction, bring it to another assistant district attorney or the district attorney himself? How would he know who was untouched and who was? He couldn't force Miriam to get an abortion, and she didn't believe the things he was telling her. Even if he had taken her away, the baby would still have killed her. John Milton would still have had his child.

No one would believe the things he had learned, and there was nothing he could do to stop them, so why did they manipulate him into killing John Milton?

The answers came a few days later. He was sitting in the cafeteria, chewing mechanically on his food, shutting away the sounds and sights around him.

Suddenly he was aware of the close presence of other men, two rubbing shoulders, one on the left and one on the right of him, and two or more standing directly behind him. He had vaguely noticed the two who were now beside him before. Whenever he did see them, he found them staring at him, smiling licentiously, so he turned away quickly. Other than that, they seemed indistinguishable from the other inmates, all of them a blur.

"Hi there," the one on his right said. His smile revealed a mouth filled with greenish-yellow teeth. His lips twisted away from them in a lustful smile.

"Bet you're lonely already," the man on his left said and placed his right hand on Kevin's left thigh.

He started to pull back, but the inmate standing directly behind him pressed his legs against his back. He was aware that this man had an erection poking him as well. His stomach churned with revulsion. The man on his left tightened his grip on Kevin's thigh. He wanted to scream, but the small crowd of inmates that had gathered behind him, on his sides, and directly in front of him blocked out any immediate rescue.

Then the half-dozen or so who were standing in front of him parted, and the inmate sitting directly across from him stood up quickly and backed away so that a tall, muscular black man could approach the table and sit there. His biceps bulged against his sleeves, and his neck muscles stretched emphatically against his smooth, thin skin. He looked invincible, hardened, a man sculptured by the system, toughened and trimmed. He had bright, black eyes with the whites around them as clear and as pure as fresh milk.

He smiled, and the men around him smiled, too. All eyes were on him. It was as if their energy, their very life force, came from him.

"Hello, Mr. Taylor," he said. Kevin nodded. "We've been waiting for you."

"Me?" His voice cracked. The smiles on the faces of the inmates around him widened.

"Or someone just like you."

"Oh," he said, looking from the man on his right to the one on his left. So he was to be passed around like some whore.

"Oh no, no, Mr. Taylor," the black man said. "You
misunderstand. You're not here for that. They can get
that any time from any one of the others," he added,
and the man on his left took his hand off Kevin's thigh
instantly. Both he and the man on the right shifted so
their bodies were no longer pressed up against his, and
the man behind him stepped back. He released a
breath of relief. "No, you're more important than
that, Mr. Taylor."

"I am?"

"Yes, sir. You see, Mr. Taylor, everyone here has
been framed, just like you." The crowd around him
laughed. They all smiled down at him. "Everyone
here had lousy attorneys." Some nodded angrily.
"Everyone needs to file for an appeal."

"What?"

"Yes, sir, you got it. Now, the irony is, we have one
of the best law libraries going, but we don't have the
skills, the knowledge you have.

"But . . ." He sat back and placed his big hands
palms down on the table. "You've finally arrived and
you'll help us . . . help each and every one of us, and
as long as you do, you'll always be known around here
as Mr. Taylor and be treated with respect. Ain't that
right, boys?"

Everyone in the group nodded.

"So. Right after you finish your lunch there, why
don't you mosey on up to the law library and meet
Scratch. He's the inmate who serves as head librarian,
and he's waiting to be of assistance to you, Mr. Taylor.
You and Scratch . . . hell, you two are going to be like
Siamese twins around here."

There was more laughter.

"You just go up there, and Scratch will tell you

where to start, who to help first. Understand, Mr. Taylor?"

They all leaned in, all eyes on him, everyone poised.

"Yes," he said. "I do. Finally."

"That's fine, Mr. Taylor. That's just fine." He stood up. "Say hello to Scratch for me." He winked, and the crowd parted, some following him, others moving off to the right and left until Kevin was practically alone again.

This was meant to be Richard Jaffee's role, he thought. That's what Paul Scholefield meant when he first approached him and told him there was an opening at John Milton and Associates. Helen Scholefield had been right: Richard Jaffee had a conscience and chose death rather than this.

And Father Vincent wasn't lying to him, either. The devil is loyal to his followers and stands by them.

He stood up. It seemed to him that everyone in the huge cafeteria stopped eating to watch him walk out, even the guards. He walked on like a man heading for the guillotine. The speed with which that blade fell would depend entirely on his own courage and his own conscience. Right now, he didn't have the nerve to bring it down.

And that was the pity of it. He was like the mythical Sisyphus in Greek mythology, punished forever with the job of rolling a boulder up a pit only to have it roll back down each time. Yet he would go on and on, believing that any existence was better than none at all.

Was it?

He knew what awaited him as he moved down the corridor toward the library. Perhaps he had always known. The evil that lurked in his heart had kept the knowledge cloaked, but it was always there.

Time to pull the cloak away and face the truth, he thought.

He turned into the doorway. The library was impressive for a prison library.

And it was as quiet as a library should be. A door opened across the well-lit room, and the keeper of the books came toward him, slowly.

Scratch.

He was smiling. He knew Kevin was coming. Of course, he knew.

As he drew closer and closer, his face became more and more familiar, until he was standing right before him.

And once again, Kevin looked into the charismatic, fatherly eyes of John Milton.